Judicial INDISCRETION

Published and Distributed By
New View Literature
820 67th Avenue N, #7603
Myrtle Beach, South Carolina 29572
annjeffries@newviewliterature.com
www.newviewliterature.com

Jenetha McCutcheon Hollis,
Quill Editorial Service

Jessica Tilles, TWA Solutions
Cover and Interior design

ISBN: 978-1-941603-03-1 Print
ISBN: 978-1-941603-65-9 eBook
Library of Congress Control Number: 2014947429

First printing April 2018

This is a work of fiction. Names, characters, business, places, events and incidents are either the products of the author's imagination or used in a fictitious manner. Any resemblance to actual persons, living or dead, or actual events is purely coincidental.

For inquires, contact the publisher.

Praise for
Judicial Indiscretion

"*I never met an Ann Jeffries novel I didn't love and her latest, Judicial Indiscretion, doesn't disappoint! Sizzling scenes, great characters, and good storyline...what more does any reader need?*" J.A. Meinecke, Author, *A Woman to Reckon With*

"*Ann Jeffries gives us seduction, romance, suspense and high-powered political intrigue in her latest installment of The Wisdom of the Ancestors. Judicial Indiscretion is a sizzling hot romance. This tale of one woman's struggle between her family's expectations and what her heart desires embroils more than the man of her dreams. The opposition doesn't play fair and her need to keep peace on all fronts while doing what is right tears at her soul.*" Rebecca Bridges, Author, *After the Reunion*

"*Ann Jeffries delivers a novel with enough intrigue and romance to keep the reader captivated from beginning to end. 'Judicial Indiscretion' is another brilliant story in her Wisdom of the Ancestors series.*" Nancy Engle, Author, *Image of Perfection.*

ANOTHER FAMILY REUNION NOVEL
IN THE WISDOM OF THE ANCESTORS SERIES

Judicial INDISCRETION

BOOK ONE IN THE CHI-TOWN GIRLS TRILOGY

ANN JEFFRIES

Ann Jeffries Titles
In The Family Reunion—Wisdom of the Ancestors Series

Southern Exposures

Another Point of View

Northern Exposures

Uncommon Choices

An Unguarded Moment

Moments to Remember

The Better Part of Valor

Walking On Uneven Ground

Ask Me No Questions... I'll Tell You No Lies

Touch Me In The Morning

All Goodbyes Aren't Gone

A Different Frame of Mind

For those who have gone on to their sweet slumber:

Charles Thomas "Tommy" Branch

Delores Jeffries Camach

Jack Gravely

Sister Beatrice Julia Jeffries

Malcolm Everett "Mac" Jeffries

Theodore Lee Jeffries, Sr.

Ellen Hughes Robinson

Byron Sims

Sandra Smith Singleton

Pattie Grace Smith

Cheryl Taylor

William Turner Ward

Verna LaNelle Griffis Ward

Thomas A Wyatt

Thank you for being in my dash.

Acknowledgements

I bow in humble gratitude to:

The Creator
My Ancestors
Jessica Tilles, TWA Solutions
The Carolina Forest Authors' Club
Jenetha McCutcheon Hollis, Quill Editorial Service
The Carolina Forest Library, Horry County, SC
Faithful Family, Friends, and Fans

The struggle for literary perfection continues and will never cease.

I remain, faithfully yours,

It is the lawyers who run our civilization for us—our governments, our business, our private lives. Most legislators are lawyers; they make our laws. Most presidents, governors, commissioners, along with their advisers and brain-trusts are lawyers; they administer our laws. All the judges are lawyers; they interpret and enforce our laws. There is no separation of powers where the lawyers are concerned. There is only a concentration of all government power—in the lawyers.

~ FRED RODELL, *Woe Unto You, Lawyers*

First, kill all of the lawyers.

~ *Henry VI* by William Shakespeare

Chapter 1

"There's a party over here! There's a party over there! Oooo Ahhh!"

Indeed, there was. A massive amount of people, most of whom were lawyers, were shouting catcalls, whistles, and dog barks over the din of loud, heart-throbbing, foot-stomping, finger popping, head locking, hand-clapping music. Multicolored strobe lights flickered in sync with the Old School funky sounds. Hot, steamy, hard bodies undulated to the driving rhythm of the beat. *"Go head! Go head! Go head!"* was another chant rippling through the space. *"Par-tay! Par-tay!"* It was a get down and it was on! *"To the left! To the left! To the left!"*

Tina Justice's body was moving like her namesake on a revival of **Proud Mary**. Cheryl Lawrence flung her impressive hips toward George Bryant. He captured her waist in his hands suggestively gyrating his torso against her rear.

"Ooowee, girl! Serve me somethin', somethin,' sister woman!" George shouted out. *"Umph! Umph!"*

"Can't handle this, brotherman," Tina teased as she snaked her body in a perfect wave from head to toe.

Fingers clicked in the air as George rounded to find another woman pressing him with a sensuous sway of her body. *"Get it, girl!"* he yelled.

Then the DJ torqued it up with another favorite body-challenging beat and the crowd went wild.

Sitting alone at the bar, Kristen Catherine Bryant, KC to her friends, slowly exhaled with total disinterest. The cool, white marble under her fingertips vibrated from the bass sound reverberating off the walls, floor, and high ceiling. She'd rather be anywhere other than this steamy, hot, ballroom at her friend, Tina's Sheridan Road mansion in Chicago. She had no choice though since the festivities were in her honor. Surprise parties, even those planned by her oldest, dearest friends, and two older brothers, weren't her thing. She much preferred sitting on an island beach listening to cool jazz, smelling salt sea air, and counting millions of stars in the endless night sky.

Thinking of the stars and sky, she recalled that her pal, Tate Kennedy, was up there right now in the wild blue yonder continuing his dream of erecting the SPACEHOME project. Another pal, Air Force General Benjamin Alexander, was making history piloting the spacecraft he and his brother, Kenneth Alexander recently designed and built which didn't need a rocket booster to lift it into orbit. Oh, yeah, she thought, teamwork makes the dream work. It worked here on terra firma, too, and as a result, she was about to embark on a new dream, however not one of her own choosing.

Long-lashed, bright brown eyes rolled to the white gold Rolex on her wrist; a gift from *"The Judge"* when she, herself, was robed and became a Federal court judge three years ago. Her father presented the watch to her hours after he held the Bible for her—her mother's Bible—and she'd taken her oath of office. The senior Judge was jubilant—in his staid, somber manner—that his youngest and only female offspring had been appointed to a federal district court in Illinois. Was that only three years ago? she distractedly mused. It seemed like a lifetime had passed.

Kristen glanced at George Bryant, her older brother, whose better than six-and-a-half-foot frame towered over others. He now had three women engrossed in his very suggestive dance moves. Their mother, Lydia Martine Booth Bryant, had been a world-renowned prima ballerina and had trained them in all forms of dance. They were young when she died, but her teaching lived on to a certain extent in each of her three offspring. Kristen shook her head in amusement and put palm to chin resting her elbow on the bar. Her eyes rounded the crowded, hardwood dance floor in the ballroom, momentarily stopping on some of the more provocative dancers' moves. If only she could be that carefree and uninhibited for just one day, she'd take it. Yet, her life had to be lived with the decorum befitting a tenured professor of law who lectured at Chicago University's School of Law, the position she had just resigned and a federal appellate court judgeship—the new position she would assume in a month and the reason for the all-out bash.

Kristen sighed again. Strickland Briggs hadn't even come to the party. *WTH*. She really hadn't expected he would or that her friends even invited him. When she turned down his marriage proposal two months ago, he had wordlessly turned on his expensive, Italian, hand-crafted shoes and walked out on her. That scene wasn't even a fleeting footnote in history before the **Chicago Times** society pages captured Strickland escorting Shannon, a high-fashion model, into one of the hottest and most exclusive night spots in town. Gossip columnists opined the affair between Strickland and Shannon never really ended. Rather, it simply went under cover, literally and figuratively speaking.

Over her two-year relationship with Strickland, he never took her anywhere except stuffy professional receptions, bar association meetings, political dinners, and office events filled with lobbyists and captains of industry. However, some enterprising members of the Fifth Estate— yellow journalists to be precise—captured rather racy pictures they claimed were Strickland and Shannon in very compromising situations.

Strickland claimed the photos were forgeries, but never took steps to clear his name. However, being seen in all the politically correct places with Judge Kristen Catherine Bryant was Strickland's saving grace, his shield against gossip and innuendo. She fit his personae—Black, upwardly mobile, young and wealthy. In short, a BUPPY.

Well, so much for licking his wounds, she thought as the music turned to the sultry voice of Toni Braxton's **Let It Flow**. The band and singers were definitely kicking it Old School tonight.

"How about a slow drag, Judge Bryant?" a man's lowered, deep-timbered voice whispered over her ear.

A leisurely grin crept into Kristen's dower expression.

"Since when do you address me as 'judge', Pete?"

"Should I call you Madam Justice?" He grinned coming around to face her.

"I'm still KC Bryant to you, pal," she smoothly answered.

"Not anymore, lady. You be 'de judge!" He teasingly laughed.

"Stop," she said, raising her hand in a traffic-sign motion. "I've had about all of *'de judge'* jokes I can take for one night."

Pete took her outstretched hand and deftly pulled her up from the barstool into his arms. "You just got it like that, my sistah," he teased while guiding her into a dance on the crowded floor.

Peter Brock, a few years her senior, had been her friend and confidant since childhood; literally since they were babes in arms. The exclusive, private school they attended together had not done its job on him the way it had settled on her like an anvil. He was still buck wild when he wanted to be, but his family's lucrative business and political connections kept him out of one jam or the other most of his life.

He was a very good lawyer now in spite of himself. He simply didn't take the legal profession or himself very seriously. Yet, he teamed up with her father, brothers, and best female friends, Tina Justice and Cheryl Lawrence, and her good friend, Federal Appellate Court Judge Vivian Alexander Montgomery, to successfully lobby for her appointment to the federal appellate court in Washington, DC, to take Vivian's place on the court. Her tightly-knit group of lawyers and supporters spent many months, almost six months, together preparing for the US Senate hearings at her father's strong suggestion, and Pete had even acted as her legal counsel whenever the need arose.

However, not many people said no to her father. Certainly, she never could. Judge Clarence Edward Bryant, Senior, intimidated everyone, except her mother and her older brothers, Clarence Junior and George. Her brothers pandered to the senior Judge Bryant's only loves—the law and sports. Her brothers, both lawyers now, George played professional football in the NFL, and Clarence Junior, professional basketball in the NBA. She, as her father's only daughter, was held to a higher standard than her brothers and had about as much athletic ability as Beyoncé.

Secretly, outside of the omnipresent eye of the austere senior Judge Bryant, she could make Beyoncé sit down and take notes. However, were she ever to exhibit any of her deftly exotic moves in public, she knew the wrath of the senior Judge Bryant would descend on her as solidly as the gavel he wielded like an ax. *Guilty!* Guilty of dreaming about something she couldn't have—a life lived in complete, sensual abandon or, at least, on her own terms.

"Why the sad face, KC? The Judge isn't here. In fact, we didn't even mention to your father we were throwing this surprise party for you."

Kristen didn't realize Pete watched her so closely while they danced. She laid her forehead against the hard-muscled plane of his broad chest for a moment exhaling before lifting her head to look up into his eyes.

"Sorry, Pete, I guess I'm still tired from all the work we did to get me appointed and confirmed to the appellate court. It seems like a lifetime ago since I've had any time to myself."

"Is that it? You just need a rest? Please tell me you're not still hung up on that weasel in a Saville Row suit?"

Kristen leaned her head back and narrowed her eyebrows as she continued to look up into Peter's handsome face searching his eyes. She didn't have to ask him who he was talking about. She knew it was Strickland Briggs.

"You never liked him, did you?"

"About as much as I like jock itch," he snorted.

"Why, Pete? What did Strickland ever do to you?" she asked, confused.

Pete looked down into her concerned expression. Then a slow, lopsided grin grew across his handsome face. "Took you away from us," he said, smiling.

"Really?" she snorted, shaking her head. "Now will the *real* Peter Brock, Esquire, please stand, place your hand on the Bible, and answer the question as posed?"

Peter's smile broadened. "Well, Judge, it happened when I was a child," he teased feigning seriousness. "I had this little girlfriend who was always tagging after me and begging me to play with her..."

Kristen pursed her lips and shook her head. "That's not how I remember it, Pete, but that's beside the point. The issue is, why didn't you like Strickland?"

"Ever the lawyer, KC."

"The question, Pete," she encouraged.

"Let's just dance, pal-of-mine."

Pete turned her on the dance floor and held her close. She waited, understanding Pete was choosing his words very carefully in how to answer her question. He was always so protective of her; as protective as her brothers and her father were. Still, she was a patient woman, and would wait until he found the words to explain his thoughts. He always told her the truth no matter what and she trusted him without question.

Kristen again glanced at her watch on her arm which rested on Peter's shoulder. In ten hours she would be on a chartered Adventurers Executive Airline flight headed for a private island where she could enjoy complete and total anonymity; her first real vacation ever.

Since the day she took her first steps, her parents designed her life in a master plan leaving little or no time or room for her to exercise any control over her own desires or destiny. Now she would be free and un-chaperoned, at least for three weeks, before her father joined her in Washington, DC, in preparations for her ascension to the federal appellate bench. She couldn't wait to step on that flight to freedom.

"The man was two-timing you, Kristen. You must have seen all the news in the society pages about him and the super model Shannon. He's a social-climbing bastard. Briggs could see, just like the rest of us, you're headed for bigger and better things. He wanted in on the action and to keep Shannon as his side piece."

Kristen's body stiffened, but Pete held her that much tighter forcing her to sway with his moves.

"I'm sorry, baby," he whispered at her ear. "You didn't deserve to be told like this, especially not tonight at a party in your honor, but I kept quiet for far too long. We all did. We couldn't stand to see you hurt."

Confusion clouded Kristen's face. "He was using me? All of the time we dated, he was just using me?" she asked searching his warm, affectionate eyes for the truth. Clearly everyone, all of her close friends, knew it, she pondered. Pete nodded again in the affirmative. "Why didn't you or any of my other friends tell me before?"

Pete blew a slow, frustrated breath and pulled her back into his arms. "The Judge had us all on lockdown. He thought Strickland had the political savvy you shy away from. That Strickland would do everything in his power to assure you a position on the Supreme Court without a breath of scandal. Your father warned me and everyone not to interfere, to overlook Strickland's affair with Shannon, and to concentrate only on getting you nominated and confirmed to the federal court."

"Even my father knew about Strickland and Shannon?" she questioned hoping it was not true.

Pete nodded in the affirmative. "Yes. He thought he was doing the right thing, KC. He wants you to be the first Black female Supreme Court Justice and a politic man, like Strickland Briggs, with the right pedigree, family background, and all the right connections would assure that would happen. You have to be very careful who you associate with, KC. Everyone has a hidden agenda, and I'm afraid, that includes Strickland Briggs."

Kristen was numb.

Chapter 2

"Ouch! Damn it! Where the hell did she put my itinerary?" a figure fumed searching the darkened office. Like a thief in the night, T. Ashton Marshall, Ash to his friends, silently moved in unfamiliar surroundings—his suite of offices on the penthouse floor in the Portland Towers. His international law cases kept him out of the country most of the time. If he worked it right, he could make his escape from Oregon again before *She-who-must-be-obeyed* knew he was even in the building, but, *damn it,* where was the plan that would free him?

Frustration, uncommon to Ashton, seized him as he fumbled in the darkness with just the aid of a pen light. The blinds were closed and the decorative, blackout draperies pulled across the windows. A sound in the adjoining office caused him to stand stark still and listen. He was in dangerous territory and, if discovered, by *she-who-must-be-obeyed,* he'd be done for. His heartbeat regained a normal pace. His ears captured no other sounds, but his time was running out. If he didn't get out of the building before *she* returned from lunch, he'd never make good his escape.

Four fingers raked through his short, dark-brown, curly and wavy hair. Damn, he needed a haircut and a shave at his favorite barbershop, but that, too, would have to wait. He knew his itinerary was left in his office. It had to be since it wasn't in his briefcase or in his office at home. Where could it be though? he wondered.

"Forget it!" he quietly hissed. His luggage was packed and stored in the trunk of his car double parked in front of the building. His tennis racket had to be picked up from the repair shop and his private Adventurer Executive Airline flight was scheduled to leave in one hour and fifteen minutes.

He rounded the desk and felt his body for his passport, credit cards, and money clip. It shouldn't be that hard to find the right chartered flight at the airport. As for his accommodations, surely an enclave as posh and exclusive as the world-renown Plaza de Masquerada would still have a record of his reservations, even if he were two days late arriving.

That _McElroy v. Wayne_ case lasted as long as the Mueller Russia probes and had caused more notoriety. When two international captains of industry clashed on the world stage and unbelievable fortunes hung in the balance impacting the economies of many nations, the world press and news media had dogged his every footstep. He couldn't even take a breath without cameras and microphones being shoved in his face. He sympathized with Bob Mueller, but in life Bob never had it this bad.

Ashton's nights were even worse. None of his lady friends—of which there were quite a few—appreciated the number of broken dates, brief interludes or rushed intimacies he was forced to have. Neither did he for that matter.

Now that he had won the case for his client and received a seven-figure legal fee, Ashton longed for the luxury of anonymity, being with a beautiful and willing woman, whiling away the hours unencumbered by prying eyes. That's why he selected the most exclusive, private, and discrete accommodations he could get. Now, if _She-who-must-be-obeyed_ could be avoided for five more damn minutes, he'd be gone.

Ashton approached the door with stealth and listened for the slightest sound. Nothing astir, he cracked the door slightly and eyed the path to the private elevator. Keys palmed in hand, so as not to make any sound, the way clear, Ashton eased out of his office, past his momentarily unoccupied executive assistant's desk and quickly walked down the thickly-carpeted hallway. His hand poised to insert the key in the elevator slot when a report sounded.

"Ashton, in my office…_now!_" the voice of She-who-must-be-obeyed pealed.

As he slowly exhaled, he rolled his eyes to the ceiling as if pleading for divine intervention. One palm met cold marble wall as he momentarily braced himself. *No rest for the weary*, he thought. Still, the sooner he got this over with, the sooner he'd be on his flight to freedom.

"Ashton!" another directive came in a voice that brooked no argument.

Ashton pushed off from the marble wall, dug his hands in his pockets, and turned slowly walking toward the well-appointed, managing partner's office.

"Yes, Mother," he respectfully said.

Sheila Duckworth Marshall's eyes breached the upper rim of her stylish eyeglasses only briefly appraising her son's attire and attitude as she continued signing a stack of papers before her. Her executive assistant stood by her side efficiently pointing to the signature line on each document and unsuccessfully trying to stifle a smile.

"I deduce from your casual attire you were not planning to attend the senior partners' meeting at two o'clock today. This is a very important meeting, Ashton. We're going to discuss bringing in another trial lawyer as a senior partner in the firm. Jillian Harris will be the first candidate to meet with the senior partners' selection committee. Also, the legal team from Foxworthy Industries will be coming in for further discussions. From the way you're attired, I'd say you weren't even planning to be in the office at all today. A fact I find unacceptable."

"In fact, you're right, Mother. I was headed—."

"You can take a vacation after you meet with the Prince of Madagascar on the mineral rights issues. Then there's that mediation in settlement of the South African land reapportionment. You're also co-counsel with Alan Lightfoot on the Alaskan Indians' claim the oil companies are not making full and complete disclosure about—."

"The oil spills and clean-up process," he finished for her, again checking his watch. "I know, Mother. I've got it covered. I've spoken with Alan about our strategy. Stark and Howard left yesterday to meet with the Alaskan Indians and a team from Alan's Washington, DC, office. I've sent Taylor, Epps, and Michaels to Madagascar to do the preliminary interviews; Anza and Collins are on their way to South Africa, with the government's approval of a preliminary approach to the discussions."

A raised eyebrow bade him to leave the door and seat himself for a more in-depth chat, but this time, Ashton didn't adjust. Again, he glanced at his watch. He had one hour exactly to make it to the airport and he still had to figure out where the flight he was scheduled to take was docked. The tennis racket wouldn't make this trip. He did have his new golf clubs in his car though. That was something, at least.

"Well, now we have the appeal filed this morning by McElroy Products, Incorporated. You'll have to prepare your arguments for dismissal of the appeal and, failing that, prepare your strategy for presentation to the federal court in Washington, DC. Since you've checked your watch several times, you must know you have enough time to change your clothes into something suitable before this afternoon's meetings. We'll likely be here until after dinner. Then we have the manufacturers' ball at eight. You usually keep several changes of clothes in your office closet so you shouldn't have to leave the building to dress appropriately for both events."

A slow grin creased his face. She must have eyes in the top of her head to notice he was marking the escaping time. She only looked up at him once since he entered her office. He approached his stately and statuesque mother as she stood and handed the last of the signed documents to her executive assistant, Doris. He hoisted a hip on the corner of his mother's authentic Louis XVI desk and folded his arms across his sportswear-covered chest.

Sheila noted his behavior with a slight motherly scowl on her comely face, but said nothing.

"You'll tell me all about it when I return, now won't you, Mother?" he asked, grinning. "I'll review all of the projects when I return. Just don't make any hasty decisions in my absence."

She met his gaze with a raised eyebrow. "Where is it you plan to go and for how long?"

Rising to his feet and towering over her five-ten height, he kissed her on both cheeks and then her forehead, before he smiled and turned to leave.

"Ashton," she fussed. "You're taxing this old woman's heart and I don't have a lot of years left, you know. I noticed you weren't taking one of the firm's jets."

"Would you pick up my tennis racquet when you pick up yours from the shop, please? We're scheduled to play in that mixed doubles, pro-am tournament in five weeks. We'll put in some serious practice time when I return, but you'll have to spot me a few points. It's embarrassing to be beaten by your own mother so often."

Sheila Marshall pursed her lips and raised one eyebrow. "I'll do nothing of the kind, young man! If you can't hold your own on a tennis court, how can you ever expect to continue to succeed in a court of law?"

"With the most celebrated female attorney in this century as my mentor, how could I fail?" he rhetorically asked over his shoulder while still moving toward the door. "Marshall and Marshall will survive without me for a few weeks."

"Just where do you think you're going, Thomas Ashton Marshall, III?" she snapped.

"Paradise, Mother, and I'll be out of touch for three or four whole weeks."

"Ashton, if your father were alive today, he'd turn you over his knee! What image do we portray when the second in command who is also the head of this law firm's International Litigation and Mediation Division is off on some junket when the firm is about to add a key player in your department? Also, it's time for you to settle down and stop all this globetrotting. You've got a competent staff of attorneys to do that. Your place is here in the office managing your employees, this firm, and preparing for the next steps and stages of your career."

"Love ya, Mom," he smiled and winked, as he slipped through the door. Then a beat later he stuck his head back in. He noticed his mother had picked up the telephone on her desk. "By the way, I've promised to fire the entire Security and Investigations Division if anyone follows or disturbs me or spies on me while I'm away."

Doris couldn't hold the soft chuckle that escaped her lips until Sheila turned a deadening glance in her direction and slammed the telephone back down in its cradle.

Ashton winked at his mother, blew a kiss to her assistant, and left his mother hurling obscenities. Rounding the corner toward the private elevator again, he bumped into someone else he tried to avoid—Jillian Harris, lead counsel for Wayne Agra Industries.

"What's your hurry, handsome?" she cooed.

"Ms. Harris," he acknowledged with a slight nod. "I didn't expect to see you here this early."

Jillian quickly scanned the area and then perused him from the bottom up. "Seems you didn't expect to be here when I arrived either. I just left your office. Why do I have the feeling you're avoiding me, Ash?"

"Nothing of the kind, Jillian," he smoothly lied. Jillian was not a beautiful woman, but one who knew how to use her feminine attributes to her best advantage. Lean, leggy and luscious, but very competitive. More competitive than any woman he had ever known. Generally, he appreciated confident women. His mother and grandmother had that trait, but they didn't exhibit arrogance as did Jillian. Aggressive was an understatement when it came to Jillian. Carnivorous came to his mind. She made her interest in him crystal clear over the past year and a half his firm represented the company she worked for. He didn't mind aggressive women either. They could prove interesting and entertaining between the sheets, but he drew the line at potential stalkers.

She was in-house General Counsel for Wayne Agra Industries. He had dodged each of her advances not wanting to mix business with pleasure, but that only seemed to heighten her interest in him rather than dull it. He didn't mind recreational sex. However, his policy was simple: He didn't sleep with his clients. In order to distract her from her personal interest in him, he brought up a professional issue. "Looks like we're going to be working together again. I understand McElroy Products filed an appeal in federal court."

"Working together isn't what's on my mind, Ash," she said fingering the exposed hair on his chest through the opening in his Polo shirt. "Unless you consider sex work. If so, I'll give it my full and undivided attention."

His ploy didn't work. "Uh, Jillian," he said removing her hand from his body. "I've got to go. I'll review the minutes from today's meeting when I return."

"When will that be?" she pointedly asked.

Something in her tone annoyed him, but he let it pass. He didn't need to get into a debate with her again over how he spent his free time. "I'll set up an appointment when it's necessary." He backed away from her and started toward the elevator.

"You know what they say, Ash, about all work and no play," she called after him.

"Jillian, I've never cared what *they* say about anything," he responded. "Have a good day."

He slipped into the elevator and was gone. He was not looking forward to working with Jillian again. Avoiding her had taken ingenuity, guile, and cunning. Traits that were key elements in defense *of* his clients, but not *from* his clients. She was his client, albeit a professional relationship, he wouldn't take it any further than that even if she weren't his client. In the mood he was in, nothing was going to stop him from enjoying a long overdue vacation, not even the ticket on the windshield of his Porsche, compliments of the Portland Police Department.

Chapter 3

"Mr. Marshall, I'm sorry, Sir. We had no word you intended to arrive today and, as I've tried to explain..." the man at the desk nervously pleaded wiping his brow with a white handkerchief, "your reservations were..."

"Get the manager!" Ashton hissed with controlled rage cutting off the distressed man in mid-sentence.

The flustered man audibly gulped, mopping more furiously. "I *am* the manager, Sir."

Ashton narrowed his eyes and steeled his gaze. He leaned dangerously close to the disconcerted man. "You won't be if you don't restore my accommodations! *Now!*"

"Sir," the man pleaded, splaying his hands in supplication.

Ashton's "you're dead meat" expression silenced him.

"Uh, yes, Sir, but, please, Mr. Marshall, you must understand we're booked solid months in advance..." he continued, looking desperate as he tapped keys on the computer's keyboard, "and, if you read the terms and conditions of your reservation, you would know..."

"Who owns this resort?"

"Uh, uh," the man stammered obviously seeing his career in the wonderful location flash before his eyes. "Uh, we do have one suite, but it..."

Ashton held a palm up and the manager hastily found, programmed, and handed an electronic key card to him. "I'll have your luggage brought to your suite, Sir, and room service will deliver a special lunch. The bar in the suite is fully stocked and..."

"Thank you," Ashton grinned. Usually it took one minute or less for Ashton to get whatever he wanted, but this guy had held out for three minutes and thirty seconds. Humph, a record, he thought. Must be losing my touch.

"Sir," the manager called after Ashton as he moved away, "I want to explain ..."

"Don't worry. You can keep your job—for now," Ashton flung over his shoulder as he marched away.

❧ ❧ ❧

Kristen tingled all over as she stepped out of the shower. The sunny, hot day had browned her almond-colored skin to a golden bronze. Before the shower's coolness left her body, she spritzed herself all over with Vanilla Berry cologne and then dusted her body with the matching scented talc. Music, filtering into her suite from a steel band playing somewhere in the distance beyond the veranda outside, caused her to momentarily pause and sway with the music. Catching a glimpse of her powdered bare torso in the surrounding mirrored and marble tiles, she laughed aloud at her naked abandon. She felt like a kid again.

Only one day in the lap of lush green and floral-scented air, cool sprinkling fountains, and sunshine warm days, she felt renewed and revived. She could live this life forever, she thought.

The night before, she danced 'til dawn with some very handsome men who didn't care who she was or what she did for a living. This evening's cabaret promised to be just as enjoyable. To think she had three glorious weeks ahead of her. Life was good. She even giggled; something else she hadn't done since she was a child.

Kristen bent forward from her waist, shook out the water from her shoulder-length, ginger-colored, crinkle-styled hair and patted the rug-sized towel through the springy mass. Righting herself, she looked into the mirror. She would never wear her hair loose and wild like this at home, she mused. With a shake of her head, she smiled because she wasn't at home.

Slipping into a one-piece, gauzy, peach-colored shift, barefooted she padded out of the large bathroom to the elegant bedroom. Pulling her reading glasses and Janice Sims' latest popular romance novel from a bedside table, she tucked the book under her bare arm, raked her fingers through her still damp hair fluffing it out as she left the bedroom, and went to the bar in the open-concept kitchen, dining, and living room combination. All she needed was a wine cooler and then she'd spend the rest of the afternoon on the secluded veranda reading the novel and watching the Pacific Ocean ebb and neap.

She bent from the waist searching for just the right flavor wine cooler in the low refrigerated drink cabinet. Wiggling her bare derriere to the enchanting music, she hummed along poorly, but joyfully, to the island beat. *What a wonderful way to spend a vacation*, she thought.

Initially, Ashton thought he must have still been dreaming as he lay still on one of the sofas catching a catnap. A wide lamp on an end table and a large potted plant had somewhat obscured his view, but the click of a door opening now had him wide awake. The vision that entered the common area from the bedroom on the other side of his suite had to be the most beautiful woman he had ever seen, and he had much with which to compare. This woman made his favorite actress, Halle Barry, look like the Wreck of the Hesperus. The barely-there shift hung listlessly around her hourglass figure and although peach colored, it gave new meaning to the phrase "see through." Full, firm, unbound breasts rode high on her rib cage. Candy Kisses peaked nipples stood at attention. Long, shapely dancer's legs seemed to go on forever and came together at a thinly-haired pubis. A full head of damp, corkscrew-curly hair askew on her head covered nearly a third of her face. Taken together, the sexy package was of a perfection only an artist could have sculpted. The vision was mind-numbing.

Quietly shifting to look over the back of the sofa, his eyes feasted as she bent to the refrigerator and wiggled her butt, but he had paid dearly for his voyeurism. His phallus, enclosed in black swim trunks, was alert and straining for release from its bondage. Something—anything—would have been preferable to the pain now clawing his gut. His blood warmed while he drew a ragged breath.

"Pardon me, but is this some sort of new room service?" he asked. "If so, my compliments to management." When she turned around he initially thought she was the former Miss America turned actress and songstress, Vanessa Lynn Williams, but then he recognized the slight difference because she looked even better than the screen star.

Kristen sharply spun dropping the novel and wine cooler, ready to fight or take flight. Both objects hit the floor with twin thuds. Her disheveled hair fell across one side of her face.

"*What? Who? How did you get in here?*" she sputtered blowing the hair from her face and then swatting at it. She inched toward the door, but then stopped, caught in the mesmerizing gaze of manly perfection. She didn't recognize him as one of the many men she met since coming to the Plaza de Masquerada. She would have remembered such a phine, truly phine specimen.

Warm, whiskey-colored eyes raked over her torso and suddenly heat flushed her face. Her appraisal of the tall, masculine physique standing before her got no less of an appraisal from her. No man had a right to be that handsome or well-built. Her eyes dropped almost imperceptibly to the bulge in his swim trunks before again making the assent through the hairy mass on his concaved abdomen and broad, muscular chest to his drop-dead gorgeous face.

"I should ask you the same question," he said, hands on firm, slim hips, a sly, lopsided grin curling his lips. "When the manager said he'd have housekeeping bring something special for lunch," his eyes washed over her with a gleam brightening his gaze, "the man must have been reading my mind."

"*Lunch?*" she bristled. "I'm not fast food, buster! If you know what's good for you—."

"Oh, yeah," he said, smirking. "I know what's good for me. You're not fast food, baby, you're a seven-course meal. Everything from soup to nuts, pun intended."

Kristen's mouth dropped open, heat flushed her skin. "You get out of my suite right now or I'll call security!" she flashed, pointing an arrow-like finger toward the exit door.

"*Your suite?*" he roared narrowing his brows. "Look, lady, you must have had a little too much sun. This is my suite, and, if you're not bringing me lunch, you'd better find somewhere else to be before I make you my appetizer for dinner."

Kristen's eyes widen in shock. No one had ever spoken to *her* like that! Her mouth again dropped open. The unmitigated *gall* of this intruder was about to make her do something rash!

"*Your suite?* We'll just see about that!" she huffed grabbing for the telephone on the bar. Her eyes never left the Adonis standing arms akimbo looking too smug and too handsome for his own good. When the operator picked up, she triumphantly said. "This is the Belvedere Suite. I have an intruder. Please send security, immediately."

Ashton's eyes mapped the face of the gorgeous woman before him. Her hair still damp, curled madly around her perfect oval face and fell across one eye. Beautiful, light eyes dancing with light, narrow nose, full lips lusciously pulled defiantly into a dimpled jaw. What he wouldn't give to suck crazily on that full, fleshy, bottom lip and see those long lashes brush together in ecstasy. She and the actress, Vanessa Williams, could, indeed, pass for twins. Yet all would end when security arrived, he was confident of that. Nevertheless, after she was ejected from his suite, he'd certainly have to make amends to her over a candle-lit dinner and a magnum of champagne that very night. Instead of making her his appetizer, she'd be his dessert…and what a sweet, tender morsel she would be.

Security arrived and stood in marked appreciation of the fine physique the woman presented as she pointed to the intruder. Something about the three men's jaws dropping open grated on Ashton. He knew what they were thinking—*damn it!* He was thinking the same thing. She was no snack, but a foody connoisseur's delight. Then the beleaguered manager appeared parting the security detail. He nervously stood wringing his hands and dancing from foot to foot until he caught sight of the woman's voluptuous body. The odds were mounting in her favor, Ashton thought, as he moved to swiftly end their malady.

"Put this on," he hissed holding out his short, terrycloth robe.

"I will not!" she spat, then turning her hardened gaze to the manager. "Get this man out of my suite!" she demanded.

The manager cowered under her blazing eyes. "Uh, I can't do that, ma'am," the now flushed manager spoke.

"Then you'll kindly remove this exhibitionist from *my* suite," Ashton interjected.

"Sorry, sir, but I can't do that either."

"*What?*" they both roared in unison.

The manager jumped at the dual, sharp reproach. "I'm sorry, but... you see, ma'am, this suite was reserved by this gentleman and your reservation was considered a standby, but you arrived first and when this gentleman did not arrive on time, we released the entire suite to you, but now he's here and, although he's late, he'd already paid in full for the accommodations. He refused a refund or to accept accommodations gratis at a later date. The terms of the agreement require that the guest notify us if he or she will be delayed at least twenty-four hours before the planned arrival date. He failed to do that, so we thought he wasn't coming. Since we're fully booked, we, well, I mean, I thought since you both have direct access from your bedroom suites and you're both single, that is to say neither of you is here with another person, you could share the common areas—the living room, dining room, kitchen, and lanai—and still maintain your privacy in the separate bedrooms and ensuites. We'll adjust your bill..."

"Unacceptable!" they both spat in unison.

"Look, I will not share this suite with a complete stranger! His failure to arrive before expiration of the agreement between this establishment and him for these accommodations is a failure on his part to fulfill his part of his contract. Therefore, you were free to re-let this suite to me, which you did, and I have accepted your offer. We have a contract. He goes, I stay."

"Pardon me, lady, but there is a grave fallacy in your argument. You see, I reserved this entire suite for the duration and paid for it. Regardless of when I arrived within the allotted four weeks of *my* contract, I was still entitled to this suite. Therefore, you go, I stay."

"Absolutely not!" she raged.

"On the contrary!" he hissed.

"Please, please," the manager tried to interject.

"*Silence!*" they both vehemently spat to him.

"There was a valid agreement in place *before* this imbecile made a mockery of my…" Ashton began.

"Your contract, mister, expired for failure to perform!"

"You never had one, lady!" Ashton interrupted.

"Stop calling me 'lady'!" Kristen retorted.

"I'll call you Lady Godiva if you want, but I don't happen to know your name!"

"You don't need to know it either to settle this! If you were a gentleman, you'd pack up your things and leave this very instant!" she fumed stamping one bare foot in a fit of temper.

"I've been called a number of things in my life, lady, but 'a gentle man' wasn't one of them!"

"Why am I not surprised!"

"Obviously, your surprise is never well hidden," he said languidly running his eyes over her barely veiled, voluptuous body. He noted her cherry-pink colored nipples which caused heat to moisten his flesh. "Neither is your arousal."

"My *what?*" she hissed. "Look, you walking groin, this is my…"

The clink of the door caused them both to go silent, turn and look around the empty common area. The manager and security guards made good their escape and nothing was resolved except neither occupant intended to leave. Both turned on their bare feet and stalked into their respective bedroom suites, slamming their doors behind them in unison.

⚬⚭ ☙ ⚮⚬

Later that evening, Ashton had just lifted the tall, cool libation to his lips when he noticed the woman, his unwanted suitemate, walk down the rock-and-earthen steps toward the cabaret revelers on the beach. He paused in mid-thought as his two female companions continued their mindless chatter. No sooner had her bare legs, sandal-clad feet, and perfectly pedicured and painted toes hit the last step when three young men closed in around her. She smiled at them, he noted, and then accepted one man's apparent request for a dance. She was proudly squired to the dance area. Her floral sarong wrapped around its precious package like a holiday gift. The rim of Ashton's glass finally found his lips, but his eyes pinned his target across the crowded, open-air, dance floor.

An hour later, two more Bahamas Mamas and Ashton had no clue what the women surrounding him, now on three sides, were saying, nor did he care. Listening was his forte. He won cases just by hearing what wasn't said. Now his mind was a boggle and the cold sweat on his brow in the hot, salty, sultry evening air, wasn't helping matters. Nor were the provocative moves of this uninvited suitemate. Her exotic, sensuous, undulating body had him and many other men transfixed, he noted. He never saw a more perfect bottom. She had danced every set with a different man, each one waiting impatiently for the next opportunity to hold her in his arms. He resembled that remark. He hadn't touched her, but his eyes held her in ways the rest of his body wanted to—continuously.

"Mmmm, I like the way you move, KC," Webster crooned in her ear. "Why don't we blow this party and go out to my yacht, The Triple W III?"

Kristen slowly exhaled in total disinterest trying to put some distance between her and a man she was unsuccessfully trying to avoid most of the evening. She stepped back from him, but his arms banded in around her like a cocoon pulling her up close to the hard plane of his body. She could smell the faint odor of liquor on his breath and his sharply abrasive alpine-scented cologne. The salty sweat from his face dripped into her eyes and burned. She had foolishly allowed him to buy a few drinks for her, but she wanted nothing else now but to be rid of him. As soon as the dance was over, she'd make her escape.

"Mmm, you feel soooo good," he said, his voice lusty and low, his hands dipping to her butt. "We should go. My yacht is moored just off shore. We can go skinny dipping and swim out or take the launch. I can't wait to get you out of your clothes and into my bed. I'll bet you're a bitch between the sheets."

That did it! Kristen tried to dislodge herself from him, but he wasn't having it. The more she squirmed to free herself, the tighter he held her laughing lowly, derisively, and sticking his tongue in her ear.

"Let go of me!" she lowly growled so as not to cause a scene.

"Naw, baby, that's not what you want. I'm what you need," he lasciviously crooned while pressing his engorged phallus against her pubis. "*I'm* going to give you what you want tonight and for a long time to come." He clamped a hand on her jaw and fingered her mouth as he tried to kiss her.

Kristen stood statute still, but Webster's hands were all over her. She forcefully pushed against his chest, but he grabbed her hair yanking down and forcing her face up to his liquor-stained lips. She turned her face away again as much as she could, but his mouth was on her neck and shoulder biting down none too gently; hard enough to leave a mark, a branding.

Her movements became more frantic, but it only seemed to serve to heighten his enjoyment of her discomfort. He derisively laughed at her efforts. Slamming his hardened ridge against her and grinding, she couldn't break free of him. *That's what comes of reckless abandon*; her father's voice rang in her thoughts.

"I said, let me go!"

Suddenly, Webster stopped his molestation. His blood-shot, somewhat crazed-looking eyes were fixed, but not on her, Kristen noticed. Something over her shoulder had his near full attention. She could feel his discomfort. His slight release of her gave her an opportunity to put some distance between them, but when she tried to wiggle free, he again pulled her closer than before.

"You heard the lady," came a reproach so quietly sharp it sent a chill up her spine. "Let go of her."

"If I don't?" Webster snorted, meanly.

"You don't want me to answer that question."

"Humph, who the hell are you?"

"Her husband," came the response.

Kristen's eyes widened in disbelief, but she didn't have the space to turn to see who was behind her.

"She's not yours," Webster scathingly laughed. "You've been over on that bar with those—."

"I won't ask again," came the cold-as-steel statement. "You've got five seconds."

Kristen could see the muscles knitting together in Webster's jaw, the rage building in his eyes, and feel the tension growing in his body. When he seemed ready to strike, one deft motion snatched her from his grip and sent Webster to his knees. The action was so swift it didn't register in Kristen's mind until she found herself being spirited away like an errant child. Her feet barely touched the ground.

Ashton had seen enough. For some reason, he noticed the Webster character put something in his suitemate's drink and suspected it was a roofie. When he wordlessly walked away from his female companions on a self-appointed mission, he noted only briefly the women's chatter hung suspended in mid-air. Something unidentifiable, but primal and territorial, propelled him through the crowded dance floor to his suitemate's back. He didn't question his motives or care what it would take to free her. He wouldn't tolerate any woman being drugged or molested. Before the full force of his action had settled on him, he forced her into their suite.

"That was totally uncalled for!" she shakily hissed pulling away from him. "You could have seriously hurt that man! What gave you the right to embarrass me that way? Calling me your wife! How dare—"

"How dare *you* put yourself in a position where the only option was to resort to violence!" His sharp reproach silenced her momentarily.

"I did nothing of the kind!" she tried to recover bobbing and weaving slightly, her words a bit slurred and lacking conviction. "I didn't deserve to be treated that way by him or you!"

"Oh, really? Prancing around in that hot, little, postage stamp you call a dress! Flirting with half the men on the beach and drinking—!"

"I don't drink! …Much," she choked out, her ire at its peak. Still, he was right, she had three Tequila Sunrises and was feeling a buzz and fuzzy. She shouldn't have felt like this after three drinks. Then she remembered Webster had given her the last one. Could she have been roofied? What do they put in those drinks anyway? she wondered. Then her vision suddenly narrowed to oblivion.

Ashton did not hesitate when Kristen tried to spin away from him and then started to fall. He scooped her up momentarily registering her sweet, womanly fragrance. Something akin to a lightning bolt hit him as he held her listless body in his arms. Her face, peaceful and relaxed sent an unmistakable signal to his manhood. If he did not bed a woman soon, he'd explode, but not the seductress he held against his chest. Burning need aside, he never took what was not offered to him freely and openly and he would not start now.

Ashton deposited his bundle in her bed and removed the sandals from her feet. That task completed, he started to turn away, but then stood for one last appraisal. The image was too jarring. He was heading back to the cabaret to resolve the ache in his groin tonight or his name wasn't Thomas Ashton Marshall, III!

⁂

Kristen stirred at the sound of a woman's throaty laugher and then muffled commotion. Her blurry eyes opened to the darkened room. Quiet, romantic music floated on the air. She registered that she was in bed—her bed—but didn't recall how she got there. Then a man's laughter again took her attention away from her confusion. Someone was in the suite. Her mind skidded through the events of the evening and halted at the point where she and her unwanted suitemate stood toe-to-toe a breath away from one another, their eyes locked in visual combat. Then all had gone dark.

Kristen rolled to her side and slowly sat up on the edge of the bed, palming her face. That muscle man made her seem like such a fool! How could she ever show her face in public again? Just because he honestly looked like the former basketball star turned actor Rick Fox, a true God's gift to womankind, he didn't have any right to embarrass her that way, did he? He should have minded his own damn business! Letting those women fawn and paw him all evening! Then treating her as if she had the plague! Oh yes, she noticed him! What red-blooded woman this side of the grave wouldn't notice how that expensive, designer, collarless chambray shirt clung to his body as if it had been painted on and his torso's muscular frame gave his Miami Vice attire life. She had the situation with Webster under control without his intervention…well almost, assuming he hadn't put Rohypnol in her drink. Her brothers and Peter warned her to never accept a drink she had not witnessed being made. In any event, the muscle man didn't have to damn near castrate Webster. Well, she would just tell him a thing or two!

Soft hands smoothed Ashton's bare chest as he sucked on the bottom lip of his evening's companion. Next, his mouth found the pulse in her throat pumping as rapidly as his own. Hot whispered words of encouragement and her nails raking down his chest to his abdomen knotted his brick-hard phallus. This woman knew how to handle a rock. He sucked in a ragged breath as she unzipped his loose-fitting trousers and slipped a hand inside. Her breathless enjoyment of what she found waiting for her heated his blood as he slowly and deliberately relieved her of her garments.

If he could just get the image of that vixen sleeping in the next room out of his mind, he could begin to enjoy more thoroughly the woman in his arms.

He hadn't been successful so far, but the woman bringing him to the height of his sexual arousal was certainly no piker. Her deep-throated moans, as he captured one small breast in his mouth tonguing the nipple to a peak, fired his sex drive. His preference would have been the soft, ample, rounded mounds of a woman, like Sleeping Beauty next door, but the molehill in his hand had not entirely lost its appeal. Anorexic women weren't high on his wish list, but this woman, at least, had skill.

Ashton enjoyed how she skillfully handled his phallus before she rolled the condom into place making it an event. His eyes narrowed to slits as he laid her on the spacious divan. Her knees raised and thighs open in hot welcome to the ecstasy so long denied him for more months than he cared to remember. It would be a long, hot, wet, exotic night. He was prepared to savor every second to a cataclysmic release. The mood was set, the seduction had done its job, and the woman was not only willing and able, but eagerly enticing him. A new millennium kind of woman he appreciated. Slowly, he began to lower himself into position.

SLAM!! went a door. Feet, strong leg, and thigh muscles pushed forcefully against his chest. Ashton found himself being catapulted through the air like a human projectile shot from a cannon. He landed face up, but spread eagle on the floor.

"Uh, excuse me. Should I have knocked?"

No longer engulfed in the heat of passion, Ashton's eyes pinned the scantily-clad vixen triumphantly standing a few feet away. Hands on hips, a devilish grin curling her lips, a saucy tilt to her head, she stood in practiced pose.

"Who are *you?*" his companion demanded standing while covering her nakedness with her hands.

He saw it coming but couldn't gather himself in time to stop it.

"His wife, of course."

"His *wife?*" the woman shrieked.

"Yes," his suitemate demurely sighed. She could have carried the lead role in **Camille** to an Emmy Award. "He does this wherever we go, I'm afraid. Sometimes he makes me watch."

Palms to his face, elbows on his raised knees, Ashton shook his head in frustration. Then getting to his feet, unmindful of his nakedness, he narrowed his eyes to thin slits at the intruder.

"You'll pay for this," he growled.

The word "pervert" uttered by his evening's companion pierced the tense air punctuated with the slap across his face that had him seeing stars.

"Melody, she's lying. I'm not…" the slamming door left his words hanging in the air, "married," he exhaled barely above a whisper.

Melody must have heard that song before and wasn't waiting for the refrain. Ashton's gaze swiveled from the door toward the gleeful countenance of the intruder.

"Why you little…!"

Retribution complete and impending danger stalking toward her, discretion being the better part of valor, and self-preservation upper most in her thoughts, Kristen did the appropriate and honorable thing—she ran. She actually giggled as she slammed her bedroom door shut and locked it a split second before he made good on his threat of justifiable homicide. Feeling triumphant and jubilant, she settled in her bed for a restful night. Or so she thought. Her eyes closed but didn't block out the vision of her suitemate's body in its aroused glory. "*Mercy!*" the word slipping through her lips before sleep claimed her again.

Chapter 4

Who ever said cold showers worked should have been prosecuted, convicted, and sentenced to life in a water-torture prison. Ashton was not coping well with his dilemma, but he had to laugh at himself nonetheless. It was his fault. There he was, fantasizing about his suitemate and conjured her up. Served him right, but oh how good she looked. "Wife," he snorted. "I'd make her a *wife* all right. Teach that show-stopper a thing or two in the process. Prancing around in nearly nothing. Even Stevie Wonder couldn't ignore her!"

Ashton spent one of his worst nights ever. Visions of the vixen invaded his sleep as much, if not more than she invaded his waking hours. That was the second cold shower today and it wasn't even dawn yet. He was up all night before, but it was usually with a woman *in* his bed—or various sundry other prone locations—but never had he spent a night simply *thinking* about a woman in another bed. Certainly not one in the same suite! "Ash, old buddy, there's something seriously wrong with this picture," he growled as he turned the shower to cold full blast.

Later that morning, after going scuba diving, Ashton relaxed on the private veranda that circled one-half of the suite's exterior overlooking the Pacific Ocean. Thanks to his suitemate, who had wisely made herself scarce so far that day, he was snubbed by the available women with whom he made an acquaintance the previous night. News certainly did travel fast at this cozy, private, island resort in the sea. The male population of resort guests, except Webster, congratulated him on his ability to have a wife in residence and still be free to philander with impunity, but

Ashton didn't share their enthusiasm for the joke. Hoping each day's private planes would bring another group of available women, Ashton resigned himself to keeping a low profile for the moment. He contented himself with a lazy, late morning brunch, and author Evelyn Palfrey's latest mystery novel.

⁂

Kristen couldn't fathom why anyone would be playing steel drums at the crack of dawn. Her eyes barely opened when the slashing pain from the sunlight creased her brow. Her mouth felt like cotton on the stalk and her throat felt like sandpaper. Her forearms covered her eyes as she fought for conscious thought. She couldn't do much more than remember her name. Her brain was mush.

When rolling slightly, the pain at the back of her neck stilled her. Had someone hit her in the head with a sledge hammer she couldn't have felt worse. *What have I done?* she chastised herself as she struggled to sit up. No sooner had she straightened her back did her body tilt at a forty-five-degree angle and her head slam back into the pillow. She groaned as the hangover grew in intensity. The more she thought about it, the more she believed Webster had put GHB in her drink. That was the only explanation she could devise for why she felt like this after only three drinks the night before. To her certain knowledge, she had an unusually high tolerance to alcohol.

When finally able to get to her feet, she stumbled into the shower. Even the soft, cool spray of water hurt and her stomach angrily growled. She hadn't eaten anything since noon the preceding day. No wonder she had a monster hangover. It was nearly noon again. "God, if you let me live through this, I promise I'll never do that again," she prayed turning her face to the cooling shower. Heaven knew she would never tell her brothers or Peter how stupid she'd been. As she toweled dry, she noted the bruises Webster inflicted on her body from his rough handling. Damn it! She was hard pressed to admit it, but she owed her suitemate a debt of gratitude!

A light, smörgåsbord brunch was already set up on the veranda when Kristen padded barefoot out of her bedroom. *Now, that's what I consider to be top-notched service,* she thought when she spied the food. She smeared cream cheese over a bagel and added lox; then a cup of fresh island fruit and coffee—black and strong with a tall, ice-cold glass of water to counteract her feeling of dehydration. She seated herself and was about to bite into the bagel when a movement caught the left corner of her peripheral vision.

"Well, good morning, my dear *wife,*" a wickedly low, sarcastic voice called to her.

Feeling totally ashamed of her previous night's behavior and owing an apology, Kristen's eyes skidded toward the voice, the bagel hanging in mid bite.

"Uh, g-good morning," she managed putting down the bagel.

"Like most wives, it seems you don't mind taking from a man without giving something in return."

"Huh?" her brows narrowed in confusion.

"First, you invade my abode, then you eliminate my ability to enjoy my vacation, wreck my reputation, and now you're eating my brunch. Still, I give you fair warning, my dear *wife,* I draw the line at you wearing my Jockey underwear."

"You've had practice with your wives wearing your underwear, I presume?" she asked more smoothly than her aching head and churning stomach would indicate. "Like last night, for example? Funny, I didn't notice your wife-for-the-night wearing any underwear, yours or her own; but then again, I'm just saying. I could be wrong."

"Practice? Oh, last night wasn't *practice,* princess. That was the real deal. Speaking of deals, you owe me."

Kristen's eyes widened, surprised, and in memory. Her father used to call her his princess. What would he think if he saw her at that moment with this Neanderthal? she wondered. She audibly gulped. "Owe you?" she cautiously asked.

"Uh huh, and I intend to collect," he said rising like a cougar stalking its prey.

Kristen couldn't run if her life depended on it, and it did, she surmised, as her stalker towered over her. Again she audibly gulped. "Uh, what is it you think I owe you?"

"Breakfast in bed," he growled.

Another gulp around the large lump in her throat and her eyelids slipped to his midsection and then flew up like window shades. The man was extremely well endowed.

Ashton enjoyed the sight of the blush that warmed the bronze tan of her skin. He intended to take his revenge on her and her response to his aggressive behavior was priceless. He lifted the plate from the table in front of her and the coffee she so carefully poured and re-entered his bedroom suite laughing.

Kristen pursed her lips and buried her face in her hands. She noticed the faint moisture covering her face. This man had the ability to make her sweat. The realization caused a tingle up her spine. Finally, she got up and made another plate of food. Before she settled in to eat, she closely listened and heard the sound of shower water running full blast in his part of the suite.

⚜

"Coming," Ashton called out as he moved to answer the knock at the door.

"Just a moment," Kristen simultaneously called out as she exited her bedroom on the same mission.

Ashton stopped in his tracks when he saw the lacy, white top over a yellow tube, wide bolero skirt hung low off her hips below the navel and tied together with a scarf. Maddeningly attractive and sexy, she was.

"It's for me," she said reaching for the doorknob with the second knock.

"Wait a minute," he said staying her hand on the knob. "Suppose it's for me?"

"I'm expecting someone," she noted.

"So am I," he replied. "After the stunt you pulled last night, I don't need to have a woman opening the door to my suite...especially not one looking like she's about to star in a hula contest."

"If it's my date, you don't exactly look like the butler, either, pal," she noted, openly appraising his European-styled leisurewear that allowed no question about his virility and rugged charms.

Crossing his arms across his ample, broad chest, he perused her body. "All right, what do we do to decide who opens this door?" he asked

"Arm wrestle," she tossed out as she quickly pulled open the door.

A long, low, sultry whistle pierced the air. "Wow, woman, you look good enough to eat and I'm ravenous," Tolliver Bunkley growled, openly appraising her. Then he noticed Ashton wearing a decidedly menacing scowl on his face. "Uh, am I early?"

Kristen smiled. "Thanks for the complement, Tolliver. No, you're not early. He's the butler," she said with a quick nod toward her suitemate. "I'm ready. I just need to switch purses. Please, come in. I'll only be a minute."

Tolliver stepped inside the suite and an awkward moment drew out as Tolliver looked from one face to the other.

"Excuse us, *Tolliver*," Ashton said, while grinning and taking Kristen's forearm to spirit her into her bedroom.

Once inside, Ashton almost held his amusement until the door closed. "Tolliver? You're going out with a man whose name is *Tolliver*?" he asked, unsuccessfully stifling a chuckle.

"What's wrong with *that?*" Kristen bristled.

"Lady, you sure can pick 'em," he said, laughing. "Tolliver?" he roared with laughter.

"Yes, Tolliver!" she fumed. She wanted to stamp her foot like a petulant child, but she refrained. After all, she was a tenured professor and a federal judge, for crissake!

Ashton tried to gather in his glee, but it didn't work. He laughed more.

Kristen rolled her eyes, started emptying her purse, and putting essentials in a smaller bag.

"Tolliver is a very nice name and he's a perfect gentleman, too," she fussed.

"About as charismatic as Dudley Do-right," he snorted.

"Well, who's making your toes curl tonight? Another Tinker Bell?" she quipped.

"Her name was Melody," Ashton sobered. "What do you mean about *my* toes curling? You're not seriously considering letting Dudley Do-wrong in there—."

"His name is Tolliver Bunkley and what I do with him is not your concern—."

"Bunkley? Oh, *please*! Tell me anything but that someone hung a handle on him like *Tolliver Bunkley*. He's got to be using a pseudonym, princess," Ashton roared with laughter again.

Kristen was nonplussed and again recalled her father's "princess" endearment. "I think he's very charming," she primly said. "He's a very good dancer and he kisses…"

That sobered Ashton completely. "Uh-uh, lady. I'm not Kevin Costner and playing bodyguard again tonight, so I suggest you wear something more conservative or stay out of harm's way."

"*Conservative?* Look, buster, I'm free, Black, and well over twenty-one! I wear whatever I please, whether you like it or not!" she flung at him with her nose in the air, "If you don't like it…tough caracas!"

He liked it, all right. The problem was he liked it *too* much. He would have loved it if the vixen was dressing that way for him.

The sight of her pique lightening through him and the thought of her with another man drew daggers from his eyes. He swept her into his arms.

"Oh, I've got your caracas, all right," he said capturing her O-shaped mouth. He knew it was a mistake the moment his mouth touched down on hers. That little bit of showmanship cost him dearly as their bodies seemed to weld together chest to thigh. She was more, much more, than he had expected and far more than he had bargained for. Her needful moan drew him erect as the kiss deepened grabbing his heart and squeezing it.

Kristen felt like she was in a minefield. Sparks were flying, brilliant lights bursting in air, and her mind a jumble of blazing erotica. She was dangerously close to threading her fingers through his hair when he broke the union. Dizzy, she stumbled back, her heart hammering in her chest and her eyes finally focused on the face that held as much shocked surprise as hers must have. He stepped back from her, his chest heaving and their gazes held for a breathless, humming moment. Then he started toward her again and suspecting his intent to ravage her mouth again, she placed a restraining hand on his firm, muscular chest wordlessly holding him off. She felt his heart hammer under her fingertips as rapidly as her own. Backing away from him, she picked up her purse, snatched open the door, and purposefully strode into the living room.

After an unsettling moment of having to reposition himself in his trousers, Ashton followed.

"Tolliver?" she called out looking around the suite and out onto the veranda, but the spaces were empty.

Kristen spun doing a slow burn and glared at Ashton whose amusement erupted into full laughter. Kristen gritted her teeth and spun toward the door snatching it open. A tall, attractive woman stood poised to knock, her wide-eyed surprise softened Kristen's ire and a devilish gleam entered her eyes. Kristen turned, hips swaying like a metronome in motion and slinking her way toward Ashton. Her arms curved around his neck and she purposefully and enticingly brushed her breasts against his chest.

"Sorry I have to go, lover, but you were fantastic…as usual," she cooed planting an earthshattering kiss on Ashton's lips and rubbing her hips against him. "You were worth every dollar." She made a show of stuffing cash in his breast pocket, winked, and slinked toward the woman whose wide eyes were joined by her wide-open mouth. "Don't worry, girlfriend, if you don't have cash, he takes checks and American Express. He even has a Square. Promise him a big tip and he'll…well, I'll let you find that out," she smiled batting her eyes and puckering her lips at Ashton's scowl. "Same time tomorrow or should I call for an appointment?" she grinned. She didn't wait for a response.

As soon as Kristen closed the door, she heard the shrilled words *"You cad! You Gigolo! You dog!"* and then the piercing slap. Kristen laughed, but her glee was tempered by the lingering taste of his mouth on hers. Only meant as retribution for his despicable behavior toward Tolliver, she had to admit to herself his kiss had tilted her universe. "Dangerous," she whispered to herself shaking her head as she went in a half-hearted search for Tolliver Bunkley.

Another cold shower was not working any better than the others had. The vixen had struck again and this time with a vengeance. If he still had half a mind left after she kissed him, assaulted him with her body, and left him slowly turning in the wind, he would have taken her right then and there! What she had done to him was no laughing matter. It bordered on criminal behavior. Like a chameleon, she changed on him before his unbelieving eyes and he could see the wheels turning in her sultry behavior as soon as Maribelle's face came into view. She's swift, he had to admit. The vixen really could think on her feet…and look shit sharp doing it, too!

Ashton stroked his sore jaw where Maribelle had clocked him. His love life was now clearly going to be nonexistent and rated "General Audiences" if he didn't make peace, instead of war, with his suitemate. Making love with her was a much more enjoyable thought though.

Chapter 5

"We should take advantage of this sovereign state, KC, and jump the broom," Dexter Morgan crooned, kissing her on one of her bare shoulders as they sat on the sandy beach watching an authentic island wedding being performed. The Pacific Island ceremony was beautiful in its simplicity.

Kristen laughed, but no way was she going to hitch herself to Dexter Morgan. Not even in her wildest nightmares. She had seen his type too many times before. Wealthy, devilishly handsome, in-comprehensibly appealing…and he knew it. Trifling, she thought, as she noted Webster's malevolent stare from across the campfire. Since his encounter with her suitemate, he kept his distance from her, but she knew he was continuously watching her. He seemed to be lurking, awaiting an opportunity to get her alone. It wasn't a good feeling and it wasn't going to happen. If she was correct and he had spiked her drink, she would not let him catch her alone or unaware again.

She also noticed how Dexter surreptitiously eyed other women while professing an interest in her. Strickland Briggs taught her a valuable lesson: Keep your eyes open. She turned her attention to her suitemate who was lounging with his back to another woman's breasts while the woman stroked his chest. That woman must have been deaf, dumb, and blind not to have heard all the whispered comments about him, Kristen thought gritting her teeth. Surely, she would never act so blatantly with a man she barely knew. Just because his prone body looked like an invitation to ecstasy didn't mean she had to accept it, but oh what a wonderful thought!

Kristen's gaze lingered too long and became too revealing. She knew she was in trouble when her eyes traced the masculine lines of her suitemate's bare physique from his bare feet to his head and met his gaze. Their eyes held for a flicker of a second. She quickly turned her head back to the tribal wedding ceremony but felt her suitemate's eyes heating her to her core.

"Hey, KC, you and that guy over there got something going on?" Dexter asked nodding toward her suitemate.

"What guy?" she innocently asked. At first, she thought he was referring to Webster who hadn't taken his eyes off her.

"The other one who's been checking you out all evening."

"Hadn't noticed anyone paying attention to me and that includes you, Dexter," she said and knowingly smiled.

His pretty green eyes and shit-eating grin widened. "Oh, I've been looking at you, all right, darlin', but the rap around this little island is you're unavailable."

"Oh, and where did you hear that?"

"Men talk, too, ya know."

"Gee, and I thought they only wrote numbers and scores on the men's bathroom wall, like juveniles," she quipped still watching the native tribal priest tie seaweed around a couple's wrists, binding them together in matrimony.

"Mumph, that's a scary thought," Dexter said, changing the subject. "All the priest has to do on this island is tie that seaweed around their wrists, give them a certificate signed on tapa, and they're hitched for life. No prenuptial agreement or anything."

"It fits the culture of these Pacific Islands. It's beautiful in its simplicity," she said more interested in how the couple looked at each other. Their youthful, scantily-clad, sun-bronzed bodies would become one as soon as the ceremony ended, she knew.

"Well, I'd have to, at least, have a prenup. Just to keep the business straight when things went wrong," Dexter intruded on her enjoyment of the ceremony.

"Prenuptial agreements are no barrier against property issues…"

"Humph, you sound like my lawyer did when I divorced my last wife."

Kristen turned her head to look at Dexter. "Your *last* wife? How many have there been?"

"Only four," he said and grinned at her before placing another kiss on her bare shoulder. "I like being married."

"Obviously, since you keep doing it," Kristen quipped.

"I like the honeymoon part," he grinned, again kissing her on her neck. "Want to try it? I hear you can get married at one of these ceremonies without a marriage license."

"Thanks for the marriage proposal, Dexter, but I'm not that brave," she said, snorting.

Ashton was about two seconds off of sending the local orthodontist a new patient. He watched with gritted teeth as that jerk, Dexter Morgan, planted kisses on his suitemate's bronze, bare shoulder and neck. Even Lola's fingers gliding up and down his chest, as they sat on the sand watching the wedding ceremony, didn't distract him. What did distract him was the kiss. Not from Lola or the one Dexter planted, but the one his suitemate planted on him three days ago. Her kiss was potent enough to wake the dead. Ashton shivered from the recollection.

"Cold, baby?" Lola crooned at his ear capturing his earlobe between her teeth.

Ashton barely noticed. His attention riveted on the vixen directly across from him on the other side of the wedding ceremony.

Ashton shifted to lift his back from Lola's chest.

Her arms possessively clamped around him. "Where are you going, baby?"

"To see a man about a dog," he said between gritted teeth.

Lola was nonplussed. For some reason he did not analyze, Ashton was uninterested in Lola or any other woman at the resort. Only one woman had his undivided attention and he simply couldn't stand to see her with another man. Abruptly, he rose and left the beach without looking back. He needed a dip in the pool to cool himself off and a stiff drink.

Every night was a cabaret. This night it was on the beach again. Food, fun, and frolic were the order of the evening. Night volleyball, midnight skinny dipping, limbo dancing, and other activities had the young, single men and women at the resort engrossed in one activity or another. Kristen, thoroughly enjoying her vacation, successfully shimmied under the limbo stick several times. Each time the stick was set a degree lower. Her agile body was one of the few to make it to the last rung. She gaily laughed as two other people matched her movements and the live music from a steel band heightened their enjoyment of the game.

What didn't go unnoticed, however, was the tall, muscular, sleek frame of her suitemate as he played volleyball in wet swimming briefs—very brief. She unconsciously licked her lips and then tucked them inside of her mouth when his body stretched full length to spike the ball. She almost missed her turn under the limbo stick as he successfully scored another point.

Not a thin man, but thick, muscular, and very athletic. Big hands, big feet, she thought registering the thick corded thighs, calves, and... mumph! Her eyes slid down his torso to his midsection. Big everything.

He had a competitive edge about him, she also noticed. Even in the friendly sport he played hard, enthusiastically encouraging his teammates. She also noted the women playing the game with him seemed to need more of his brand of encouragement. They purred and cooed, flapping their eyelids so much they might have raised a sand storm in Japan.

Humph, she thought, *guess he'll score again tonight in more ways than one.*

Ashton had to expend his energies somehow. The sight of his suitemate shimmying under a limbo stick was jarring. He was ready to switch sides in the volleyball match just so he could play with his back to her. Anything was preferable to the sight of her voluptuous body. The neon, hot-pink bikini she wore against her sun-bronzed skin was no wider than dental floss. And those long legs and sculptured thighs! What he wouldn't give to have them clamped around his back tonight!

Give me strength!

As the evening closed in around them and the hour grew late, Ashton noted how that character Webster kept edging himself nearer to his suitemate. Something about Webster made Ashton uncomfortable, so he made a point to position himself beside his suitemate near one of the many campfires along the beach. From this position he could also keep an eye on Webster.

"Does my wife have a name?" he asked sitting sideways to her on the sand with his legs stretched out behind her.

Kristen pulled her legs to her chest and wrapped her arms around them. "I wouldn't know," she said, laughing. "Which one is she tonight? Point her out or give me her telephone number. I'll call her and ask her for you. I can be discrete though. I won't mention you have a harem."

Ashton smiled and shook his head. "Does everyone have this much trouble getting to know you or is it just me?"

"I'd say you know me better than most considering we're virtually living together, dear husband," she said, laughing.

"Good, then I'd like to call a truce, dear wife."

"A truce? Were we at war?"

"No, I surrendered like most obedient husbands who believe happy wife, happy life," he said and laughed. "Now, I'm Ash to my friends," he said extending his hand.

"To your enemies?"

"Ash," he said. "We won't be adversaries anymore, of that I'm sure. We're beyond that now. With a little work, we can even learn to live in peaceful cohabitation. Now, do I continue to call you 'lady' or are you going to give me your name?"

"KC," she said taking his hand and shaking it. His hand was warm and soft much like the way he was making her feel. That was different, she thought. Usually she didn't have much of a reaction to meeting men, but he enlivened her when he released an earth-shattering smile.

She had a confidence about her he liked; something akin to the strong women who he called mother and grandmother. He had known many women, but a woman with inner strength appealed to him on a level in above sexual. KC was the type of woman he would take home to meet the family just to announce the engagement and wedding date. Now that *was* a novel thought. He hadn't found anyone he thought he wanted to make Mrs. Thomas Ashton Marshall, III, but as they talked, KC, with her clean, crisp, clear smile, lightning-fast wit, utterly charming humor, and guileless demeanor, was shaping up for a starring role.

"Is KC your real name or a pseudonym?" he asked studying her beautiful face and profusion of shiny, butterscotch-colored, corkscrew curls.

"A name my friends call me."

"I see. So, we're going to stick to the resort credo of not revealing who we are or what we do?"

"That's what Plaza de Masquerada stands for, isn't it? The Place of Masks. Here you're not obligated to divulge more about yourself than you want to."

"This little island paradise does have its charms and very charming women."

"And me," she added with a broad smile. Kristen wasn't leery of the genuinely warm, sensitive man who she found positively awe inspiring. In fact, she knew, despite his good looks and charm, he was not pretentious or posturing for effect.

"Careful, my dear wife, you've already charmed most of the men on this island. I could be the jealous-husband type, you know?"

"I seriously doubt that. In fact, I doubt you'd feel insecure about anything you did."

"Now you're really pushing the envelope," he said, laughing.

"No, not really. You know, it's funny, but I like you," she said frankly enjoying his company and their easy repartee. "Over the last two weeks, you've taken a lot of intrusions on your privacy from me, but you've been very good-natured about it. You also deserve my thanks for getting me out of a sticky situation with that Webster character."

Ashton laughed enjoying the sound of her voice and her enchanting manner. "Aside from your difficulty with Webster, you were having so much fun at my expense; I couldn't deny you the vacation you obviously needed."

"Was I that obvious?" she asked without guile.

"I'm very observant. Probably not many people notice how desperate others are to let loose and enjoy themselves, but I've noticed you. You dance like a professional with such energy and zest, but like someone who loves the art; not someone who works at the art. Your style is somehow familiar. I've seen it before, I believe."

"You know, you're not only very observant, you're very perceptive. I do love the art form." For a moment she wondered whether he had seen her mother perform. She and her mother had similar styles and body size. They even looked alike. Although much more fair-skinned, her French Canadian-born mother had often been mistaken for the actress Vanessa Lynn Williams. However, Ash didn't look quite old enough to recognize the resemblance between her and her mother, so she relaxed. Her mother retired from the stage when Clarence, Jr., her oldest brother, was born more than thirty-five years ago. She guessed Ash was around that age himself. So, he had to have seen her mother's movies and/or shows to recognize her style. If he recognized her mother's unique dance technique, that knowledge would lead unswervingly to her identity.

"It shows." Ashton couldn't remember the last time he enjoyed having a conversation with a beautiful woman who was without pretense or posturing. Nor could he remember wanting a woman more than he wanted KC. Sex with her, however, wasn't the overriding factor. He wanted to know her. What made her happy? What made her sad? What was her favorite food or color? It didn't matter what she did professionally or who her family was. It only mattered that she was unattached and he liked her regardless of who she was or what she did. Instinctively, he knew they would, at least, become good friends, and at most, the possibilities were endless and mind-numbing.

As with every previous night, couples who wanted to take part in an island wedding ceremony stood waiting for the tribal priest to join them together. Once the ceremony was completed, young people dressed in scant native costumes entertained the couples. Their agile bodies performed in sync for the guests sitting in a wide circle on the beach. The music was hot, rhythmic, and enticing.

One young man in his teens pulled Kristen to her feet and started seductively gyrating his torso around her. Other young men did the same with the female guests, while young island women pulled male guests to their feet. Though she protested, laughing, it didn't take Kristen long to mimic the rhythm of his steps and hula body movements. She added a little more double-timing her movements and becoming more erotic and urged on by the crowd. She was so good at her deft movements, the young people began to imitate her seductive style—her mother's style—and suddenly she was the center of attention...and she loved it.

Her mother was a great professional dancer, revered, and world-renowned. As a child, Kristen was an eager student studying all forms of dance, including modern, jazz, and classical ballet. After her mother's untimely death, Kristen sacrificed the career as a dancer she wanted all of her life and bowed to her father's will to go into the law as did her older brothers. It wasn't that she didn't love the law or being a professor and an attorney or judge, it was that she loved dancing more.

Kristen let herself feel the movement, the music, the enchantment of the soft, salt sea air, moonlight, and stars and the encouraging crowd which swept her to a place where not only her mind and body danced, but also her soul and her imagination. The soft-as-sugar sand under her bare feet gave spring to her steps, the steel band gave life to her body, and the look on Ashton's face gave fever to her blood.

Never had any woman so totally captivated and entranced him as did the vision who danced in the firelight surrounded by young adults. She was at one with the mood and music. Her body moved as if boneless, twisting, gyrating, stretching in a harmony unmatched on the professional stage, yet something in his memory said he knew her. Her hands were graceful, imparting the meaning of the music.

Absently, Ashton wondered whether she was a member of the Alvin Ailey Dancers or the Dance Theatre of Harlem or a diva on holiday from some other world-renowned dance troupe. From her voice, he believed her to be an American, perhaps from somewhere in the mid-west. For the moment, however, all he could do was watch in rapt attention. His body could feel every movement as if she resided in his soul. Every tilt or rapid gyration of her perfect, luscious hips pulled hard at his groin.

She moved toward him swaying her hips in a manner that called up her African roots, Spanish definition, and Hawaiian erotica. She was every woman. Incomparable. Ashton let out a breath he didn't realize had lodged in his chest. The air closed in around him, the music faded from his conscious thought, and the crowd was nonexistent. His vision narrowed. All he heard, felt or saw was the woman before him—KC. In that instant something in him—call it fate, destiny, or kismet—told him she was *The One*. She was not just any woman, not every woman. She was *his* woman. The woman he was meant to spend the rest of his life with.

KC didn't know or understand why her body chose that night to play out every erotic fantasy she had ever dreamed or learned, but she didn't care. She loved it. Seeing the darkening, fixed stare in Ash's smoldering gaze bolstered her confidence and she danced with reckless abandon only for him. Never before had she moved so sensuously or enjoyed it more. Nor had any man ever looked at her the way Ash looked at her as she danced and held his undivided attention.

They were communicating on a level beyond the sexual as if their souls came together and became one. He stood up, not breaking eye contact, and slowly moved toward her as if drawn by some invisible tether.

The intimacy in their locked gazes was mind-numbing and palpable. They made love to each other only with their eyes, but it was the most satisfying union either of them had ever experienced.

The music ended. They stood a breath apart, their eyes still locked, searching the depth of their souls. Kristen's heaving chest rose and fell; a light sheen of moisture covered her body. The ocean breeze cooled her to the point where she trembled. Ash moved to take her mouth with his when suddenly she was snatched from him by the adoration of the crowd. He was so painfully aroused he could barely move from the spot where they had stood nearly chest to breast. When the crowd engulfed her, he shook his head as if coming out of a dream or a trance into reality. She was no dream though. She was flesh and blood. A woman, who had, in the space of a few weeks, captured his heart, mind, body, and soul. His spirit danced with hers to an age-old rhythm. He let her adoring fans express their adulation. He would have the rest of his life to love her.

From that night on, Ash and KC spent their time together, often alone together, and rarely with others. They were inseparable. They went parasailing over the deep blue water, water skiing, scuba diving, and golfing. Long private walks along the beach, intimate, candlelight meals on their lanai, hiking in the lush, hilly terrain, sailing a skipjack to a secluded alcove on the windward side of the island, and sunning on the sand. Neither one had talked about their families, background or what they did professionally. It seemed to fit their easy friendship not to delve too deeply into each other's lives. Yet, they pined to know everything about the other. Their comfort level with each other grew and soon they were so attuned to each other, they were completing the other's thoughts on a wide variety of subjects, but the law was something neither raised as a topic of discussion.

One night, as they sat with a group who was having a lively conversation, Ash heard the music turn to something low and plaintive. He smiled at the group but leaned close to Kristen.

"May I have this dance, KC?" he asked.

Kristen slightly smiled and wordlessly rose from her seat. She glided into his arms and moved to the sultry sound. In her high-heel sandals, her forehead was at his chin as they moved around the dance floor in perfect harmony. Their bodies in perfect symmetry. He released her hand and placed both of his around her waist pulling her closer into his embrace. Her free hand floated up around his neck and joined her fingers together at his nape. His hair was curly, soft, and wavy. Kristen didn't know or care why she felt so drawn to this man. Her body melted into his so perfectly she lost all sense of reason. No longer was she Kristen Catherine Bryant, Judge of the US Federal Court of Appeals. Tonight, she was a woman in need of a man. Before the number ended, they left the dance floor.

"I'm not so sure this is a good idea," KC sucked in through clenched teeth as Ash's mesmerizing eyes looked at her.

"You're right," he said, desire clear in his gaze.

"You know, people will talk because we left the party so early," she half-heartedly commented.

"Two in the morning isn't that early," he said, his brows drawn together. "Of course, we do have to keep up appearances."

"You're right. However, people would talk no matter what we do or say," she declared.

"We're already the source of a lot of speculation. Still, we don't have to talk to them anyway. Why isn't this a good idea?" he asked.

"I need you so badly I might not be able to hold out for the long haul," she admitted.

"We managed for nearly three weeks," he offered.

"Good point," she agreed.

Throughout the conversation, KC and Ash were disrobing each other and savoring every moment of discovery between kisses. Finally, their nude bodies slammed together. Later, after several simultaneous cataclysmic eruptions, Ash exhaled in her ear. "Now that you've had your way with me, will you marry me?"

KC laughed and Ash joined her.

Chapter 6

Constantina "Tina" Justice elbowed Cheryl Lawrence in the ribs in an exaggerated manner. "Isn't that Judge Kristen Catherine Bryant?" Tina asked in a loud, stage whisper. "Or is that one of those famous fashion models?"

With one finger, Cheryl pulled her fashionable sunshades down to the end of her nose, peered over the top rim while smacking her chewing gum in an energetic fashion, then drawled, "Naw, de judge, she don't be glowing like that!"

"Yeah, you're probably right. Must be this hazy, hot, humid DC air. Maybe she missed her flight."

"Nah, not de judge. She don't be missin' noffin'."

Kristen saddled up to the limousine where two of her best friends since birth, Constantina "Tina" Justice and Cheryl Lawrence, lazily leaned against the hood of the car. Kristen heard their teasing remarks as she approached them and knew what she was in for. She struck a pose, arms akimbo and shifted her weight to one leg. She casually looked from side to side seeming to ignore them.

"You know, you 'ladies of the night' could get arrested for turning tricks in front of Dulles Airport in broad daylight," Kristen distantly commented.

Tina's and Cheryl's heads slowly swiveled, but dramatically, toward each other.

"Did you hear what that heffa said?" Tina asked Cheryl.

"Yeah, I heard, but she said it with class," Cheryl answered.

"You know, you ladies, correction, *hussies*, should give up the law and take that act on the road. You've got jokes."

Tina said, gyrating her head on her neck. "Probably make more moolah than we're gittin' with our current GS-level, nine-to-five gig. I've got needs."

Both women turned their cool appraising gazes on Kristen and looked her from the bottom up, sucked their teeth, and then rolled their eyes. Their cool appraisals of each other soon broke into slight grins, then full smiles, and then uproars as they group hugged each other.

"You two are sick puppies, ya know," Kristen said and warmly laughed.

"Yeah, but we're *your* sick puppies. If you hadn't brought us here to this bastion of male testosterone and fertility, you could have gotten rid of us. Not anymore. You're stuck with us," Tina said around a decidedly unladylike snort.

Tina, Cheryl, and Kristen had been best friends since long before adolescence pimpled their skins. All three going to the same private schools, then Spelman College together, law schools in different parts of the country, but remaining best friends. Before encouraging KC to run for the federal judgeship, Tina was a senior law clerk for an Illinois State Supreme Court Judge while Cheryl was Junior Counsel on the Ohio Senate Ethics Committee. Both Tina and Cheryl were highly-respected attorneys who could have had any position in public service or private practice they wanted. Young, energetic, and idealist, both gave up their jobs, lobbied for KC's appointment to the federal bench, and then agreed to clerk for her.

"I don't know why you look so radiant, KC, but I could use some of it," Cheryl commented. "Just where did you go on this secret getaway of yours?"

Kristen almost blushed at the remark thinking about the passion-filled night she had spent with her suitemate locked in lovemaking that rivaled the birth of the universe. At least it felt that way to her. Still, what did she know? She hadn't had a lot of experience with which to compare. A few crushes in college and law school and then an ill-fated relationship with Strickland Briggs, but no man made her body hum with desire… until Ash accomplished that miracle. He was appropriately named, she thought. He made her body burn to ashes. He had actually wrung tears of joy from her eyes and untold satisfaction for her love-starved body. He was definitely experienced at lovemaking. That was what those women were after him for she now knew. Fleeting intimacy didn't a relationship make, she cautioned herself. It was only a brief fling. A roll in the hay. A one-night stand. He was probably making some other woman's toes curl at that very moment having counted her among his many conquests. It hadn't been so simple for her to kiss and leave, but the thought of watching him seduce other women had her heart in a vice. She could not stay and watch that happen.

"All right, KC, who is he?" Cheryl asked when Kristen brought herself back to the present.

Who was he indeed? Kristen wondered to herself. They had made love with wild, lightening-hot abandon, even pledging…she didn't want to think about that bit of insanity. It was entirely too painful. All she knew about him was the name "Ash". Not even whether that was his first, middle or last name or even a pseudonym. Plaza de Masquerada kept its clienteles' identities a secret and, for that, considering her uncharacteristically lusty behavior, she was grateful. Now her task was to forget that mind-blowing experience and move on with her life. Easier said than done.

Kristen struggled back from her erotic vision, leaving Ash to her secret memories. Leaving him in bed in the predawn hours before he awoke was one of the hardest things she ever did. However, getting away from that Webster character was a godsend. She was convinced he had spiked her drink and warned the resort management before she left the island. He had a creep factor that made her uncomfortable, but his yacht, The Triple W III, wasn't in sight among the other sleek vessels when she left the island.

"He who?" she absently answered her friend.

"Don't give me that 'he who' bull, KC. I've been around. I've never seen your eyes sparkle like they are right now, and you've got this funny faraway look about you."

"Maybe one of us ought to see an optometrist," she said finding the countryside of greater interest through the darkened limousine window as the chauffeur drove toward the city.

"This heffa isn't going to tell us who hung her moon?" Cheryl asked.

"Mum-hum, she be tryin' to play us," Tina intoned in the vernacular she slipped into and out of easily. "Ain't gonna be that way, my sistah. We gonna get the 411. Sooner or later, KC, we're gonna hear about this brother or my name ain't what it is."

Kristen shrugged. "Nothing to tell."

"Right," Tina and Cheryl facetiously said in unison.

"Still, we do have something to tell you, KC," Tina said on a more serious note.

Kristen's head turned from the window toward her two friends and looked from face to face.

"What is it?" she asked.

"Well," Cheryl began with a deep sigh, "while we were at your old office arranging to ship your things from Chicago to DC, Strickland Legend-In-His-Own-Mind Briggs, Esquire, showed up looking for you. Said he wanted you two back together and wanted us to tell him where you were. Tina told brotherman that we didn't know where you were, but that, even if we did, we wouldn't tell him."

"Strickland was looking for me?" KC asked in disbelief. Her friends nodded in the affirmative. "That's crazy."

"That's what the man said," Tina confirmed, "and he was serious as a heart attack. He was thoroughly pissed off he couldn't find you. Apparently, he was making plans to join you on your vacation."

"Everyone knows he's seeing what's-her-name, the model, Shannon. You must have misunderstood what he wanted."

"Not likely. He made the record clear. He wants you back."

Back for what? she wondered. She didn't love him and he knew it. Why would he want to go back to something that didn't exist?

People stopped Kristen in the halls of the grand old court house building on Constitution Avenue in Washington, DC, to offer their congratulations. Everyone from the security guards to high-priced lawyers shook her hand as she tried to make her way to her new office. Her progress was slow, but she finally reached her chambers with the high, wide, double mahogany doors and fingered the gold plate affixed to the wall.

Judge K. Catherine Bryant, it read.

Well, she thought with a deep sigh, *there's no turning back now,* although she desperately wanted to turn around, board an Adventurer Executive Air flight back to the Pacific Island paradise of Plaza de Masquerada. Back to Ash, whoever he was. Back to the arms of a man who she barely knew, but with whom she had shared something so magical, so wonderful, so precious the thought of him constricted the muscles in her flat abdomen and squeezed her heart.

She could have gone on loving him for a lifetime, but it would not and could not be. Her life was moving in another direction with no room for love and certainly not for lust. As the cold, hard, gold, metal plate proclaimed, she was Judge Kristen Catherine Bryant, newest member of the U.S. Federal Appellate Court for the District of Columbia Circuit; a court that sits just below the US Supreme Court. Ninety-four US district courts report up to one of thirteen courts of appeal. Her job, as one of three appellate court judges, would be among the most difficult tasks she took on in her career. In her new role, she was no longer the woman who did the Dance of the Seven Veils for the stranger, Ash.

Flanked by Cheryl and Tina, Kristen opened the doors and all commotion in the office ceased. Awed eyes raked over her in awkward silence. Eleven people in the outer chamber seemed to all hold their collective breath.

"Good morning," Kristen said and smiled.

"Good morning," her staff tentatively answered.

She glanced around the too-still room at faces she had known for many years, and some new ones, but her smile grew brighter when her Chief of Staff, Peter Brock, Esquire, approached her.

"You look…radiant, Judge Bryant," he said with what she believed was a curious expression on his handsome, pecan-brown face and wavy, close cut, dark-brown hair. "Simply beautiful, Your Honor. Welcome to Washington."

He took her leather briefcase from her hand and guided her to the next chamber. Tina and Cheryl moved toward their own offices adjacent to the stately reception area.

"Obviously, it was a good vacation," Pete remarked as he closed the door. "Meet anyone interesting?" he asked.

Kristen curiously eyed him. "Most people would first ask where I've been, how was the weather or the accommodations or the food, so why did you ask who I may have met?"

"A. If any of the above was distasteful, you would not have stayed. B. You wouldn't tell me or anyone else where you were going before you left, so I don't expect you to tell anyone, including me, now where you've been. C. You look marvelous, like a happy bride on her wedding day; and D. It had to be the company you kept on this hideaway vacation considering the fact that you just got off a very long flight, several days early." His eyes washed over her.

Kristen was nearly struck dumb by his insight, but she quickly recovered to camouflage her physical demeanor lest Pete realize how close he had come to the truth she fought so hard to hide.

"This time, my dear friend, your usually astute, deductive reasoning has led you in the wrong direction," she lied. She never did it with Pete before and it hurt her that she couldn't share her happiness and her heartbreak with her closest friends. Still, unknowingly, his reasoning had hit the mark. Her heart constricted as Peter's face first masked with confusion and disbelief and then dissolved into an unreadable façade. He let her hand drop from his and folded his arms across his broad, strong chest. He nodded toward her closed office door.

"He's waiting for you, KC," Pete quietly said.

"Father? He's here?" she incredulously asked.

Pete nodded. "You'd better go in. He's been here waiting for several hours."

"How did he find out I was coming back today? I only called Cheryl and Tina yesterday to tell them about my change in plans. I was at the airport when I called."

"Your father has been in town for a few days making the rounds of people he knows on the social scene. Remember, he graduated from Howard University and the law school. He has quite a few friends in this town. He was in your chambers every day scrutinizing your staff and organizing your schedule."

"That's your job, not his," she fussed.

"Nevertheless, when he arrived today he asked where Tina and Cheryl were. One of the assistants told him they went to the airport to meet you."

Still she couldn't read Peter's expression, but now she understood the reason for her staff's tentative behavior. Her father intimidated most people even if he wasn't presiding over a trial. She moved toward the large carved mahogany doors and was almost tempted to knock. She did so many times before whenever she entered her father's study at home in Chicago. She shook off the thought. After all, it was *her* office, not his study. She was no longer a child, but a woman. An Appellate Court Judge. She deeply inhaled, briefly closed her eyes, and regally raised her head. Shoulders back, head up, she pressed against the door and entered the well-appointed, inner chamber which would be her office for the duration.

"Father," she acknowledged as she walked to her desk, found her seat, and put her purse in the bottom drawer. She picked up a few telephone messages and smiled at the one from her friend, Vivian Alexander Montgomery. Then she checked her calendar inking in the place, date, and time Vivian suggested. She would add the engagement to her electronic calendar after she finished reviewing the more pressing matters on her schedule.

When her father did not turn from the window, she looked up from her calendar at his broad shoulders, lean figure, and stiff stance. With his hands laced together at his back, she felt like a child waiting for him to scold her for some infraction of his unyielding code of responsibility, behavior, and ethics. She wanted nothing more than for him to turn, open his powerful arms to her, and beckon her into his embrace. Yet, why should she want or even need that now? He had not held her in that way in more years than she could remember.

When she was a child, he was so warm, so loving. He would prop her on his knee and tell her silly stories to make her laugh. Or he would read to her or tickle or tease her. Mother would chide him for spoiling his little "princess" and he would have agreed and spoiled her more.

Still, the warmth left him when her mother died. Now where her father was caring, he was calculating. Where he was warm, he was cold and distant. Where he had smiled, he now frowned. Loneliness, the pain of losing his wife, and anger at the manner in which she died, Kristen surmised, changed him. No one in their family or among their close friends recovered from the woeful absence left in their lives when Lydia Martine Booth Bryant died by random gunshot, but though the pain had been experienced by them all, it had never been shared.

"Father?" she asked again.

Clarence Bryant's eyes surveyed the picturesque landscape that was Washington, DC, but he saw nothing to delight him. It was a city of much beauty, but not for him. He had once lived there in college at Howard University and in Howard's Law School on the Dumbarton Campus. He had rich and lasting memories of meetings the first woman he ever loved while they matriculated through undergrad and law school together. He never forgot his first love even after he met and married the young, Canadian, prima ballerina Lydia Martine Booth. He worked summers in the Washington, DC, metropolitan area and knew the political landscape well. Scandals lurked behind the white, pillared façades, but his daughter's name would never be whispered in shame...not if he had anything to do with it.

"Kristen Catherine, your recent behavior is unacceptable and I will tolerate no more!" He turned to see her stunned expression. "No more! Do you understand me?"

Chapter 1

Ashton whipped into his office not even acknowledging the chorus of greetings that followed him from the moment the parking attendant took his car to the point when he slammed his office door in his executive assistant's face.

He snatched the cordless telephone from its cradle, punched in two numbers as he paced the floor.

"Get in here, *now!*" he roared.

Not waiting, he dialed another number.

"I want to know who owns Plaza de Masquerada, how much they want for it, and what day this week we can close the deal!" he barked.

Again, not waiting for a response, he called another number.

"Girard, get the CEO of Adventurer Executive Airlines on the line, pronto!" he demanded.

He tossed the telephone onto the glove-soft, gray, leather sofa across the well-appointed room, dug his hands into his pockets, and continued to pace.

"*Where the hell is she?*" he bit out to the expansive, empty office.

A knock on the door and it opened. Slade Richardson wordlessly stepped in. He took a seat crossing his right ankle over his left knee and casually laced his fingers behind his head. Slade, the epitome of patience, had seen Ashton, his boyhood best friend, in various states of agitation. It was a familiar behavior pattern Ash used to clear his mind and plot his strategy. Ashton was always at his best when under pressure. It never failed to work to their benefit. In Slade's view, Ashton was one of the best, most brilliant civil litigation attorneys in the country and a master at international mediation law.

Always together in many places throughout the world, Slade and Ashton pulled off some minor and major miracles for their clients. Though their careers were vastly different leading to this point in their lives, Ashton's and Slade's thoughts and positions on many issues were attuned. They were closer than brothers and read each other like yesterday's news.

It was not difficult for Slade, Code Name: Cobra Kahn, to surface leaving his invisible life with a super-secret organization; a secret entity created by the nations who constitute the G8; France, Germany Italy, Japan, the United Kingdom, Canada, Russia, and America. The President of the United States, no matter who that person is, holds the secret leadership role for twenty-five years. The sole purpose of the unit is to secure peace worldwide within that time frame—by any means necessary. When the goal is achieved, all nations will disband their military forces and weapon systems and then the task is over. A small unit would be formed to police the nations and assure no other aggression occurs.

When his friend and mentor, Delta Dawn, decided to leave, Slade also left. These days, Slade was an outlier; someone called back into The Nursery, The Nations United in Security and the World Security Network when the need arose, but otherwise lived a public life.

Ashton came looking for Slade and found him at a most inopportune moment, holed up with a very seductive and willing woman in a secluded chalet in the snow-filled Jura Mountains of France. Ashton asked Slade to head the law firm's Security and Investigations Division for a salary reaching high into the six-figure range. Actually, it wasn't a request. It was more a question of *when* was he going to take the position and move back to their hometown of Portland, Oregon.

The job for Slade became nearly as suspense-filled as his previous life was. Often finding himself, or any of the twenty-two hand-picked men and women he now managed, undercover investigating industrial espionage, computer fraud or sandbagging agents who sought to overthrow small countries who were clients of the law firm. Other times they may be doing deep background checks on witnesses for major cases or companies involved in hostile take-over mergers, Slade knew what to expect when Ashton called him—expect the unexpected. This seemed different somehow. Ashton, he knew, didn't take no for an answer on anything, but something or someone must have said no by the look on his friend's face. Well, he thought, it was going to be a long day. He'd call Marie or was it Candice or whoever, and cancel his evening as soon as Ashton's plan was formed. Then he thought, oh hell, it was Candice Jordon, sister of Cecile Jordon Dixon. He had been trying to get close to her for years. Ow he may have to blow off this long sought-after evening with her.

"I want you to find a woman for me," Ash bit out still pacing.

Slade reached in his pocket, pulled out his iPhone, and held it up to Ash. "Here, take your pick."

Ashton merely cut his eyes at Slade but didn't stop his pacing.

Slade got the message. "Age?" Slade asked turning on a small computer notebook with a micro recorder that he carried in his breast pocket.

"Thirty something."

"Height and weight?"

"Five eight or nine. Weight? I don't know. One twenty to one thirty, I think but stacked. Hour-glass figure."

"Distinguishing marks?"

"Cherry-shaped birth mark on her right inner thigh."

"Description?"

"Beautiful."

Slade looked up at his pal. "Could you be more specific? Beautiful like Beyoncé, Angela Bassett, Mariah Carey, what?"

"More beautiful than any of them. She looks like the actress, Vanessa Williams, but better."

Slade whistled. "The former Miss America?" At Ashton's nod of agreement, Slade said, "Nice. No wonder you're looking for her. Connection?"

"None, but she may be a professional dancer, recuperating or vacationing at Plaza de Masquerada..." Slade's head came up again, but he didn't indicate the island meant anything to him, though it did. Ashton didn't notice Slade's changed comportment. "Before I left the island, I had the suite sealed. Get someone to the resort today to dust for finger prints, DNA samples."

"Time frame?"

"I want this information yesterday."

"Done," Slade said unlacing his fingers and standing.

"Slade."

"Yes?"

"This is critically important."

"I gathered as much," Slade said as he walked out of the door. "She must be one helluva woman."

Ashton looked at his closed office door. "She is," Ashton said again to an empty room, "and she's mine."

Later, Ashton sat in his office looking out through the floor-to-ceiling glass windows at the panoramic view of the City of Portland, Oregon, and the point where the Willamette and Columbia Rivers diverged. On a clear day he could see Vancouver, Washington. He accomplished little or nothing all morning while he set in motion and orchestrated much activity.

How could she leave him like that without a single word of explanation or goodbye? After what they had shared, nothing in his life or experience compared. He closed his eyes against the vision of her in ecstasy wrenching every ounce of being from him. He was irrevocably hers. No other woman could measure up. He had to find her. He would never rest until he did and, once he found her, he would never let her go.

She was a highly-intelligent, self-possessed woman who had captured him and now possessed him completely. Yet, the facts remained: She had loved him, and left him, stealing away in the dead of night. When dawn came, she was gone. He had only closed his eyes for a few moments after loving her for more than twenty-four hours.

They had a light dinner and two bottles of wine. Fed each other and drank from the same glass. Bathed each other in the hot tub and oiled each other with fragrant lotions. Touched each other—"

"Earth to Ash," a voice pulled him back from his erotic memories.

Ashton swiveled in his chair and turned to see Jillian Harris and his mother, Sheila Duckworth Marshall, standing in front of his desk. Slowly, he got to his feet.

"Hello, Mother," he said rounding his desk. He engulfed her in his arms kissing her on her forehead. "Jillian," he acknowledged with a nod.

"Ashton," Sheila said searching her son's eyes with concern, "are you not well?"

"I'm fine, Mother," he said, slightly smiling.

"I'm not convinced," she said laying a hand against his jaw. "I thought you said you needed a rest, but you came back early. You said you would be away for four weeks. You look worse now than you did before you left here three weeks ago. You don't look as if you've had much sleep."

"I assure you I'm fine and I never said exactly how long I intended to be away. I just have something on my mind."

Sheila cocked her head to one side and narrowed her eyes. "It certainly couldn't be any of your cases. Nothing there you can't handle with your eyes closed. Did something happen while you were away?" she asked.

Ashton noticed Jillian's rapt attention to his conversation with his mother and sought to end his mother's line of questioning before it strayed into dangerous territory and too close to the mark.

"Did you pick up my tennis racket?" he asked.

Sheila suspiciously eyed him because of his abrupt change in the conversation. She would let it rest, for the moment because they weren't alone, but she knew her son. Something was wrong and she would know what it was and the reason for it. "Yes, I picked up your racquet and you owe me thirty-four dollars for having it restrung."

"Put it on my tab."

Motherly concern was one thing more lethal than Sheila's legal skills and Ashton knew his mother would press him again at her earliest opportunity.

"Come to the house for dinner Saturday night. I planned this dinner party to coincide with your return."

"Saturday? Perhaps. I'm waiting for some information to come in and, when it does, I will have to leave the city at a moment's notice."

"Saturday night is important, Ashton," she impatiently, sighed.

"I'm sure it is important, but I just got back into town. I haven't even been home. Usually, I enjoy your parties, but—."

"Cocktails at six sharp, Ashton. Black tie."

"I will not promise—."

"Esmeralda will be there."

"Grandmother?" Ashton asked, his mood considerably brightening.

"Yes. She'll be in town working on one of her Save the Yak campaigns or some such thing," Sheila said facetiously with a corresponding dismissive flip of her hand.

"All right, I'll be there, if I can…but only for a short time to see grandmother."

Slade knocked and entered but was brought up short by the sight of Sheila and Jillian.

"Mrs. Marshall, Ms. Harris," Slade politely acknowledged. "Sorry for the intrusion. Ash, I'll see you later…"

"No, no," Sheila said bidding Slade to enter. "This is not a private conversation. In fact, I want to confirm you'll be at dinner Saturday night, Slade."

"Uh, security for your dinner party will be handled by Johnson, as usual, Mrs. Marshall, but I don't believe I can make it."

"Are you working on something I'm not aware of or are you and Ashton up to no good—again?"

Slade grinned at the woman who was a surrogate mother to him but did not answer her question.

Sheila's head cocked to the side and swiveled toward Ashton. "Just as I thought. Well, cancel whatever it is you two boys are scheming. The ladies of Portland can do without you two for one night," she said.

"Uh, Mother, would you and Jillian please excuse us? Slade and I have some important matters to discuss," Ashton said guiding them to his office door.

"For now, but you two be at the house on time and we'll discuss these 'important matters' further."

Sheila crossed the threshold ahead of Jillian who leaned into Ashton.

"You're mine after dinner," Jillian whispered before she followed Sheila out of the door.

That was not going to happen, Ashton mused. If Slade had good news for him, he'd be on his way to find KC before this day was over. He'd bring her back to meet his mother and grandmother. Sheila's dinner party would provide a perfect occasion to announce his marriage.

"Lady's on a mission, Ash," Slade said nodding in reference to Jillian Harris.

"Mission impossible," Ash snorted then waited for the results of Slade's investigation.

"Not much to report," Slade said, digging his hands into his pockets and squaring his shoulders. "Whoever she is, she's never been fingerprinted in AFIS, the Automatic Fingerprint Identification System, and the DNA results only indicated that you and she had one helluva—."

"I know," Ashton interrupted raking four fingers through his unusually long, dark-brown, curly hair. "Nothing in the registration records?"

"Plaza de Masquerada doesn't keep ordinary records, Ash. You know that. That's probably the reason you chose the place for your vacation. Bit coin transfers only. Cash and carry, then all records erased and untraceable. They have video security, but only to insure safety, then it's destroyed. I couldn't get enough for facial recognition since she's apparently not in any system."

"Damn!" Ash bit out. "What about wastepaper traces?"

"Not even a Kleenex. The suites are sanitized when a guest departs. Obviously, you know that since you had the suite sealed. Seems to me the lady didn't want to be found or she's casting herself in the role of Cinderella."

Ashton turned his obsidian gaze onto Slade. "You'll find her, though, won't you?" he asked, confident of Slade's skills and abilities.

"This one is that important to you?" Slade asked already aware of the answer.

"Treat it as a matter of life or death," he answered not breaking his gaze.

Slade's thoughts bunched. "It will take a little time, but I'll find her. There were private planes that left the island and yachts galore. I'll see what satellites were operational in the area during that time. I'll track them down."

"Thanks," Ashton said assured that, no matter where on the tiny globe KC went, Slade would find her.

"On another note, were you aware that, after you left the island, two women went missing?"

"No, I wasn't. Any idea who they were or what happened to them?"

"One was a female Air Force pilot with a wealthy family background and the other female producer with a nationally televised cooking show."

"I may have met them, but they don't ring any bells for me. We weren't handing out business cards or resumes."

"Are you sure the woman you're looking for left of her own free will?"

Ashton's brows bunched. "Do you think differently?"

He shook his head. "It looks like she packed up and left according to the night concierge who arranged for her unscheduled transportation to the airport. After turning over her luggage to a porter, the driver left. It's a small airport, but she could have left in any number of private planes. There were no scheduled commercial flights in or out of the island resort during that timeframe."

"Then you're on the right track with satellite surveillance and the flight plans filed by the pilots of the private planes."

Chapter 8

On Saturday evening, the Marshall Mansion and grounds were lit to perfection as limousines rolled up the long driveway two abreast under the north porte-cochère. Luxury cars were beginning to line up aided by motorcycle-riding police almost a quarter of that distance waiting to disembark their passengers. The mansion sat on a bluff near the affluent Magnolia section overlooking the convergence of the Columbia and Willamette Rivers. Fashioned and built to resemble the U. S. Supreme Court building, it made a formidable impression on the landscape and on anyone fortunate enough to glimpse it from the main road a mile away.

Ashton wheeled his Porsche into the service entrance and keyed in an entry code at an iron gate. Slowly, the gate cameras turned to frame him and then the gate opened. He drove the quarter-mile distance and parked amid a full caravan of caterers, florists, musicians and other service providers. Security was thick with armed guards and guard dogs because of the caliber of the guests scheduled to be in attendance, including the Vice President of the United States and the Governor of Oregon, but Ashton easily moved in the familiar surroundings of his youth.

Entering the kitchen, he snatched a few shrimp canapés and then spied Millicent "Millie" Turner, the majordomo of the house, issuing her orders and overseeing each aspect of the service. She flashed him a quick glance as he unsuccessfully tried to avoid her while stuffing another of the delectable tidbits into his mouth.

"Uh, not so fast, mister," she bade him to come to her with the crook of one finger.

Ashton stopped in his tracks and turned back to the woman who had taught him how to brush his teeth, comb his hair, and had often changed his diapers when he was a baby. She took a broad view of him, then straightened his black tie, and wiped an errant crumb from his mouth.

"You know, Ash, you never could do this right," she said fiddling with his tie and collar.

"That's why I always come to you, Miz Millie."

"Should have a pretty and pregnant young wife to feed you and dress you. Not these old hands. Found anyone who knows how to dress you rather than undress you yet?"

"Only you, Miz Millie. Now if you'll divorce Walter, you and I can slip away to some secluded spot and get busy."

She blushed. "Go on with your fresh self," she fussed, stifling a giggle. "Now where is my nephew? If you're here, he's got to be somewhere in the vicinity. You two are like Frick and Frack."

"Slade's around here somewhere, I suppose. I saw his car parked outside."

"What are you two up to tonight?" she asked with one raised eyebrow and hands on her slim hips.

"Not a thing, Miz Millie. Scouts honor," he said holding up two fingers with an innocent, boyish grin on his face.

"Humph, you and Slade never were Boy Scouts. Grown long before your time. Now Sheila says you two are up to something and we want to know what it is."

"Innocent until proven guilty."

"Innocent? The hell you say," she laughed and popped him on the butt with her clipboard.

Ashton laughed. "Mmmm, that's a start, you sweet thing."

"You're too fresh for bread, young man," she laughed as he hugged her and kissed her on the cheek. "Don't think I forgot about this secret you're hiding."

Millie, like Sheila, had a memory as long as an elephant's and a steel trap for a mind. Even in her fifties she was a beautiful woman born in India but raised in the United States. He'd have to be swifter than them both, but his most difficult test was still ahead of him.

Esmeralda.

The Queen of Causes was encircled by many admirers as she held court captivating her subjects with stories of her exploits to save so many species of animals and pristine places in the world. Seventy-one years young, she easily could pass for forty-five. Bedecked in authentic African garb, she was picture perfect. Thick, long, hair micro-braided and beaded, her face clean, clear, and wrinkle free with soft, supple skin. She defined the phrase "the twenty-first century grandmother."

Ashton clipped a glass of champagne from a passing waiter's tray and eyed his beautiful grandmother across the crowded room with a combination of awe, reverence, and pride.

"Hello, lover," a sultry voice whispered at his back.

"Jillian," he acknowledged, not turning.

She rounded him and stood blocking his view. Her hot, bright red, *haute courante* evening dress shimmered in the glow of the massive overhead chandeliers and splendidly wrapped her perfect body, but Ashton was totally unimpressed.

Her feral smile cooled him even more. Perfectly manicured and painted fingernails matched her stunning attire and complemented her cream-colored complexion. His thoughts, however, were on the sun-kissed, almond-bronze-skinned beauty who so closely resembled the former Miss America turned actress and songstress. She had captured his heart and soul so completely and then left it crumbled and broken before the dawn's early light. He had to find her, his KC to understand why she left him, and he knew, with the same clarity of thought and flawless, deductive reasoning that buoyed his career so rapidly, he had to get her back in his life.

"You seem distracted, Ash." The husky timbre of Jillian's voice brought him back to himself.

"Distracted, no. Determined, yes," he said with a steady grinding of his teeth.

"I know that feeling well," she lazily cooed while taking a sip from his glass of champagne.

"You do, do you?" he asked more as a statement than a question.

"Yes. I'm also on a mission," she hauntingly said, "and I can be downright tenacious when I go after something I want."

"So can I, Jillian," he absently said. "So can I."

"Don't you want to know about my mission?" she asked, while leisurely stroking his chest.

Ashton looked down at her fingers on the crisp, white, tailored shirt that covered his finely-tuned torso and then raised his eyes to hers. "Keep it a secret, Jillian," he grinned. "I wish you the best of luck."

"Luck has nothing to do with it, Ash," she grinned. "I make things happen. I never leave anything to chance."

"Oh, really?" a voice said at Jillian's back.

Jillian turned, annoyed at the interruption, but immediately her face slipped into a façade of serenity.

"Dr. Marshall," Jillian acknowledged, "It's so nice to finally meet you. I'm Jillian Harris. I work with Ashton," she said extending her hand. "We're very close."

Esmeralda Marshall, PhD., briefly took the hand offered to her, and smiled. "If you work with my grandson, Ms. Harris, I'm sure he's paying you an outrageous sum of money for whatever it is you do for him." She let the statement hang for a humming moment. "There's a table for donations set up beside the bar. If you hurry, I'm sure one of my assistants will accommodate you, and that you'll be very generous with your donations. You see, my dear, I don't leave anything to chance either."

The dismissal was both scathing and polite, but nonetheless a dismissal. Jillian took the veiled insult and the cue, nodded in deference to Dr. Marshall, and sauntered away. Silently, the unflattering things she thought about Esmerelda Marshall didn't show on her face. If she was to have the grandson, and she would, she would have to put up with the old witch and his bitch of a mother.

The smile on Ashton's face raised a corner of his mustache as he folded his grandmother in his arms and kissed her forehead. "You know, grandmother, you get more beautiful every day. Are you still my best girl or did some undeserving gentleman steal your heart away from me?"

"Gentleman?" she snorted. "After living with your grandfather for fifty years, God rest his wicked soul, only a real man could come close to stealing my heart." Her demeanor softened to a smile. "No, my favorite grandson, you still have my heart," she said laying her palm to his face.

"Good, despite the fact that I'm your only grandson. I wouldn't want to have to fend off your many admirers," he said smiling devilishly while kissing her palm.

"Well there is Slade after all. However, it looks like I may have to return the favor," she said, taking his arm. "That one is trouble," Esmeralda said nodding toward Jillian Harris as they sauntered into the cavernous library and sat on an ornate fifteenth century settee to chat. "What's her name," Esmerelda asked holding her grandson's hand as they sat side by side.

"She just told you, grandmother. Her name is Jillian Harris," he answered.

"I heard her. I'm not senile. I don't mean that one. I mean the other one."

"Who?"

"The one who's got you browbeating some hapless corporation into selling you an island resort you really don't want. The one who's got you cracking a whip around an office you barely visit between complex and convoluted cases. The one who took some of the sparkle from your eyes and fire from your heart. That's the one I'm talking about, not the walking piranha with the big...glands. So, now, tell me, what's her name?"

"You know, grandmother, I think you missed your calling. Maybe you should have been a lawyer, instead of an investigative reporter and college professor."

"Maybe I ought to send you back to law school if you think you're going to avoid my question with a bit of your court-room, diversionary tactics," she said, smiling knowingly.

She had him cold, he knew, but she above all knew him completely, and with his human frailties, still loved him fiercely.

"KC," he said knowing he could not avoid his grandmother's pleasing personality, quick assessment, and unyielding gaze.

"So, where is this paragon of a woman who has you so uncharacteristically stymied? I want to meet her."

"Where ever she is, I'll find her."

They gazed into each other's eyes and Esmerelda put a hand to his jaw.

"Ashton, women aren't the same now as they were in my youth. They have their own agendas now. Not every woman wants a home and family the way you do."

Ashton squeezed her hand. She did know his desire to lead a normal life. She was aware of his relentless search for the one right woman who would make his life complete. What she didn't know was he had found her or so he thought.

"I'm happy for you, Ashton," she said squeezing his hand in return. "You'll find her again, I'm sure, but if you need my help, let me know. I still have a few friends in interesting places."

Ashton was taken aback. He had not given her enough credit for being so deftly astute and having such keen insight. She guessed his secret, he now knew, and had given him her blessing.

Esmeralda regally rose from the settee and took his arm again. "Now, I hear you were handsomely paid for that last case you won. I'd like some of those ill-gotten gains of yours for Green Peace. A million sounds like a nice round figure," she said and victoriously smiled as they slowly strolled arm-in-arm back into the grand ballroom.

"Whoa, grandmother," he chuckled. "My client may want their legal fees back. An appeal has been filed. Looks like I'm going to have to argue this case before the federal appellate court in Washington, DC, in the next few weeks."

"You'll win, Ashton. You're like your father and grandfather, unstoppable."

"I hope so, grandmother. I hope some of that Marshall tenacity got passed on to me through my genes. My father and grandfather married two of the three best women this world has to offer."

"Don't try to smooth talk me, Thomas Ashton Marshall, III. I've had the best smooth talker in your grandfather," she said, smirking. "Your daddy was cut from the same cloth. Now, about that donation…"

Ashton stopped walking and grinned at his grandmother. "Smooth talking, huh? Grandmother, who talked me into doing *pro bono* work for the Sierra Club, the Aborigines in Australia, the Save the Whale Foundation, the Brothers for LA's Save the Children program, intervention and mediation for the Arabs and Israelis, and that stint I did for the Serbs, Croats, and Bosnians on land apportionment? I've contributed well over a million in legal resources for each case and now you want another—."

"You keep talking and it will be one point five million," she smugly said. "By the way, I want you to handle this little case—."

"Ladies and Gentlemen, thank you for attending this most auspicious occasion," Sheila Duckworth Marshall announced into a microphone quieting the throngs of people. "It's an honor to have the Vice President of the United States of America, the Governor of our great state, and so many other notable people here tonight. It is also my pleasure to welcome back my son, Thomas Ashton Marshall, III, who, as you've no doubt read in the printed press and seen on the television news media, has returned victorious from yet another very long and arduous case."

The applause filled the expansive, grand salon ballroom and Ashton, still squiring his grandmother, nodded to those around him. The crowd pushed him forward toward his mother who was standing on a platform.

"By his side, throughout that ordeal," Sheila continued, "is similarly a woman who needs no introduction. A daughter of a fine family of our great state and formerly lead, legal counsel for Wayne Agra Industries, Ms. Jillian Harris."

The applause again rose and Jillian joined Sheila and Ashton at the center of attention. "I say formerly because Ms. Harris will continue her illustrious legal career and fine trial work as the most recent senior partner at Marshall and Marshall…"

Sheila continued, but Ashton didn't hear another word his mother spoke. The news Jillian Harris would be working for him as a senior partner nearly flattened him. He glanced at his mother who winked at him while she continued talking. Then as Sheila ended her speech, she raised both his hand and Jillian's in a triumphant gesture, brought their hands together and stepped back. Jillian was beaming as she held Ashton's hand high. The applause from the crowd was deafening, but it didn't drown out his pique. His mother had some explaining to do.

Jillian brought his hand down and placed it behind her back flattening his palm on her butt. The gesture intimated something more than a work relationship. He knotted his hand into a fist, but she held his wrist behind her with her left hand while she shook hands with her right. When Ashton tried to dislodge himself, she dug her nails into his wrist enough to draw blood but continued smiling at the gathering crowd around them.

Ashton's discomfort was great, but he endured the torture until he could stand no more. Finally, he extricated himself from her grip and sought out his mother. Finding her engrossed in a conversation with some of their clients and the governor, he abruptly excused them both and escorted his mother into a smaller, empty salon closing and locking the door behind them. He leaned his back against the door, folded his arms across his chest, and crossed his legs at the ankle. He waited for Sheila to open.

"Isn't it wonderful Jillian will be working with us?" Sheila rhetorically asked. "She's such a dynamic lawyer, we're lucky to get her. She'll be a great asset to the firm and to you. She's, uh, single, you know. Comes from a highly-respected Oregon family—"

"Has all her own teeth, passed the physical, did she, Mother? Can bear a house full of little Marshalls, no doubt. Is that why you hired her without my knowledge or consent and literally behind my back?" he tersely asked.

Sheila raised an eyebrow at his tone of voice and then her nose in the air. "You were consulted, Ashton, but you chose not to participate in the decision-making process. Rather, you flew off to heaven knows where and—."

"Mother," he interjected in a directed tone, "you have ninety days to undo what you've done—."

"*Or what?*" she flashed.

"Or you can change the firms name to Marshall and Harris for all I care because this Marshall," he vehemently said with his thumb to his chest, "will be out of here!"

"Don't threaten me, Ashton!"

"That's no threat, Mother, it's a promise," he countered with equal force.

"You wouldn't!"

"Don't press it. You won't like the result."

"This is your firm as well as mine! It's your heritage! Your three-times great grandfather started it and your father gave his life's blood to make it what it is today. You can't turn your back on your family, Ashton! It's time for you to step up and fill your father's shoes. Stop all this globetrotting, whoring around the world with Slade. It's time for you to settle down, get married, and raise the next generation of Marshalls." Sheila paused, taking a deep, calming breath. The next few moments were going to be very important and she wanted to ease her son into her plan without him invoking his stubborn streak.

Turning to face him, she was composed and in control. "This last case has given you great notoriety and name recognition in all the right circles. Most of the influential people who constitute this state's political infrastructure are here tonight. They tell me they are very impressed with what they have seen of you. The party chairman and some of the other movers and shakers want to meet with us to discuss your future in the political arena. There's never been an American of African descent as governor of Oregon, but the political party and even the pundits believe you are a shoo-in for that post and Jillian can make it all happen for you. Her family is politically well-placed and extremely active in the party. They own television and radio stations throughout the state and in other parts of the northwestern United States. They believe, as I do, a match between you and Jillian would be an unstoppable combination. She's aggressive, intelligent, attractive—"

"Ninety days, Mother. You have ninety days to get Jillian Harris out of this law firm or you can start adoption proceedings to make Jillian legally your daughter because that's the only way she'll ever be a Marshall!"

<h1 style="text-align:center">Chapter 9</h1>

Later, Ashton lay on his stomach across his round bed trying to recall every detail of KC's behavior. *Maybe he missed something…something important. Had she done or said anything that could help lead him to her?* His usually clear thoughts jumbled in his mind. All he could recall was hearing her sparkling laughter, seeing the clear, clean, fresh smile on her beautiful face and the gleam in her shining eyes. He adored the way she tilted her head when she was about to unload one of her zingers on him. How she felt beneath him, on top of him, beside him. How complete he felt inside her. The devilish play…

The telephone rang, interrupting his mental escape.

"Yes!" he answered, resenting the intrusion.

"You alone?"

"Yeah," he growled. "You got anything yet?"

"I'll see you in a few."

Ashton hung up and sat on the edge of his bed rubbing his face in frustration. His nude body was moist just thinking about KC and his hardened phallus stared back at him as his constant reminder of his need for one woman—KC. He hoped Slade had good news. If so, he'd be at the airport and on his way in no time. He already had one of the law firm's jets on standby.

Grabbing and putting on a pair of loose-fitting, drawstring, sweat pants commando-style, he went to the security system to turn it off and then to the front door to unlock it. Not that he needed to. Slade's company installed the system. He had keys to his place and codes to his security system although he really didn't need them. As a former Navy

SEAL, Slade could access Fort Knox without difficulty if he wanted to and exit unnoticed.

Ash headed for his game room. Bending forward searching for a beer in the tall cooler, his thoughts went immediately back to KC. He remembered how she wiggled that perfectly-shaped bare bottom of hers and his groin immediately constricted. With his arms outstretched and leaning against the wet bar, he tightly closed his eyes against the vision. Needing something stronger than a beer, Ashton grabbed a few ice cubes, filled two tumblers, and left one on the bar. He poured two fingers of Stoli and shot it down in two quick gulps wincing as it burned going down his throat. Shaking his head, he poured another. This was no cure for what ailed him, he recognized. Then padding barefoot to his music center, he downloaded eight tracks onto his iPod. Soon the soulful sounds of Paul Taylor's **On the Horn** filled the room. Stretching out on a wide, fawn-brown, leather, contour chaise lounge, he braced one arm over his eyes and rested the ice-filled tumbler against his hardened ridge in an effort to stifle his need.

The music spoke to his soul. The needful horn stirring his loneliness and biding him to relax. The need he felt for her was so deep, but his grandmother's words of wisdom came back to him. *If she's for you, she'll come back. You can't make anyone love you if they don't want to.* She'd said that to him as he was leaving the party before dinner was served. Maybe Esmerelda was right. Maybe he should just forget about KC and move on with his life.

Life? What was it anyway? He had success, a career that was carefully planned. Wealth was something he was born into so he didn't have to struggle to make ends meet. He could go anywhere and do nearly anything he wanted. Was that life? If so, why hadn't he found love? The love of a good woman. Sex was one thing, it was easy, but love, well, that was an entirely different matter. He thought he had found the one thing that had eluded him in a long list of loveless affairs and brief encounters.

Love, thy name is KC.

The doorbell brought him out of his thoughts. He reached for the telephone.

"It's open. I'm in the game room," he said, then resumed his prone position. Shortly, the scent of perfume jarred him into an alert position. He opened his eyes and narrowed his gaze.

"What are you doing here, Jillian?" he asked, his frustration apparent in his tone.

"Aren't you even going to offer me a drink?" she asked running her fingers over his bare chest.

"You shouldn't drink and drive, and I'm sure you'll want to get on your way soon."

"I'm in no hurry and the chauffeur is being well paid to wait. I could send him on his way and spend the night here with you," she said. "You left the celebration so abruptly; I thought maybe you weren't feeling well. I told your mother I'd come by and check on you on my way home."

"As you can see, I'm fine. Now you can leave."

Jillian ignored his suggestion. "I love your house, Ash," she said fluidly moving around the room looking at or touching the priceless art. "It has your flare. Very manly though. Stylish as it is, it needs something."

"I have a housekeeper, so that position is taken. Beyond that, I like things just the way they are. Now, if you'll excuse—."

"Looks like you're expecting company," she said pouring a drink for herself in the glass he left on the bar. "Anyone I know?"

"You said you were concerned with my well-being. As you have witnessed, I'm not ill—"

"You didn't answer my question."

Ashton pinched the bridge of his nose and closed his eyes. He felt like physically ejecting her from his house, but he had never touched a woman in anger before and he wasn't about to start now.

"Ash," she cooed.

Ashton felt her presence next to him before he felt her body straddle his.

"Jillian, please…"

"Please what?" she asked kissing his chest and biting at his flat nipples. Her hair feathered his skin like KC's had done. Her fingers roamed his body and her nails raked him. The Stoli, the music, and Jillian's aggressive approach to his lowered defense made him want KC even more. His mind went back to the night he made her his and she made him hers. The bonding was only the cherry on the icing. He could visualize her face, her physique. He could smell her sweet allure. How it felt to hold her in his arms and how she loved him. Oh, how they loved, he lamented in his silent thoughts. The vision was jarring.

"KC," the name slipped from his lips. "KC," he moaned again.

"*Casey?*" Jillian bit out snatching herself away from his body.

Ashton shook his head in frustration. "Go home, Jillian." He sat up and swung his feet to the floor.

"Who is *Casey?*" she demanded.

"Who she is, is none of your business, Jillian."

"Look, Ashton, I'm working with you now, so—"

"Not for long!" he said rising to his feet.

"What does that mean?" Then, as his meaning dawned, she said, "If you're trying to sever my professional agreement with Marshall and Marshall, I'll sue the pants off you!"

"I didn't ask you to join the firm, Jillian, so sue!"

"No, you didn't, but your mother did! She's the managing partner and she hired me!"

He had done it again. He successfully diverted Jillian's attention away from the identity of KC. Even to the point of distorting her name. Now if he could only make Jillian angry enough to leave him alone.

"Then sue her!"

Jillian puffed up, slammed the drink on the coffee table, and snatched her coat and handbag from the billiard table.

"I'm not through with you!" she shrieked.

"Tell it to someone who gives a damn, Jillian!"

Her heels clicked a staccato beat on his hardwood floors before the front door was slammed shut behind her and Ashton slowly exhaled.

"You haven't lost your touch," a low voice said from the opposite doorway.

"How long have you been here?" Ashton asked not turning.

"Long enough. That little spitfire was about to toast your marshmallow for you, brother man."

"I'm not that sweet or that desperate. What did you find out?"

Slade shrugged his shoulders. "Not much before…"

Ashton turned his questioning gaze on Slade. "Before what?" he asked.

"Well, seems the boss wants me to handle an investigation in Japan. Something about a client and bank stocks. The client is being hacked. Sheila cornered me at the party tonight."

"Damn!" Ashton spat. "Send someone else. I need for you to keep working on finding KC for me."

"Sheila wants me to personally handle this case in Japan and you know as well as I do that, what Sheila wants, Sheila gets."

Ashton knew all too well Slade was right. Sheila would be obeyed or the sun wouldn't dare to rise. "How long do you think you'll be away?"

"Two weeks, maybe three. I've got a jet on standby at the airport now."

Four fingers raked over Ashton close-cut hair. "She's up to something."

"Tell me about it," Slade snorted. "As indicated by tonight's soirée, Sheila's got plans for you, my man."

"I know. That's why she hired Jillian."

"Sheila respects Jillian's drive and ambition, though according to my aunt, she doesn't like her very much. Probably thinks she can keep you in line. Staff is making bets on whether Jillian Harris is going to be Mrs. Thomas Ashton Marshall, III, within a year."

"Which way are you betting?" Ashton asked his friend.

Slade poured a drink for himself and raised it in toast. "She has a snowball's chance in hell of pulling that off."

Ashton raised his own glass and touched it to Slade's. "You'll win that bet."

Chapter 10

Days later, the tirade was still ongoing and this time it had lasted nearly an hour. Kristen felt mentally, emotionally, and physically drained by the experience.

"Father, I've done nothing to be ashamed of."

"Behaving like some strumpet in public! I'd say you have a lot to be ashamed of! Do you know or understand what an impeccable reputation means in this town to a woman in your position? This city could make you or break you! You could destroy everything that we've worked for! Years of careful training, grooming, and positioning could go right out of the window and your reputation would go down the drain. You're headed for the United States Supreme Court, Kristen!"

"Father," she breathed in frustration rubbing her throbbing temples. Her headache was getting worse. "I haven't done anything professionally to be ashamed of. My private life, such as it is, is just that, private. I've said this over and over so many times it's beginning to sound like a mantra. Now, I don't know or understand why you want to keep hammering at me about dancing with Peter at a private farewell party over a month ago at Tina's home in Chicago, but I've had enough."

Kristen was thankful her father only learned about the farewell party and not about her reckless behavior at Plaza de Masquerada. He would have a coronary if he learned she shared a suite with a man… A complete stranger and then had fallen into bed with him. The shock of it all had not even settled in on her yet, but the memory of Ash lingered every moment since she left him. She tightly shut her eyes to block out the vision of Ash. His keen mind and easy wit had attracted her to him. His sexy smile and deft moves had drawn her in, but his lovemaking had imprisoned her like nothing she ever knew before. The thought was not only vivid in her mind's eye, but also palpable.

He loved her so tenderly, yet completely. She touched him in ways she knew would have been declared illegal in forty-nine out of fifty states. She loved every millisecond of being with him…but she left him. Walked away in a manner that said there were no tomorrows for them. The tears she shed on her flight to DC were unwelcome and unstoppable. Yet she had sweet, poignant moments of her memory to last her for a lifetime. Her heart broke in a million pieces knowing she would never see him again and she would never love or be loved like that again.

"*Kristen?* Kristen, are you listening to me?" her father's sharp reproach brought her back to the present along with the burgeoning headache.

"Yes, Father," she said pushing herself away from her desk. "I heard you. I'm sorry if you're disappointed, but—."

"I don't understand what's gotten into you lately. You've been acting as if you're sleepwalking. Your attention span is that of a three-year-old. You're…"

Her telephone rang and, relieved, she pressed the blinking light on the console.

"Yes, April."

"Judge Bryant, Judge Montgomery is here to see you."

Kristen's face grew into a smile. "Please have her come right in," she said disengaging the intercom. "Excuse me, Father," she said rounding her desk and crossing the expansive office. She opened her office door and waited. Soon her college school chum ambled in. "Vivian," Kristen broadly smiled as they warmly embraced.

"Hey, kid," Vivian Alexander Montgomery beamed.

They hugged for a while without speaking and then Kristen backed up mindful of Vivian's burgeoning pregnancy.

"You look wonderful, Vivian," Kristen said and warmly smiled.

Vivian laid a palm against Kristen's face. "And you don't, KC. What's wrong? I thought the vacation would have done you some good."

"It did, but it's been a long week. I got back into town a little over a week ago and it's been nonstop since I arrived. I can't thank you enough for everything you've done."

"What good does it do to own an island resort and an airline if I can't share it with my best friends? I hope you were treated well…oh," she noticed Kristen's father and moved to acknowledge him. "Judge Bryant," she said extending her hand, "I apologize. Did I intrude?"

"No, no, of course not, Judge Alexander-Montgomery," Clarence Bryant said briefly extending his hand to palm hers between both of his. "If it were not for your decision to take an extended leave of absence from the federal court, Kristen's opportunity to sit in your place may not have come up as soon."

"Kristen would have gotten here on her own volition," Vivian smiled at Kristen with knowing eyes, "if she had wanted it."

"Of course, she would," he said, grinning. "Well, I'm sure you two have lots to discuss. I'll leave you to it," he said to Vivian. "Judge Alexander-Montgomery, always a pleasure." Then turning to Kristen, "We'll continue this discussion tonight at dinner," he said then left the room closing the door behind him.

Kristen slowly exhaled, the room seeming to fill with air again with her father's departure.

"That bad, huh?" Vivian asked cocking her head to one side and looking at Kristen.

"Worse," she said as they walked to a sofa holding each other around the waist.

They sat for a moment not talking.

"He's so intense sometimes I feel like I want to just scream." She bowed her head and shook it in frustration. "I can't make a move without his blessing. He has choreographed everything I've done since I arrived. If I have to give one more lunchtime keynote address, lecture or attend another dinner party or tea party, or do another breakfast interview, I'll go insane. I haven't had one moment to myself. He still thinks I'm some dim-witted, wide-eyed child who just wanted to grow up to be a dancer like my mother and have a family."

"You don't want those things anymore?"

Kristen abruptly rose from her seat and raked her hands through her hair loosening the tight French twist and letting her curly hair fall to her shoulders and down her back. She wrapped her arms around her waist and slowly paced coming to a stop in front of one of the large windows in her office. She stared blankly. "Do you remember our senior year at Spelman? The performance we did for Spring Festival?"

"Yes, I remember. You danced the lead role in **Firebird**. You did so well you were offered opportunities to dance professionally. You gave a brilliant performance, KC," Vivian quietly said, "and you were very happy."

"I wanted so much to do it, too. I wanted to dance. I was so excited. I wanted my family to be proud of me. I wanted—."

"Your father's approval. I remember. You were heartbroken when he didn't support your dreams."

Kristen turned her head to look at Vivian. "Didn't approve? Well, that's putting it diplomatically," she snorted. "He went ballistic," she said closing her eyes and rubbing her face as if to block the memory. "He forbade me from ever dancing in public again. Made me swear I'd never defy him."

"You never have, KC. You kept your promise," Vivian said holding out her hand to Kristen.

Kristen crossed the room, took her friend's hand, and sat down beside her. "No, I defied him. I danced in my room every chance I got. All the years I was in law school, I'd go to a dance studio and work out with professionals. I even taught a beginner's class of little seven-year-olds when father thought I was studying for the bar exam. Working with those children reminded me so much of my mother. Vivian, if you could have seen her dance," she wistfully said. "She was poetry in motion."

"I've read about her, of course, and I've seen some of her videos and movies. She was something very special, KC."

"One of the world's best artists," Kristen proudly said remembering her mother. She shook off the moment. "Well, Mrs. Montgomery, what about you? I can see you're very pregnant again."

Vivian laughed. "KC, no one can be just a little bit pregnant."

Kristen laughed, too. "I wish I were in your shoes with a husband who loved the ground I walked on like Chuck does with you. Still, sixteen babies?" she said feigning wide-eyed astonishment.

"Twenty-four, KC. You've got to keep up. The Alexander-Montgomery household does not stand still. Chuck and I completed adoption on another set of twins two months ago. He performed the surgery on the four-year-old girls to separate them. They were born in Guatemala, but their parents didn't want them because they were conjoined at the hip. They are primitive people, in the village where the girls were born, who believed the joined twins were some type of bad omen. The villagers were going to let the girls slowly starve to death. A friend of Chuck's, Dr. Evan Cain, found the twins just in the nick of time while he was working on the *Ship of Hope* and arranged to have the girls brought here for the surgery at Chuck's hospital. Evan obtained a parental rights release and Chuck and I adopted them. We have so many children now we're running out of godparents," she said and laughed.

Kristen's smile narrowed. "Still, you're happy, aren't you?"

"Deliriously happy," Vivian slightly sobered and Kristen could see the glow of a very contented woman.

She shook her head. "I don't know how you do it, Viv. You're one of the wealthiest women in the world. You've authored so many books on the law. Run major corporations. Argued some of the toughest legal cases. Become the youngest woman to sit on the federal bench. Adopted more children than the fabled Old Lady in a Shoe."

"I still can't cook," Vivian said, laughing.

Kristen heartily laughed too. Then they sobered.

"Kristen," Vivian began.

"Uh-oh, am I going to get a lecture from you too? You only call me Kristen when…"

"No, no lecture," Vivian said. "Still, I wouldn't be able to call myself your friend if I didn't level with you. We've been friends since undergrad. True, we haven't found much time to get together more often until now.

However, when you called me and said you needed a change of pace, I sensed you didn't just mean you needed a vacation. You sounded like someone who needed to change her life.

"You're an excellent attorney and you've distinguished yourself on the Federal District Court," Vivian continued. "Your lectures at the University of Chicago and your Law Review articles are well respected. You're a better jurist than most I've seen, KC, but I believe it's because you had to be. Not because you wanted to be a judge. Your father didn't give you any choice in the matter. When I suggested you move up and take my place on the appellate court bench, I had hoped getting out of Chicago and away from your father would help you decide what it is you really want."

"It's a little late for me to consider dance as a profession now, Vivian. I'm over thirty-years-old. Well past my prime to go on the stage."

"Maybe not as a performer, but certainly you have a lot to contribute to the art. When your mother left the stage, she began to teach. She taught children from disadvantaged neighborhoods the beauty of the body in motion. Some of her pupils are now rising or established stars in theaters around the world, but there are so many more children who would benefit from learning the discipline dance teaches. I should know. My daughter, Linda, is after all, a prima ballerina, and she would love to work with you. Couple that with your legal training and I see a new dance company bigger than the Dance Theater of Harlem taking the world by storm."

Kristen smiled. "Actually, I was thinking the same thing recently. On your island, in fact. There were so many young native men and women who danced for us in the evening. They would make a very good and unique dance troupe." She sighed and shook her head. "You remembered my dream, didn't you?"

"Yes, and it doesn't have to be a dream, KC. You can make it a reality… not your mother's reality, but your own, if that's what will make you happy. It's what she trained you to do; to dance the way you did most of your youth."

"It's also what took her away from us. That stray bullet in a drive-by shooting. If it were not for her need to reach out to children in dangerous, disadvantaged neighborhoods, she would still be with us and father wouldn't have reacted so bitterly against my wanting to follow in her footsteps instead of his."

"Kristen, if you shared your father's views, you could have become a prosecutor, but you didn't. Your father is a highly-respected man, but you stayed away from the criminal side of law for which he's made his mark. You know he's a prosecutor's dream and a defense attorney's nightmare because he shows no compassion, no mercy, zero tolerance where violence is involved. Every kid or young adult convicted of a violent crime who faces him in a court room gets the maximum allowed sentence."

"I know. Sometimes when I read his cases, I believe he's out on some sort of vendetta to convict whoever it was who killed my mother, but you're right. I don't have a taste for the criminal side of law. The best I could do to honor his wishes was to practice civil law instead."

"Still, how long can you keep doing something, even on the civil side, your heart, mind, and body aren't into? You're a dancer, Kristen, who happens to be a judge on the federal court. Not the other way around. Not someone looking to make her mark on the Supreme Court."

Kristen looked at Vivian and narrowed her eyes. "You knew?" she asked in surprise. "You knew what my father is planning for my life?"

"Certainly, I knew."

"Yet, you still worked to get me appointed to take your place?"

"Yes, KC. Life is too short to wake up with regrets and it's about having choices, options. Opportunities to make the right decisions for you. Not for your father or for your mother, but for Kristen Catherine Bryant."

Before she answered, Cheryl and Tina knocked on her office door and peeked in.

"Is the coast clear?" Tina asked spying the room.

Kristen laughed. "Yes, Father has left. It's safe to enter."

"Girlfriend, that man makes me nervous. Thank goodness I never had to argue a case before him. He'd find *me* guilty," Tina said.

"You would be, too," Cheryl said with a deadpan expression.

"Thanks, friend," Tina said rolling her eyes at Cheryl. Then to Kristen. "You okay, KC?" "Yes, I'm fine."

"Good, so let's dish the dirt. What's happening, Viv? I know you have the best investigative team in town!"

"Only because I don't tell you anything," Vivian said, laughing. "I could get impeached."

They all laughed, ordered in lunch rather than going out, and talked for an hour more.

"So, let me see if I got this straight. Savannah Logan married Nathan Flack and they have two children. Dakota Sinclair married Savannah's brother, Jefferson Alden Logan, that phine ambassador. And it turns out that Dakota Sinclair is really LaiLoni Skai Hawkins, the kidnapped daughter of Jake Hawkins and JaiHonnah Reise Hawkins' sister. And Savannah's old flame, Roderick Baylor, married JaiHonnah Reise Hawkins and they have five children. And Roderick's sister, Kelley, married JaiHonnah's father, and he's an ambassador to Africa. Your brothers, that heartthrob, Kenneth, former California Governor, married JeNelle Towson, now junior US Senator from California, and that sexy Benny, your astronaut brother married Stacy Greene, now a Navy Admiral, and Gregory married…"

"Hold up, Gregory's not married, not yet at least," Vivian said.

"You mean that fine young example of a gift-to-womankind is still on the loose?" Tina asked with renewed interest.

"*Loose'* describes my baby brother exactly, but he already has a mother, Tina."

"Vivian, there's only," she silently counted on her fingers, "a few years between his age and mine," she said feigning innocence.

"Light years, Tina. Gregory isn't ready for you yet."

"He's a former professional basketball player and now a stockbroker, Vivian. He's used to taking risks."

"Only calculated risks, Tina, not calculating ladies," she said, laughing and was joined by their friends.

Cheryl poured more tea for them all.

"Well, I don't understand how our crew from Spelman could find these phine, upwardly mobile, dedicated Black men and KC, Tina, and I can't."

Tina jabbed Cheryl in the ribs. "Chuck's not Black, Tina, he's white. Very white."

"He is?" Vivian asked in mock surprise. "Jeez, why didn't someone tell me that before I married him?"

"Because with someone who looks like Johnny Depp it wouldn't have made a bit of difference if we had, Vivian," KC laughed.

"You're right about that," Vivian said and winked.

"Well, he is a hunk, I have to admit. If you had to cross the color barrier, you sure picked a good one."

"Thanks, Cheryl, I'll tell Chuck you approve. I'm sure it will make his day."

"Obviously, he's been making your nights, girlfriend. Sixteen babies and one on the way."

"Twenty-four," Vivian and Kristen said in unison.

"You've got to keep up," said Vivian while they all laughed.

"So, Viv, is it really true that Judge William Whiting had an affair with Audra Kirkland?"

"Regrettably, it is, or he may have had a chance to fill my spot, but he lied to the police during an official investigation. That put an end to his career options."

"I read his wife, Charlotte Townsend Whiting, Kirked out and held Capri McAllister Kennedy's executive assistant hostage."

"Sad, but also true," said Vivian. "Fortunately, no one was hurt."

"I think of Capri's husband, Tate, and your brother, Benny, being up in space working on the SPACEHOME project. Nothing can compare with that," said KC.

Tina and Cheryl rose from their seats.

"Well, on that positive note, back to the grind. Lunch time is over and the boss," Tina said nodding toward Kristen, "cracks the whip if we're late."

"About that, you're right," Kristen said.

"Hi ho, hi ho, it's off to court we go," Cheryl sang.

"You know, it's not a bad gig. We do get to see some super fine specimen strut their stuff, like the formidable Thomas A. Marshall, III. Now that's something worth working for!" Tina demonstratively intoned.

"Marshall? I don't think I've heard of him before," Kristen said.

Three pairs of eyes swiveled toward her and she noticed.

"What?" she asked looking from face to face.

"BFF, everyone has heard of him. He makes Clarence Darrow, Johnny Cochran, William Jennings Bryant, and Bob Mueller seem like ambulance chasers!"

"Yeah, I'd like to chase his…" Tina said.

Kristen held up one hand. "I get the picture."

"I don't think you do, KC. He can't be comprehended in a picture; he's got to be experienced! Victoria's Secrets will be dropping all over DC when he hits town. Denzel Washington-eat-your-heart-out gorgeous!"

Vivian laughed. "Thomas is very good looking, but he doesn't look like Denzel to me. He could pass for Rick Fox's twin."

"You know him, Viv?" Cheryl asked astonished. "Of course you do. You know everybody."

"Yes, I've known him for many years. He and I argued two cases together before the International Court in The Hague on mineral rights issues. He's an excellent attorney and expert on international case law."

"All I want to do is carry his briefs," Tina crooned.

Kristen shook her head, the double entendre clear. "It's his legal skills he'll have to use in court."

"Well, KC, I'll bet you lunch that while that man argues his case in your court, even *you* will want to hold night court with him," joked Cheryl.

"Speaking of those who should drop dead, your former boyfriend is lead council for the plaintiff," Tina mentioned.

"Strickland Briggs?" Kristen asked, surprised. "Seriously?"

"Yep, his name is on the legal brief you assigned to me and Tina to read. He's lead counsel for McElroy Products Incorporated. Looks like your first case as a federal judge is going to be interesting."

Kristen narrowed her eyes. She turned to Vivian. "Maybe I shouldn't sit for this case, Vivian. Until about three months ago, Strickland and I were involved."

"I don't believe it's a problem, but, in an abundance of caution, bring the possible conflict to the attention of the Chief Justice Harold Hathaway. He's a good man and I trust his judgment. Let him rule on the question of impropriety."

"You're right. I'd better do that before this session begins in a couple of weeks."

Chapter 11

Later that evening, Kristen sat writing notes at a desk in the library in the home she was renting from her friends Vivian and Vivian's brother Benny. She looked up to see her father reading the newspaper across the room from her. He hadn't continued to barrage her, and, for that, she was grateful. He would be staying with her only a few more days, then returning to Chicago for the start of his own judicial session. She would welcome the peace and seclusion the large, spacious house in the fashionable Georgetown area would afford her. Another thing she had to be grateful to her friend, Vivian Alexander Montgomery, for. The house was fully furnished and sat on the edge of Rock Creek Park. Vivian had once lived there while she was a student at Georgetown Law Center. Kristen, Tina, and Cheryl visited Vivian while they were all in law school and Kristen always loved this house and the surroundings. She was thrilled when Vivian suggested she stay there for as long as she wanted. The house majordomo, Anna Jones, literally lived next door with her husband, Fenster Jones, a world-renown violinist.

She absently wondered whether Ash would like this house. He seemed to be able to handle himself in any surrounding though. Then she wondered what his surroundings were like. Whether he liked old-fashioned things or was modern architecture and furnishings more his taste? Resting her elbow on the desk, she palmed her face. The September sun started to set, and she recalled, as she stared out the window, how the sun set in a brilliant array of colors on the veranda as she and Ash made love. The waves were breaking against the shore, the cooing of doves, and the smell of exotic tropical plants and salt air mixed in the sweet smell of hot, steamy love. It was paradise.

Ash stroked her breasts, kneading them, and then taking them into his mouth one by one to lath them with his warm, wet, rough tongue. She cradled his head against her breasts, arching her back to offer up herself to him. His name escaped her lips as he set her body ablaze again and again. His kisses silenced all but her deep moans of pleasure as their tongues danced to the urgent beat of their hearts. Their hips joined the ancient rhythm as she matched him stroke for stroke, clinging to his moist body and to the edge of sanity. Nothing separated them, not even the breeze blowing in the open door to the veranda and across their damp bodies. They moved together whispering words to each other that singed them both and took them to another level of ecstasy. It was as if they read each other's needs and thoughts even without the words. Words that became unintelligible the higher into the euphoria they climbed, but she heard the words that transfigured their union —"Marry me."

"Kristen?"

"Uh, yes, Father?" she said snapping back from her memories.

"What is on your mind? Didn't you hear the doorbell?"

"Uh, no, Father," she said frowning at her watch and then rising from the desk.

A light rap on the library door and it opened.

"Mr. Strickland Briggs," Shelton, the butler her father hired, announced.

When Strickland stepped over the threshold, Kristen froze in her place. Her head snapped toward her father who rose from his seat, broadly smiling at Strickland, and extending his hand.

"Strickland, my boy," Clarence beamed. "I'm so glad you could join us for dinner."

Kristen was nearly struck dumb. She had no idea he was even in town or that her father invited him to dine with them.

"Judge Bryant," Strickland smoothly acknowledged her father. "Always a pleasure to see you, Sir. Thank you and Kristen for inviting me."

"Your parents, they're not with you?" Clarence asked.

"They'll be here shortly. They're having cocktails with Senator Tollson and the leadership of the conservative wing of the party. I, on the other hand, couldn't wait to see my bride-to-be," he said moving toward Kristen. "Hello, darling," he said bending to kiss her mouth. Kristen turned her head and his kiss landed on her cheek. "With that wonderful tan, you're more beautiful than I remembered. I've missed you so," he said pulling her into his embrace.

"The feeling is definitely *not* mutual," she lowly hissed while pushing away from him.

"You'll feel differently after we're married," he quietly said holding her. "Isn't she beautiful, Judge Bryant?" Strickland said, again kissing her near her ear.

Kristen wanted to slap that smug, shit-eating grin from Strickland's lips. She eased out of his arms and stepped away from him meeting her father's smile as she did.

"Yes, she is lovely, Strickland. Just like her mother. You're a very lucky man, if I do say so myself."

"Father, you have to know this is very improper. Strickland has a case pending before my court and Strickland and I—."

"Are going to be very happy, once this minor matter is over," Strickland cut in. "I've promised the Judge we'll be very discreet and I'll take very good care of you, darling. I'm opening an office for my parents here in Washington, so you and I can be together while we're planning our wedding. I've taken on a few new clients, but that won't interfere."

"I'll rest a lot easier knowing you two are together again." Clarence broadly smiled. "You can introduce Kristen to Washington society and the political powers that be. You two, along with your parents, will make a dynamic team, I'm sure of that."

Kristen was temporarily lost in her father's excitement. She knew with Strickland on the scene, with her father's blessing, he would attempt to drag her to every social and political event in Washington just as he had done in Chicago. Strickland and his parents had long been on the

Washington "A List" and still swiftly climbing the politically conservative ladder nationwide. She also knew and understood what it was her father wanted her to achieve and if anyone could clinch a Supreme Court nomination and appointment for her, Strickland and his parents certainly could. Yet, what was in it for him? she wondered. The stakes must have been high for Strickland to disregard her rejection of his marriage proposal, flaunt his affair with a high-priced fashion model in her face, and then return to her as if nothing had ever happened.

Another knock at the door took her mind away from her father and Strickland.

"Mr. Peter Brock, Esquire," Shelton announced.

Kristen crossed the room and went into Pete's arms.

"Brock, I didn't expect you this evening," Clarence said miffed, Kristen knew, because of her show of affection for Pete.

"Kristen asked me to dine with her tonight. I didn't know you were going to be here either, sir," Pete smoothly said extending his hand.

"I see," Clarence said clearing his throat. He shook Peter's hand. "Of course, you know Kristen's fiancée, Strickland Briggs."

"Briggs," Pete acknowledged with a nod, but with no other show of recognition for the reference to being Kristen's fiancée.

"Brock," Strickland returned the stiff greeting.

"If you'll both excuse us, I need to have a private word with Kristen—about the office," Peter offered.

Kristen was grateful for Peter's insight that she needed to get out of the room. She preceded him into a solarium filled with tropical plants and flowers.

As soon as they entered, Pete folded his arms across his chest and stared at her. "Fiancée? Really?" he asked. "When did this happen?"

Kristen gritted her teeth and fumed. "Beats the hell out of me!"

"Well, someone certainly should know something, KC. The man is acting as if your wedding is already a *fait accompli* and why did you invite me to dinner, if you knew Strickland was going to be here. You know I don't like the man. I thought we were having dinner alone tonight."

Kristen paced with hands on hips. "You knew father was here, Pete," she said with a wave of her hand.

"Oh, so you wanted me to be a buffer between you and your father? Someone to draw his fire or cool his dictatorial behavior toward you? Is that it, KC?"

"No, not entirely, Pete," she said still pacing, but deep in thought. "I didn't know father invited Strickland *and* his parents. I didn't even know they were in town."

"Oh, so the plot thickens. No wonder Washington has been buzzing."

Kristen stopped in her tracks and sharply turned toward Pete. "Buzzing? Buzzing about what?"

"It's not common knowledge yet, but Senator Tollson is going to step down at the end of his current term of office and Briggs is looking to step in and up. Strickland's parents are using their considerable political clout as lobbyist to position him to run for Tollson's vacant senate seat in the next election. It certainly wouldn't hurt his chances of winning if he announces he's going to marry a federal court judge with your *bona fides*. Certainly no one will be able to overcome that combination in the State of Illinois."

"Senator? That's crazy, Pete. Strickland hasn't held public office before. Why would anyone think he could be a contender? He's barely ever been in a courtroom. Moreover, why would anyone risk a vote on someone who has no track record in public service or politics? He's a completely unknown entity."

"Untested, perhaps, but certainly not unknown. He's been in the public eye in Illinois politics for some time as you should remember. He took you to every political shindig possible over the last two years. Imagine what he could do for your career when you make a bid for the US Supreme Court. Positioning, KC," he said tapping a finger to her forehead. "If he's in the Senate and you're on the Supreme Court, could the presidency then be out of reach?"

Kristen's eyes widened in shock. "You can't be serious!"

"As a February morning in Chicago, Madam First Lady-to-be or the first female Chief Justice of color."

Kristen heavily sat on a stone bench between the lush green foliage. She felt like the wind had been knocked out of her. *Where had she been when this conniving had been going on?* she wondered. *Was she so wrapped up in a cocoon she didn't see it all coming? No wonder her father insisted, despite the presence of a house majordomo, that she have a cook, a maid, and a butler. The chauffeured car, making the right connections, wearing the right clothes, and marrying the right man. It wasn't only the Supreme Court he was positioning her for as she thought, it was to be the wife of the President of the United States.* The realization made her shudder and involuntarily wrap her arms around her waist.

Pete sat down beside her. He wrapped his arms around her and she buried her face in his chest fighting back her anger and frustration.

"I'm surprised you didn't know this, KC," Peter softly said.

"I had no idea, Pete. I've been so naive," she choked.

"You're still that little girl dancing across the stage in your first recital," he said laying his head atop hers.

"You resented me because your parents made you come and watch when you'd rather be hanging out with your home boys and my brothers," she choked a smile.

"Yeah, well, for once my parents were right," he said kissing her forehead and caressing her face. "You were pure magic, even at eight years old," he said lifting her chin to gaze into her eyes, "and you still are magic to me…"

Kristen blinked, surprised by the look of heat she saw in Peter's eyes. It wasn't brotherly at all. It smoldered with a longing, a lust that threw her thoughts into a prism. The moment was pregnant with unspoken truths.

"Uh, excuse me, Madam," Shelton interrupted causing them both to break their hold on one another and look toward the man standing in the doorway. "State Senator and Mrs. Briggs have arrived and your father asks that you join them in the library for cocktails before dinner."

Kristen pinched the bridge of her nose. "Yes, thank you, Shelton. Please tell Judge Bryant I'll be there after I freshen up."

"Certainly, Madam," he said with a nod as he backed out of the solarium closing the atrium door behind him.

Kristen couldn't look Pete in the eyes for fear of what she would see there.

"Pete, I don't know—."

"Maybe I should leave, KC."

"No, no," she hurriedly said looking up into his face. "Please, Pete, I need you. I mean, I need a friend to help me get through this. I have to have time to think of what to do before this goes too far."

"'Goes too far?' Are you referring to Strickland or to me?"

Kristen inhaled a ragged breath and stood. "Pete, please. I can't think under this much pressure at the moment. I'm not up to battling with my father, Strickland, and his parents alone tonight. Just stay with me now and help me out until I have time to focus on what to do."

Pete nodded and put his hands on her arms. "Just so you know, KC, Strickland Briggs isn't your only option." He gently kissed her on her forehead, dug his hands in his pockets, and walked away.

Kristen watched him leave the solarium and then robotically walked up the back stairs to her bedroom. She flopped on her bed, deep in thought. Her friend, her father, her ex-lover, everyone was pulling her in too many directions. She wanted to run away. Run back to the Polynesian island in the sun. Vivian would make it happen if she asked her, but she knew Ash would not be there waiting for her. Even if she wanted to go to him, she wouldn't know where to start looking. All she knew about the man she had loved was the name Ash. She didn't even know whether that was his real name. What they had shared had meant everything to her, but maybe it had meant nothing to him. She was just one of his wives-for-the-night, but to be in his arms momentarily would shield her from the public spectacle her life would become if her father and Strickland had their way.

What of Peter Brock? Dear Pete, her friend and confidant for so many years. She had no clue he felt anything stronger than brotherly affection for her, but now it was clear that again she had been so naive. She loved Peter Brock, but only as a sister would love her brother. Certainly not with the unspoken, but blatant passion she saw in Peter's eyes. She turned on to her stomach and wept. In her deep despair, only one name escaped her lips. "Ash."

The Briggs left along with Pete and her father went to his bedroom to read. Kristen stood by the fireplace in the library trying to sort out how to handle the hectic orbit swirling around her. She drummed her nails against the marble mantle while Strickland poured another drink for himself.

"Cognac?" he asked.

"Answers would be appreciated more," she said turning to face him, arms folded.

He shrugged, "What do you want to know?"

"I want to know why you're putting on this act, Strickland? Why you let my father and your parents believe we're in love with each other?"

"Love? That's a laugh. The only person in love is Peter Brock. Man, the look on his face tonight was priceless," he mirthlessly laughed. "Frankly, I never liked the guy, but he's useful. His family is very well positioned, wealthy. God knows they've had to pull him out of one misadventure or another most of his life. If his behavior was more discreet, your father would have given more consideration to Peter as a suitable husband for you. As it stands, Peter Brock can only stand and stare. Take him as a lover if you want after we're married."

Kristen pointed an arrow-straight finger at Strickland. "You're crazy!" she spat.

"Oh, so you don't want him? Well, I'm not surprised. I almost feel sorry for the jerk. He's been in love with you so long and still can't get into your panties," he gulped down his drink. "Well, I know what he's missing and believe me, baby, it ain't much."

"Good. I'm glad you find me as physically repulsive as I find you. Now you can stop this charade and get the hell out of my life!"

Strickland mockingly laughed. "No, I'll marry you, Kristen. I'll even bed you now and again. Maybe melt some of that frost from around your edges. 'Physically repulsive?' Naw, I don't think that," he derisively laughed. "When the time is right, we'll have the proper number of children and be viewed as the couple most likely to succeed, and we will succeed."

"What, when you're president? What a crock!"

"Laugh if you want to, Kristen, but I'm going to get there and you'll be by my side."

"I don't love you, Strickland, so what makes you think I'd marry you?"

Strickland poured another drink for himself. "You're so naive, Kristen. Do you think there has been a president and first lady who actually *loved* each other? Trump proved that theory of love doesn't exist. Well, maybe the Obamas, but …" he shrugged. "What kind of dream world are you living in, Kristen? It's all an act and you're good at acting. Look at the Clintons, open philandering when he was governor and the scandal with Monica Lewinsky; Bush and his paramour at the State Department; Nancy Reagan and her rumored infidelities with Frank Sinatra; Carter, who publicly admitted he lusted after other women in his heart. Right. Dare we mention Kennedy in the same breath with Marilyn Monroe?

"No, you'll marry me, Kristen. First, because it's in your best interest to do so to become a justice on the Supreme Court. Secondly, because you know I can make it happen for you with my connections and those of my family. Finally, and probably more importantly, because it's what your father wants you to do and you'd never do anything your father didn't like. So take a lover, Kristen, but keep it discreet. More discrete than Lady Di or Fergie did. You'll find I can be a real Prince Charming. What daddy doesn't know won't hurt him. Still, we're in this for the long haul."

"You're despicable! Get out of my sight, Strickland!"

He checked his watch. "Yeah, you're right. It is getting late and Shannon will be wondering where I am. Appearances, you know. By the way, as you already know, I'm representing a new client and the case has been assigned to your docket. Don't try anything funny when you write your opinion granting my motion for a stay of the lower court's decision. Just a nice, clean opinion. This is a very important case for me. That's why I've taken it on. Senator Tollson thinks it would get me instant national notice."

"I will not compromise my ethics for your image, Strickland! Not now, not ever!"

"Don't be foolish, Kristen. I don't want this case appealed to the Supreme Court on reversible error or because of judicial indiscretion. No, I can take this character, Thomas Marshall, and the publicity, too, when I beat him. He's been in the limelight long enough. After this case is remanded to the lower court to be retried, I'll drop it and move on to something bigger with more visibility. Marshall can wallow in that legal morass at the lower court level, but I'll be on my way to the Senate of the United States. We'll announce our engagement after the case is out of your purview."

"All I have to do is withdraw from the case, Strickland. I will not become involved in your scheme to ascend to the throne!"

"What can you say, baby: That we had a relationship. That we were lovers? So what? I'll simply acknowledge it's true, but you broke it off three months ago. Also true. I'll be the jilted suitor with nothing to gain or lose. The spotlight will be on you to be unbiased in your deliberations on this case. That you are a capable, female jurist entitled to respect? The national women's rights groups and organizations around the country will hold you up for public adoration. I'll spin it to make sure they think you're a saint. They'll call you Saint Kristine Catherine. You'll be squeaky clean, as usual. Counsel for Wayne Agra Industries won't challenge that because it works in their favor. If privately they believe you harbor some ill feelings against me, all the better. In fact, if you try to withdraw, they will demand you hear the case. Moreover, you will bend over backwards to be fair and impartial. Never one for letting down women, you will rise to the occasion. Back out? In this day of the #Me Too movement? I don't think so. You do that I will make you regret it. You and your father!"

Chapter 12

Three weeks later, Ashton sat in his home staring at the national news on television. The press and news media were making a field day out of the pretrial publicity on the _Wayne v. McElroy_ case. He was thankful he wasn't in the center of the fray. Jillian Harris' face was very prominently displayed on the news reports, however, along with a relatively unknown attorney, Strickland Briggs. A loud knocking at his door had been going on for some time. So had the constantly ringing telephone. Press and news media, he figured, wanting to quote him, no doubt. He ignored it all. He only wanted one thing: To find KC.

Every lead he followed led him nowhere. She was still as much of a mystery now as she was over a month ago. Slade was still in Japan and the other investigators were tied up with other legitimate cases. He also made no progress in tracking down the ownership of Plaza de Masquerada or Adventurer Executive Airlines. Everything was shrouded in blind, irrevocable trusts. Whoever owned the island property and airline didn't want to be known and had covered his tracks well.

Finally, the knocking got to Ashton. He picked up the telephone intercom.

"Whoever you are, I'm busy!"

"So am I and I'm also angry! Open this door, Ashton!" his mother's words pealed through the telephone.

Ashton pushed a button on the telephone console and lay back across the chaise lounge. Soon his mother came to stand over him. To say she was merely angry was a gross understatement. She was livid.

"Just what do you think you're doing, Ashton? You haven't been in the office, you won't answer the door or the telephone, and you aren't handling your cases or your department! You didn't even put in an appearance at the pro-am tennis match for your favorite charity! What's wrong with you? Poor Jillian has her hands full with this case, the media attention, and the client isn't happy about your absence!"

"Isn't that what you wanted, Mother? Didn't you want Jillian Harris in the firm?"

"I wanted you two to work together…as a team the way your father and I worked together. He would never leave me high and dry the way you've left Jillian out there!" she said pointing to the television pictures of the scene outside of the court room.

"It's only a hearing on the Petition for Stay, Mother. The trial, if there is one, won't come for months. Jillian is a very able litigator. She can handle this part of it without me."

"The client doesn't share your views and, after all, they are paying handsomely for your services. You could, at least, go to Washington and show your face instead of moping around here pining over some floozy!"

Ashton pinned his mother with his eyes. "She's no floozy, Mother!"

"I was being diplomatic. Call a spade a spade, Ashton! What kind of woman has a three-week affair and then moves on to another conquest? Ever since you came back from that vacation of yours, you've been acting as if you're moonstruck. No one woman deserves this much attention, if she isn't interested in being here with you! You should spend your time with someone, like Jillian, who wants you and wants to be with you!"

"You don't know what you're talking about. This woman is very special to me. She's not what you think she is, and I resent the characterization."

"Of course, I know what I'm talking about! Do you think your father didn't slip every once in a while? Have lovers outside of our marriage? Of course, he did, but he never left me because I understood him and I stood by him. You're no different. Women gravitate to you in droves because you're strong, handsome, rich, and powerful just like your father and your grandfather, back through the generations of the Marshall family, but Esmerelda and I held on to our men. Jillian is good for you. She will be good to you and give you the family you want. She will stand by you no matter what. This other woman is obviously not committed to you or she'd be with you now."

Ashton rose from his seat and approached his mother. "I'm sorry, Mother, I never knew that Dad disrespected you that way."

"It's not important now," she said dismissing his concern with a wave of her hand. "What your father and I had I'll cherish for the rest of my life. We had you. What is important is that you get back on track. You have a future, Ashton. You're the last in the Marshall dynasty. You have to settle down with someone who understands and supports your drive and ambition. Someone who understands how to use power. Someone who can give you a family."

What he wanted to tell his mother was he already found someone to share his life with, but he didn't want to carry on an argument with her. The sooner this case was over, the sooner his life would be his again. So, he simply acquiesced and agreed to go to Washington.

⁂

"I'm glad you showed up, Ash," Jillian said after a long session in preparation for appearance in court the next day. "Maybe we can spend a few days touring the city after this is over. I haven't spent much time on the East Coast. I'm sure Sheila wouldn't mind us taking a mini vacation."

"Stay if you want to, Jillian," he said, barely paying attention to her as he continued to read the case files.

"And you? Wouldn't you like to stay here with me?"

"I have other things to do. I am going to look up an old friend of mine while I'm here then I'm heading out."

"Still tracking down this illusive woman, I suppose."

Ashton ignored her question and continued reading. Then something in the files caught his notice.

"What's this entry about a relationship between one of the judges on the panel and counsel for McElroy?" he asked reading the file more closely.

"Oh that. It's nothing," Jillian dismissively said. "Apparently this new judge, Catherine Bryant, and Strickland Briggs were an item a while back in Chicago. She dumped him."

"So why is this on the record?"

"Apparently, she wanted the chief judge to rule on the question of propriety. Nothing to worry about. In fact, since Judge Bryant dumped Briggs, there's a likelihood she doesn't harbor any amorous feelings toward him. It would be even better if she hated his guts. Then we'd have one sure vote in our favor to quash this foolish appeal petition. If this goes against us, which I'm sure it won't, we could have a basis on which to claim judicial indiscretion, have the matter vacated, and start over with a new panel of judges. "

"That's not the way I work, Jillian, and you know it."

"You're the one who has the background investigations run on everyone related to a case, Ash. I've watched you use every trick in the book and even a few that weren't to win for your client. This just came up as a matter of record and it's an ace in the hole if it's needed."

"Smart move on this Judge Bryant's part, though, putting it on the record. Your 'judicial indiscretion scenario' goes right out the window," he absently said. "No, if we're going to win this, it has to be on the merits of the case, not on some technicality. The lower court tried the pertinent facts, the record is complete, and there is no basis for appeal. My oral argument will confirm that and counsel for McElroy can't retry the facts of the lower court's decision. This is open and shut. I should be out of here as soon as court concludes tomorrow."

"We're ready no matter what," Jillian said walking around behind Ashton and massaging his shoulders. She bent and kissed his ear running her tongue teasing around the lobe as her hands slid down his chest. "You've been working since the moment you arrived, Ashton," she seductively whispered. "Why don't we relax together in a warm bath?"

Ashton lifted her hands from his body, stood, picked up his jacket from the back of the chair, and slipped his arms inside. "We're ready for tomorrow. All of the loose ends are tied up. Enjoy your bath and have a good night, Jillian."

"Ashton, you can't run and hide from me forever. Sooner or later, you're going to realize we could be great together. We make a good team. I could even find myself in love with you."

"Don't hold the thought, Jillian. I won't *ever* find myself in love with you."

With that, he turned and left the office space in the hotel.

⁂

"Well, Judge Bryant, are you ready to hear your first oral argument on this bench?" the kindly, silver-haired chief judge said, smiling.

"Yes, Judge Hathaway, but I still have certain reservations about sitting for this first case on today's docket."

"Not to worry. I have the upmost respect for Judge Vivian Montgomery. She championed your selection which is enough for me to believe you're more than capable of handling your responsibilities. Besides, there are three of us on this panel. Counsel for both parties were given ample notice of your prior association with lead attorney Strickland Briggs and neither party has raised an objection to your presence. You've sworn you can evaluate matters that come before this court fairly and equitably and without prejudice. This is only a Petition for Stay of a lower court's decision. It shouldn't take that long to hear the arguments and this matter should be over quickly. Then we can move on to other matters on the docket. I can promise you they'll probably be more interesting than this first case today, no matter what the press and news media want to make out of this."

Kristen smiled. "Then I'm ready and very eager to get started."

"Good. Then let's have at it, shall we, Judge Bryant."

⁂

"*All rise! Hear ye! Hear ye! Hear ye!*" the Clerk of the Court announced in a loud, clear, booming voice. "*The United States Federal Court of Appeals for the District of Columbia Circuit will come to order! Chief Judge Harold Thomas Hathaway, Judge Richmond Jenkins, and Judge K. Catherine Bryant, presiding!"*

Chapter 13

Ashton was still jotting notes when the Clerk of the Court bade them all to stand. He automatically rose from his seat but didn't immediately look up. When he did, he did a double take, his heart jolting. He blinked several times, not believing what he saw before him. It couldn't be her! his brain told him. This had to be a case of mistaken identity. He had KC on his mind these past weeks so much that now his mind was playing tricks on him. He was seeing her in every woman. The woman seating herself before him, whose hair was pulled back away from her face in a severe French roll, rimless glasses, and a face naked of enhancements, looked ten years older than his KC—but yet… He shook his head to clear his thoughts. The black robe. That's it. Maybe, if it didn't cover her body like a tent, he could see her legs, but that was impossible now. It took all of his restraint to keep from rushing forward.

He had to do something!

"Be seated," the Clerk of the Court announced after the three-judge panel settled in.

Everyone in the courtroom complied—everyone except Ashton.

From her chair, Jillian urgently tugged on his arm, trying to signal him to take his seat, but Ashton ignored her. "Ashton, sit down! What's wrong with you?" she hissed. She stared at him, suddenly aware something was wrong.

Without looking down, Ashton pulled his arm away from her. He stared at the panel of judges, but his gaze was riveted to only one judge. "Your Honor, may I approach the bench?"

Kristen thought that, like Lot's wife, if she looked up, she would surely turn to a pillar of salt. That voice. The timbre. Only one person had a voice like that, the passionate memories that were folded into the sounds from his throat. She took off her reading glasses that blurred her distance vision. She paid for that gesture. Her audible gasp in the cavernous, silent courtroom turned heads as she blinked back her shock and struggled to regain her composure. There, standing behind the highly polished oak table across the cavernous courtroom was the man she had… the thought galvanized her. She fumbled with her glasses. Trembling hands could not be stilled. Her mouth went dry. Slipping the eyeglasses back on her face, she read the cover of the brief before her again. Ash. Thomas Ashton Marshall, III, Esquire. Something was wrong. It had to be a mistake. This man couldn't be the same man, but when his eyes riveted on her, her body froze.

"Mr. Marshall, the Clerk hasn't even called your case yet. You'll have an opportunity to speak, I assure you," Chief Justice Hathaway smoothly said.

"Yes, Your Honor, I'm aware of that, but I believe it's imperative that…" he froze seeing the look of panic on Kristen's face. Her light skin went even paler. He momentarily lost his train of thought just looking at her; wanting to touch her. Her lips parted and her tongue slide over them in a nervous gesture. A jolt went straight to his loins and the memory of them together flashed before his eyes. Even in the presence of the austere surroundings, he wanted to capture that devilish, pink tongue of hers as he had done more than a month ago. He wiped his face with one hand and felt the moisture just looking at her caused, but she was sweating, too, he could tell. She had picked up the glass of water in front of her three times. Her hands were shaking. He couldn't determine whether she was seeing the same vision as he was. Visions of them together loving each other.

"Yes, yes, what is it, Mr. Marshall? Approach the bench," Judge Hathaway ordered in obvious frustration.

It all came back to him in torrents, his mind working fast. The pretrial discussion that Jillian handled. He fumbled flipping pages in his trial book to find the court's decree. *Had he read it right? Had KC been in love with and/or engaged to opposing counsel, Strickland Briggs? Was that why she wouldn't tell him who she was, where she lived or even her full name?* He had to have answers and the only person who could answer him was sitting in judgment outside of his reach.

"Mr. Marshall?" the Chief Judge asked again.

"Uh, yes, Your Honor," he said, slowly moving toward the elevated dais. His arousal was painful.

Kristen thought she would faint at any moment. He was more magnificent than she remembered. His power, navy-blue, pin-striped suit, a crisp white shirt, navy and gray Hermès silk tie, did its job on his tall, well-muscled body. The man knew how to dress for success and she knew how to undress him. He looked every bit the legal icon everyone said he was and much more. She tried not to make eye contact, but his riveting gaze didn't allow her to look away. An automatic response to being so close to Ash, she felt the poignant constriction in her womb. Quickly, her eyes skidded around the courtroom feeling as if all eyes were on her. A glance at Strickland, also standing before her, confirmed he was carefully studying her. Her eyes skittered to her father sitting in the back of the courtroom with Strickland's parents. The courtroom was packed and the news media sat in the spectator section. She diverted her attention back to the legal briefs in front of her. She didn't know what else to do. Her eyes skipped to Pete whose narrowed gaze told her he knew something was amiss. She noticed Tina and Cheryl whispering to one another, frowning. She recalled they had been chatting all morning about Thomas Marshall and how drop-dead gorgeous he is. Vivian was right. He did look like the athlete-turned-actor and businessman Rick Fox. She wanted to drop dead at that very moment. If anyone in the courtroom knew she and Thomas Ashton Marshall had…she couldn't even think the words. Then she heard him speak.

"Your Honor, with the Court's indulgence, I would like to request a continuance."

"A continuance? Mr. Marshall, are you ill?"

"Uh, no, Your Honor, not exactly, but something has come to my attention that, I believe, directly bears on this case. I need time to review the merits of the matter."

"Is it so important you cannot proceed at this time?"

"Yes, Your Honor, it is."

"How long will you need to address this matter, Mr. Marshall?"

"A few days, a week at most."

The judge looked toward Strickland. "Any objection, Mr. Briggs?"

"Yes, Your Honor. If Mr. Marshall is ill equipped to argue this case, after having ample time to prepare, I don't want to waste the Court's precious time nor that of my client's because of his ineptitude. He should allow the Petition for Stay to pass unchallenged and the Court can proceed to return the case to the lower court for rehearing."

"Mr. Marshall?" the Chief Judge asked waiting for the retort.

How could KC be involved with a prick like Strickland Briggs? Ashton wondered. He didn't usually take an instant dislike to a person, but Briggs was quickly at the top of his shit list. He had to thank Briggs for providing a distraction though. His adrenalin began to kick in. Oh, how he loved the smell of fear in his opposing counsel. He'd take particular pleasure in destroying this man.

"I assure you, Your Honor, this matter does not arise out of any inability on my part to adequately prepare for this hearing. Rather, as I have stated, new information has just come to my attention. There is, therefore, no basis to acquiesce to Mr. Brigg's request. His request is an unnecessary and premature assumption that the Count could proceed to trial before all pertinent issues are fully explored. My request may, in fact, relieve the Court of the need to hear oral argument on the lower Court's decision. Thus, saving time and the Court's resources. The defendant maintains the lower Court's decision is full and complete."

Briggs fired back. "If that is the case, Your Honor, then Mr. Marshall should be required to make a full and complete disclosure of this 'new information' before you rule on the question of a continuance. If this new information puts my client at a disadvantage, then the plaintiff deserves the right to prepare a defense."

"Your Honor, I will make a full and complete disclosure of this information, *if*, in fact, it appears to be pivotal to this matter. At the moment, however, as this issue has recently come to light, I have not had an opportunity to evaluate it."

The judge heavily sighed, holding up both hands to forestall the legal jockeying. "Mr. Marshall, you ask this Court to grant a continuance while you investigate this alleged new development. Yet, you do not state what this new development is—."

"Precisely the reason to reject his request, Your Honor—," Strickland interrupted.

Judge Hathaway silenced Briggs with a glance. "Mr. Marshall, the Court does not favorably look upon delaying tactics."

Briggs presented a cool façade on the outside, but he was fuming on the inside. He'd bet real money Kristen had something to do with this somehow. It wasn't the type of thing she would do, but he had her over a barrel. She was such *a "lady"* and Miss Goodie Goodie he knew she'd find a way out of his plans for her. He'd make her pay. Oh yes, she'd pay. Before he gave her the vanilla loving she wanted, but now he'd whip her into the supplicant he deserved. Shannon wouldn't be his only love slave. She'd learned to respond to the whip and soon the strong Kristen Catherine Bryant would kneel before him and respond to his needs. Fifty shades? Ha! He had that and more!

Hathaway continued. "Counsel may step back while the Court considers this request for a brief continuance," he said and exhaled a frustrated breath.

Counsel for both sides returned to their seats while the Chief Judge quietly discussed the matter with Kristen and the other judge on the panel. Minutes passed while the judges conferred. Then the Chief Judge spoke.

"Mr. Marshall, the Court is aware you primarily practice before the World Court in the Hague, and you rarely practice before courts in this country. Your record before the World Court is somewhat flamboyant, but, nevertheless, unimpeachable. I will not look with favor on any such future requests. That aside, this Court will allow you some latitude, *pro hac vice.* Your request for a continuance is granted, but only for four days. You will return to this courtroom four days hence in the morning at nine o'clock."

Strickland leapt to his feet. "Your Honor! This is wholly improper! Mr. Marshall has not made his *prima facie* case for a continuance and I demand—!"

"*Mr. Briggs!*" came the sharp reproach from the Chief Judge. "In *my* Court, you do not *demand* anything! You will be allowed to prepare a response should Mr. Marshall bring to the Court's attention evidence that is pivotal on the question of a Stay of the lower court's decision. I have considered your arguments, ruled on the question of a continuance, and I am satisfied with these proceedings as they currently stand. Court will begin in fifteen minutes," the judge said banging the gavel.

"*All rise!*" the Clerk of the Court instructed.

Kristen didn't know whether her legs would carry her out of the courtroom. She stood and kept her eyes trained on the door that would lead her to safety. As soon as she was out of the courtroom, she headed for the ladies' room, nearly knocking over a secretary as she bolted through the door. She splashed cold water on her face and held her hands there wishing this day had never happened. Her breathing was labored and her hands shook. If she didn't know better, she would swear she was experiencing a full-blown panic attack. She wouldn't have voted against the continuance if her life depended on it—and it did.

Leaving the courtroom in a hurry, Ashton was in a near daze. He broke through the crush of reporters issuing a terse "No comment," to each question. Jillian was right on his heels as he entered the limousine. "To the hotel," he barked to the chauffeur and then loosened his tie and unbuttoned his shirt at the collar.

"Do you mind telling me what the hell just went on in there?" Jillian snapped. "What new information do you have that I'm not aware of? Also why were you fixated on Judge Bryant? You two were staring at each other like—."

"Don't interrogate me, Jillian! I'm not on the witness stand! I'll drop you at the hotel. I have something to do. That's all I'm going to say about this!" he sharply said.

Jillian sat back in the plush limousine. She was livid. The first thing she was going to do was find out what the hell was going on!

Chapter 14

The limousine ride out to Prince George's County, Maryland, didn't take long in the late morning traffic. Shortly, it pulled into the gate leading to a beautifully-restored and refurbished, antebellum mansion. Horses romped in the fields as the limousine passed up the long, blacktopped driveway between rows of brilliantly-colored Live Oak and tall, dark green, cone-shaped pine trees standing sentry in a straight line on both sides of the drive. Ranch hands moved cattle from one grazing field to another. Other ranch hands rode tractors baling hay. Harvesting equipment crawled across the vast expanse. The ranch was a veritable beehive of activity on a particularly dry, cool, September day. When the limousine pulled to a stop in front of the huge, white mansion, Ashton opened the door, before the chauffeur could get out of the car. He hurriedly stepped out and jogged up the long, wide stone steps to the front door. He knocked and then paced waiting for the door to be opened. When it did, identical twin girls, who couldn't be much older than three or four years old, stood looking up at him. His heart melted at the sight of their wide eyes and open smiles.

"Well, hello, ladies. My name is Thomas Marshall. Is your mother at home?"

"Yes," they said in unison. "Do you want to speak to her?" one of them asked.

"Yes," he said, smiling.

"Tom Cat," a warm, familiar voice washed over him.

"Vivian," he said, smiled and swept her into his arms. "Only you call me that."

"With good reason, you will recall." She giggled. "I certainly didn't expect to see you at my door."

"I planned to visit you and Chuck tomorrow, but something came up. I need to talk with you."

"Certainly, come in," she said. "Now, Laurel, Laura, this is Mr. Marshall."

"Mommy, why did you call him Tom Cat if his name is Mr. Marshall?" Laura asked.

"That's a long story, honey," Ashton smiled stooping to their height.

"Goodie, we like stories. Daddy and mommy read stories to us all the time so does out big sisters and brothers. Would you tell us one?" Laurel gleefully asked.

"Aren't you two young ladies supposed to be helping Mrs. Miller bake cookies for your daddy?" Vivian interjected with a warm smile.

"Yes, Mommy," the two little cherubs sighed and then scampered away. "Bye, bye, Mr. Thomas Tom Cat Marshall," they waved.

"They're adorable, Viv," he said rising and watching the girls disappear down a long hall.

"Yes, they are and quite a handful, too," she said, laughing while slipping her arm into his and guiding him into a large library. "I'm not moving quite as fast these days and they race to open doors or to answer the phone. That's Chuck's doing. He tells them they have to take care of me and they take his instructions seriously."

They sat on a sofa and Vivian placed a pillow at her back and put her feet up on an ottoman.

"You and Chuck are still adopting children, I see, and the man is also keeping you very pregnant," he said, laughing.

"Very happy, too," she said rubbing her burgeoning tummy.

"Where is that big galoot anyway? I haven't seen him in years."

"At his hospital not far from here. He had an early surgical schedule this morning and then rounds. He usually makes it home around lunch time. Then, he has office appointments starting around two in the afternoon. His private practice office is right across the road next to the general store and barber shop. How is Esmerelda? I haven't talked with her since the last meeting of the One Thousand Black Women."

"Still as active as ever," Ashton distractedly answered.

"All right, Tom Cat, enough with the small talk. What's up?" Vivian asked with a knowing smile.

"Vivian, you know me too well."

"Not *that* well," she teased, "but well enough to know when something very important is on your mind. So, let's hear it."

"Do you know Judge Bryant very well?"

"KC Bryant? Sure, I do. KC and I were in undergrad at Spelman College together. In fact, we were roommates. We've been close friends for many years. I lobbied for her to step in for me while I'm on sabbatical. I hope she'll want to stick around after my year-long leave of absence is up. Why do you ask?"

"I'll level with you, Vivian, because we've been friends for a long time. I need to talk with her...privately. Do you know where she lives?"

"Yes, but you can go to her office, Ash. She moved into my old office at the Court House. It's about as private as it gets."

"I can't do that, Viv. I'm too easily identified and I have a case pending before her."

"I'm aware that you do. I had lunch with her when she first came to Washington and she's been out to the ranch for dinner with our mutual friends. Does the reason you want to see her have anything to do with your case?"

"Not directly, no. It's personal. If I go to her office, the visit would have to be made a part of the official record. What I have to discuss with her I can't make a part of the record."

"Is this so urgent you can't wait until the matter is over before you talk with her? As I understood it, the matter pending before the court is a Petition for Stay. That should only take a day or two to resolve."

"It is, yes, but I must see her immediately."

"Mrs. Montgomery," a voice came from the library door.

Both Ashton and Vivian turned to look at the housekeeper.

"Yes, Mrs. Miller?"

"You have a call on line two. It's Judge Kristen Catherine Bryant. She says it's important or I wouldn't interrupt you."

"Thank you, Mrs. Miller." Vivian turned to look at Ashton. "This is shaping up to be a day full of surprises."

Kristen impatiently waited for Vivian to come to the telephone. When she did, Kristen nearly burst. "Viv, I'm in trouble. I need to see you. Court has ended early for the day. Can I come to your place now?"

"Whoa, KC. Take a breath. Does your trouble have anything to do with T. Ashton Marshall?"

Kristen was taken aback. She heavily sat on the sofa in her office. "Yes, but how did you know that?"

"Short story. He's here now. He wants to talk privately with you."

"I…I don't know," she mindlessly stammered. "I don't know if it's a good idea to see him."

"Well, as I told you, I've known Ashton for many years and he's not going to just let whatever is going on between you two rest."

"I'm on my way."

Kristen didn't remember much about the drive to Vivian and Chuck's ranch. She was so distracted she had to use the GPS in her car to get her there. She barely remembered the details of the cases argued after the break. Thankfully, they were short and she had an excellent legal staff who would review the issues and prepare preliminary opinions. Now, if the rest of her life could be handled that easily, but, deep in her heart, she knew it couldn't. She was certain of it when she pulled her Lexus up behind the limousine parked in front of Vivian's mansion and saw the tall figure standing and waiting on the veranda. He moved toward her car without expression and opened her car door as soon as she turned off the ignition. His gaze was so unnerving and riveting her abdomen knotted. She unbuckled her seat belt and swung her legs down to the ground. Ashton extended his hand to her and she took it.

Ashton's breathing nearly stopped when their hands touched. He wanted to pull her into his arms and kiss her until there was no tomorrow, but he held back. She looked so beautiful and yet so weary and worried. Her eyes didn't sparkle and he wondered whether he was the reason. Wordlessly, he guided her away from the mansion along a cobblestone path that wound through the forest to a guest cottage near a lake on the property. Once inside, Kristen went to the far wall not turning to look at him. He held his breath, but the words came out anyway.

"Kristen, I love you."

He saw her body shake with pent up emotion. When her hand went to her face to stifle a sob, he went to her in a flash pulling her back to his chest enveloping her in his arms. "I love you," he urgently whispered at her ear, kissing her neck then spinning her within the circle of his arms and capturing her mouth in his. He swallowed her sobs until she began to respond to his urgent need for her. Slowly, as he held her, the magic began to return. Tentatively, her arms circled him, while she went up on her toes to meet him as he bent to her. He inhaled her sweet, intoxicating scent. His hands raked through her tight French twist pulling the pins away until her hair sprang free and fluidly fell through his fingers. Maddening sensations streaked through him as he molded her body to his. His phallus strained the fabric of his designer suit.

"I love you," he repeated, and liquid fire coursed through her body. Kristen tried to hold back, but it was futile. She felt her body tremble with the lowered timbre of his voice. He swept her up in his arms and carried her to the bed. He set her feet on the floor and held her as he undressed her. His mouth followed each bare spot as it was uncovered until she wore only a lacy bra, matching panties, a garter belt and sheer hose that disappeared into her high-heeled pumps.

"Ashton," she breathlessly said, "please, we can't do this."

"Why, because you're a judge? I won't accept that. I didn't fall in love with a judge. I fell in love with a woman. A beautiful, passionate, and sensuous woman," he said tossing his jacket on a chair. The rest of his clothes quickly followed suit until he stood bare before her. "My woman," he said when he again took her in his arms and kissed her breathless. "I was nearly out of my mind because I thought I had lost you," he said kissing her ear. "Do you think I'll permit your position to stand in the way of what we have? Nothing, and no one will ever do that. I'm yours, Kristen. Only yours," he said removing the lacy bra that covered her ample breasts. He took one hardened nipple in his mouth and stroked the tip with his tongue until Kristen moaned from deep in her throat. His mouth blazed a trail down her stomach to her abdomen. Her intoxicating scent and moist panties driving him near the edge of sanity. His hands slipped the panties down her long legs and his mouth covered the place where they had been, leaving the sexy garter belt, hose and high heels in place.

Kristen thought her knees would buckle until Ashton laid her on the bed and covered her body with his. Spontaneously, she kicked off her shoes and raised her knees as he began again to raise her to another level of ecstasy. When her first orgasm gripped her, she held on to Ashton's shoulders, digging her fingers into his flesh until they were numb. "Ash, Ash," she moaned climbing yet another peak to ecstasy.

"Kristen," he moaned, "How I love you." Then he slipped inside her.

The urgency of their need for each other brightly burned in the little cottage by the lake in the woods. The afternoon slipped into evening and the two lovers lay together totally spent. Ashton pulled Kristen close to him half covering her body with his as he touched her gliding his hand down her side to her bottom and then to her firm thigh.

"Why did you leave me?" he asked, his mouth at her throat.

Kristen cradled his head in her arms lovingly stroking him. "I had no choice, Ash. What we had was like a ship-board romance, like two ships passing in the night. We had no past and no future. We only had a present."

"We made a commitment, Kristen. Kristen," he repeated. "It feels so good to call you by your name. Kristen Catherine—."

"Ash, please." She breathed him in, tightening her arms around him. "Don't do this."

He raised his head to look into her eyes. "Don't do what, Kristen?"

"Don't make this harder than it has to be," she said turning her face away.

Ashton narrowed his eyes and with a hand at her chin, turned her face back to his. "What are you trying to tell me, KC?"

"I think you know."

"Know what?"

"We can't see each other; that we can't be together like this ever again."

"The hell you say! The only thing standing between us is this damn _Wayne v. McElroy_ case, and I intend to eliminate that problem _tout suite_."

"Ashton, please listen to me. It's not only the case. You don't understand. This is very complicated."

"Then explain it to me. Some people think I'm, at least, literate."

"I have...obligations."

"So do I, and your point is?"

"I've just been appointed."

"Fine. You want to continue on the federal bench, that works for me. I'll close up shop in Portland and move to Washington. I can open an office here. In fact, I have more than one reason for wanting to make a change at this particular time."

"Ashton, you're not listening to what I'm trying to tell you. You're creating solutions to problems you don't understand. I have a plan for my life. One I can't share with you."

Ashton raised his upper torso, his arms straddling Kristen's bare body.

"Can you share it with Strickland Briggs?" his directed gaze searching her eyes. "Is that what you're trying to tell me? Is there still something between you?"

"No, not exactly, but my father..._Oh, God_," she said looking at her watch. "_Father!_ I have to go, Ash. My father will have the police looking for me if I don't get home immediately." She sat up, but Ashton refused to let her leave the bed.

"Call him from here, KC. We can shower and then we'll go to see your father."

"No!" she nearly shouted. "We can't do that."

"Kristen, I know our being together may come as a shock to your father, but he'll get over it."

"You don't know my father."

"No, but I'm not concerned about meeting him."

"You should be."

Ashton laughed. "Tough, huh?"

"Does the name Clarence Edward Bryant mean anything to you?"

"The Hanging Judge? Illinois State Court?"

"Yes, the same."

"I don't care for the man's positions in criminal cases or his politics, but I'm in love with his daughter, not him. So that means we'll only visit him on Father's Day." His eyes narrowed. "Wait a minute. If he's your father, then Clarence Junior and George Bryant are your brothers. I remember when they played professional sports. We have several mutual acquaintances in the sports and entertainment industry. We can visit them, too," he chuckled. "Meeting my mother will take a bit of intestinal fortitude on your part. However, considering how easily you handle me, I have no doubt you will persevere over She-who-must-be-obeyed. Now about that shower…" he said pulling her more firmly beneath him for another round of lovemaking.

Another hour elapsed before Kristen left the cottage and headed back to Washington. She had convinced Ashton he shouldn't accompany her home, but that was the only thing he agreed to. She quickly discovered Ashton was a very tenacious man, but he stayed at the ranch to have dinner with Vivian and her husband, Chuck Montgomery.

The headache started as soon as she entered the house.

"*Where the hell have you been?*" her father thundered. "You had a house full of important guests waiting to celebrate your first day on the federal bench and you chose not to put in an appearance. A few of your office staff are still waiting for you in the library."

"Father, please. I have some very important matters to consider and I can't discuss this with you. My friends and associates will understand."

"Does this have anything to do with that young upstart, Thomas Marshall? His behavior in court this morning was reprehensible. Why was he looking at you that way?"

"Father, I'm sorry. I can't talk about this now."

"Then we'll discuss this in the morning before I leave for the airport. Good night."

"Good night, Father," she said relieved he had not pressed her further.

As soon as her father was up the stairs and out of sight, Kristen expelled a long, weary sigh. Her shoulders dropped and she cupped her face then drilling her fingers through the length of her hair.

"Looks like you need a friend," Pete said stepping out of the shadow of the dark hallway, his hands dug deep in his pockets.

Kristen's head snapped up and she robotically moved toward him.

"Just hold me, Pete. I need…someone to just hold me for a moment."

Pete's arms enveloped her as she laid her head against his chest. She felt the gentle pounding of his heart as she tried to gather her wits about her. What was she going to do? She was deeply in love with a man she could not have.

"Tough day, huh?" he quietly asked and kissed the top of her head.

"The worst," she mumbled against his chest.

"Vivian help you sort out whatever it is that's bothering you?"

Kristen's head rose and her eyes narrowed in question as she gazed into his eyes.

"Your telephone log. Her number was the last one you called before you disappeared this afternoon. I called her and she confirmed you were there and you were safe, but she said you were unavailable."

"I, uh, had something I needed to discuss and…"

Pete put a quieting finger to her lips. "One of Vivian's daughters answered the telephone when I called and the little girl confirmed that a Mr. Marshall was also there."

"How did you know?"

"Considering his behavior in court this morning and yours, well it didn't take a Harvard lawyer to figure out something was going on between you. Something that had nothing to do with the case."

"Pete, I can't—."

"Talk about it," he said finishing her thought and nodding his apparent understanding. "Be careful, KC. This could spell trouble for you…and for him. Strickland Briggs may be a pig, but he's not stupid. He's beneath contempt, but he's not beneath using you or anyone else to have his way."

"How well I know," she said and sighed easing out of his embrace.

Just then she heard giggles and looked over Pete's shoulder.

"Mumph, mumph, mumph, KC," Tina teased. "You sure do have a way with men!"

A slight smile curled Kristen's lips. "I wish," she said, but she noticed the unsmiling face of her friend, Cheryl, who quickly turned and walked back to the library.

"Something must have happened. Thomas Marshall either got a hard on for you or he thought he saw his Maker. The man was nearly speechless as soon as he saw you and you looked like you were going to faint. We tried to warn you he was gorgeous, KC."

"Uh, yes. You did and you were right of course. He is striking," she said, briefly cutting her eyes toward Pete. If everyone thought it was just his handsome face and powerful physique that had startled her, then for the moment, no further explanation was necessary.

"How about something to eat?" Pete smoothly asked, guiding her toward the dining room.

"I don't think I could swallow a bite."

"You haven't eaten since breakfast, I'll bet," Tina said grabbing her arm and helping Pete guide her.

They strolled into the huge, formal dining room and Kristen's eyes widened in surprise. The remnants of a lavish buffet spread over three tables. China, crystal, and silver gleamed. A silent Justice is Blind ice sculpture stood melting in the center position surrounded by red roses, baby's breaths, and greenery at her feet.

"It's lovely, Tina," Kristen said and hugged her friend. "Thank you."

"We know you hate it when we do this, but we wanted to surprise you. Pete and Cheryl helped, of course. Don't worry. We didn't try to cook. We used this fabulous caterer, Greenfield Brothers. They're really good and drop-dead handsome. The food was not only delicious, but also plentiful which was a good thing because everyone was here. My family, Peter's parents, and Cheryl's parents flew in from California where they had been on assignment for their respective television shows. Your brothers, Clarence Junior and George, had to get back to Chicago. They couldn't stay, so they asked we give their baby sister a kiss for them. I personally collected the one from George," she said, grinning.

Kristen shook her head. She knew of Tina's interest in her older brother, but didn't realize until that moment how interested she was. The look of longing in her eyes told the story. Tina was hooked, but, with Tina, being hooked on a guy was usually temporary.

Kristen partook of the buffet nibbling on a selection of delicious tidbits and slowly walked into the library. She found everything she tried was delicious. Peter mentioned the Greenfield Brothers are friends of Vivian's. She wondered whether Vivian knew of this surprise event and chose to let her spend the time with Ashton. Likely so given that Vivian would have been on the guest list along with her husband Chuck.

In the library, Cheryl sat alone talking on her cellphone, but looked up and smiled as Kristen entered the room. Cheryl quickly ended her conversation, but Kristen noticed her friend's smile didn't quite reach her eyes.

"Congrats, KC. You looked good up there on the bench today."

"Thanks, Cheryl. It was truly an experience."

"I'll bet," she absently said.

Kristen moved closer and sat beside Cheryl. "Anything wrong?" she asked.

"Wrong? Why would you ask that?"

"Because I've known you a very long time and although I know you're happy for me, you aren't asking a million questions the way you normally do."

Cheryl smiled. "It's your day, KC. You're rightfully the center of everyone's attention, especially that fine specimen of a man, Thomas

Marshall. I've known you long enough to know you don't like the limelight. I'm just giving you a break from the barrage of questions everyone's been asking. Besides, the press and news media are going to be asking a lot of questions. I'll save mine to prep you for your news conference. Don't forget you're scheduled to do MSNBC and CNN in a couple of days."

"You're crazy if you think I'm falling for this. You're chattering about inconsequential things, Cheryl, and it's totally out of character for you. Now tell me. What's going on with you?"

Cheryl abruptly stood up. "Not tonight, KC. I've got a hot date waiting for me. I need to get my freak on," she said, laughing.

"We will talk, Cheryl," Kristen said in a directed tone.

"I know," Cheryl said straightening her stylish fall, avocado-colored outfit. "I think…" she started, but when Pete and Tina walked into the room, Cheryl stopped talking. "Look, hon, gotta go. See you tomorrow," she said giving Kristen a quick kiss on the cheek and then rushing from the room.

She breezed out of the room so quickly that Kristen didn't even have a chance to answer.

"What's up with Cheryl?" Kristen asked Pete and Tina.

Tina listlessly shrugged and plopped down beside Kristen. Pete said nothing at all.

"Will someone please tell me what's going on?" Kristen asked again.

"I guess we could ask you the same question," Tina said. "Do we have something to be concerned about with you and Thomas Marshall?"

Kristen looked away. "No. Nothing at all."

Chapter 15

Early the next morning, Ashton finished breakfast in his suite at the McCoy Regent Hotel while talking on the telephone tying up loose ends. He was amazed he could sleep at all. Weeks of worry about and want of Kristen had taken its toll on him. The sheer joy of knowing he had found her made him rest easier.

"Yeah, man, so you can call off the search," he said, to his friend, Slade.

"Glad to hear it," Slade said. "So, what's next?"

"I'll head back to Portland after court in a couple of days, close down my house, and have a few things shipped to DC. In the interim, until this case is over, I'll find someplace for me and Kristen to live and then I'll set up offices here in town. Vivian offered the use of her Watergate condo to me."

"Sounds like you're moving at the speed of light as usual," Slade said, laughing.

"That's not fast enough for me, good buddy."

"What about the lady? How does she feel about this?"

"She loves me, Slade. I'm in love with her. That's all I need to know."

"Counselor, you didn't answer my question. What is the lady prepared to do?"

That Ashton and Slade were friends, closer than brothers, for many years was evident in the way they read each other's thoughts and between the lines. Ashton was never able to keep anything from Slade, but this time he had to. He was not feeling as confident about what Kristen would do, but he did know he wouldn't let her disappear from his life again. He had to admit, even if only to himself, that Slade's mention of missing women from the island gave him pause for a time, but he breathed easier now that he found her again.

The memory of them together increased his breathing. She was so nervous when they entered the cottage; pacing back and forth like a scared rabbit afraid of being caught in a snare. Her eyes were wide and wary, but he also read the passion in them when he approached her. He opened his arms, and, for a moment, he thought she would bolt from the room, but then she hadn't. Something in her seemed to still and then she walked into his embrace. Her body trembled like a fragile bird. He folded her in his arms while his heart exploded with joy. His bliss was so great, so complete it brought tears to his eyes. His arm around her back and his other hand laced in her perfusion of corkscrew hair removing the pins that held her lustrous crowning glory captive, her sweet natural scent raising his nature to its peak. Nothing in his life felt so good, so right, so natural as holding Kristen in his arms and against his needful body.

They held each other for what seemed like an eternity, but it had only been minutes. Then he couldn't wait any longer. He had to taste her sweet mouth. Slowly he released her just enough so he could look into her beautiful, but worried eyes. Her arms gently and tentatively circled his neck and she rose up on tiptoes to meet his mouth. Slowly, at first, they kissed in short, luscious, butterfly passes. Then their lithe tongues joined in frolicking together and stoking the flames of their passion for each other. His body was rock hard when she uttered a soft moan and her arms tightened around his neck giving him unobstructed access to her body. The only sound in the cabin was their hot, wet kisses when he began to remove her suit jacket. His soon followed without releasing the tender hold they had on each other's mouth. He barely felt her soft hands remove his tie and one by one undoing the buttons on his shirt, but her touch against his bare skin, plying his hardened raisin-like nipples nearly drove him over the brink. They made quick work of the rest of their clothes never saying a word, but instinctively knowing what each needed.

When he laid her on the bed, his urgent need to be inside her overridden and erased his conscious thoughts to protect themselves. He was not prepared to make love to her, not expecting to be with her that way, but love her he did. Love her with every ounce of his strength and being. Over and over again they reached climaxes riveting them together in passion's age-old rhythms. He couldn't seem to get enough of her. They took each other so many times he had lost count and thrown caution to the wind. He would never regret their impromptu joining, even if their lack of caution produced a child. He wanted that, a baby with his beloved KC. In fact, he wanted a houseful of sons and daughters with her. That would be the next topic of conversation they would share. How soon they could start a family?

Closing his eyes, Ashton recalled the memory of his mouth on her sweet, taught nipples, the swell of her breasts when he cupped them, the depth of her navel as he tongued it, the soft fur of her pubis as he nuzzled it, and then the hidden center of her passion at her inverted Y-axis as he pleasured it. After her next orgasm, she took him to ecstasy when she kissed her way all over his body, teasing his chest and abdomen and then conquered his raging phallus, totally eclipsing his ability to breathe. The sweet, erotic torture culminated when he brought her body under him and slowly by inches sunk into her hot, wet, and tight womanly core. Time spun out of existence. Over and over and over again they reached plateaus, lingering there only to reach higher and higher in a rhythm as potent as the birth of the universe. Their bodies though sated, still hungered for more, matted together, yet their drive for yet another fulfillment went beyond the bounds of human endurance until they collapsed from sheer exhaustion. Hours passed and yet, again, they clung to each other until it was time to go.

Distantly, Ashton heard the knock at his door when Slade brought his attention back to the present.

"Are you going to answer my question?" Slade asked.

Ashton wiped the perspiration from his face with one hand. "No, but hold one," he hoarsely said clearing his throat. "Someone's at the door."

Ashton rose from the sofa in his hotel suite and padded barefoot to the double doors. Tying the belt of his robe more securely around his waist, he opened the door and immediately regretted it.

"*Where have you been?*" Jillian Harris vehemently flashed marching into his suite. "I waited all afternoon and evening for you to come back! I called that damn limo so many times, the driver refused to take my calls! He wouldn't even tell me where you were! Now I want some answers, damn it, Ashton, and I'm going to get them! What is your connection to Judge Bryant?"

The truth was on the tip of his tongue, but instead he said, "I'm on a call, Jillian. We'll have to talk later."

"I'll wait!" she hissed.

Ashton shrugged and shook his head. "Suit yourself, but how I spend my time is not open for discussion." Returning to the telephone, he picked up the receiver. "Sorry about that."

"Sounds like you've got your hands full," Slade commented. "Watch yourself with Jillian, Ash. She's trouble."

"Tell me something that I don't already know," he snorted.

"Look, I won't press the issue now. I'll catch up with you later, but we're going to finish this conversation."

"Before you go, has there been any more information about the missing women?"

Slade hesitated. He was asked the same question by his former line handler from The Nursery. As a result, he was re-activated to look into it. "I'll let you know when I hear anything."

Ashton knew he would. "You know where to find me." Then he hung up.

"Well, I'm waiting," Jillian said as if she was speaking to an errant child.

Ashton knew he had to give her some clarification for his behavior in court, but at the moment, he couldn't think of a plausible explanation. He made a decision, though, that he could tell her about. Still, handling Jillian was going to take skill. At the moment, all he wanted to do was be with Kristen. He had to get by Jillian first without risking a blip on her radar. Moreover, he had to come up with a justification for the continuance. Quickly a plan formed in his mind.

"Coffee?" he asked rising to pour another cup for himself.

"I've already had breakfast, Ash. What I want to know is why you pulled that razzle-dazzle move in court yesterday. You did not say anything to me about needing a continuance or anything about new information coming to light. We were ready to proceed. I have to say our client is not very happy about this."

She was right, he had to admit. His client didn't deserve legal representation that was not top notch, particularly for the price they were paying for his time. At the moment, he was having difficulty separating his professional obligations from his personal life. He knew he couldn't go back into that courtroom and have his client's best interest at heart. Nor could he see the distress on Kristen's face knowing he was the cause.

"Jillian, you're an excellent litigator. You've been my second chair through the entire proceeding at the lower court level. You handled the pretrial pleadings and motions. You're sharper than I am in U. S. civil law and you know these circumstances as well, if not better, than I do. This is a winnable case and you're the one to lead the defense team."

Jillian's mouth dropped wide open. "*What?*" she shrieked. "You're walking out on me and leaving me to handle this work alone?"

"You're a senior partner in Marshall and Marshall. You're never alone. I'll put in a call to Ben Knight and Von Little and have them come to DC to work with you. They're both excellent civil trial litigators and have the most experience with corporate cases. I've managed both of them. They can back you up and do an excellent job for you."

Ashton noticed it took Jillian only a few seconds to get her bearings before suspicion narrowed her eyes. "Exactly what are you going to do?"

Ashton dismissively shrugged. "What a good manager does, I'll manage from the sidelines. Not that I think you'll need my help with Ben and Von as your second chair."

Actually, it was a golden opportunity for Jillian and Ashton could see the play of emotions on her face, the dawning of her realization that this case would catapult her career into the highest echelons of the legal profession. Not many women had an opportunity to head a legal team for a client with billions of dollars at stake. One thing for sure, she was as tenacious an opponent as he had ever seen. She would carve up Strickland Briggs with malice and forethought. The man wouldn't know what hit him. This would be child's play for her and he could see she relished the thought. When her eyes began to shine and her lips curved into a feral smile, he almost pitied Briggs…almost.

Briggs, the pompous ass, would not like being beaten by a woman. No doubt he would underestimate Jillian's legal skills and abilities, but Marshall and Marshall's client would get the best legal representation with Jillian, a known entity to them, rather than him, leading the legal team. Because of that, he felt no remorse at dropping off the case now. Better still, it would relieve Kristen of a burden he knew she carried. It would also release him to concentrate his time and energy on preparing for his future with her. Because, as sure as the sun rose in the East and set in the West, he knew he and Kristen were going to have a future together.

Until this case was over, she technically was outside his reach. Their intimate relationship would have been considered wholly improper if he hadn't stopped the court proceedings when he did. He would not jeopardize her career with any hint of scandal or worse, judicial indiscretion. That could, at a minimum, get her censured by the court, or possibly disbarred. His career was always important to him, too, but nothing and no one was more important to him now than Kristen.

"Ashton?" Jillian called to him. "Have you heard a word that I've said? I said I would do it on the condition that you clear it with the client."

Ashton grinned. "Consider it done."

Chapter 16

"April, do you have my notes on _Wyatt v. DeBerry_?" Kristen asked as she, Pete, Cheryl, and Tina sat around a conference table in her office library on Saturday.

"Hold it," Cheryl said raising both hands and then standing. "Are you on some kind of kamikaze mission, KC? We've been at it since early this morning. We're reviewed nine cases today. It's Saturday and, so far, you haven't given us or yourself a break…not even to have lunch. It's nearly three o'clock and I need to clear my head before I tackle another case."

"I'm with you, Cheryl," Tina added slumping back in her chair and tossing her pen on top of another legal brief. "I need more than a break. It's been one hellified week. I need an escape."

Kristen checked her watch and looked around at the tired expressions on everyone's faces. There were small mountains of legal briefs stacked before each person at the table. The time had nearly flown by.

"How about you, Pete?" Cheryl asked.

"I'll stay as long as KC needs me," Pete said not looking up at Kristen or Cheryl while he wrote notes on the case they just finished briefing.

Although he jotted notes as he spoke, Kristen's heightened awareness of Pete's feelings for her told her there was more in that statement than just his dedication to the job. She hadn't given a lot of thought to the situation because, although her mind had been on Ashton most of the week, she still didn't know what she was going to do about Peter. He was a good friend, the best. Just as much and as close as Cheryl and Tina. He could be working anywhere he chose. His legal skills were excellent and she knew several law firms offered high six-figure salaries to him, but he chose to come and work with her as not only her senior legal counsel, but also as her Chief of Staff. She owed him so much for always standing by her and she loved him as she loved her own two brothers, but she could not be his friend and his lover. There was only one man who she could give herself to, and that man might never be hers. The thought of that made her so sad she needed time alone.

"Look, why don't we knock off for a few hours. We could meet back here after dinner. Say about seven. I'd like to, at least, cover these last three or four cases. That will put us ahead by a couple of days."

"You're not coming with us?" Tina asked.

Kristen took off her eyeglasses, rubbed her eyes, and wearily smiled at her friends. "No." Then turning to her Executive Assistant, she said, "April, would you order a tuna on whole wheat and a tomato soup for me, please?"

"Make that two, April," Pete added. "Chips and some fresh fruit, a couple of sodas."

Kristen turned to look at him as he continued to write. "Pete, you don't have to stay. Why don't you take a well-deserved break and go with Cheryl and Tina?"

"I've got too much left to do," he said without missing a beat.

"I'm outta here," Cheryl flung over her shoulder with a bit more vehemence than Kristen thought necessary. She had noticed a subtle change in Cheryl's demeanor, but hadn't had time to address it. If something was wrong with her lifelong friend, she was going to have to make time to figure it out.

"Hey, Cheryl, what's the rush? Wait for me," Tina said following her out of the door.

"I'll stay, too, Judge…I mean, KC," April said.

Kristen didn't require formality from her staff, a fact they were all having a hard time getting used to.

"That's not necessary, April. If you'll order the food, you may leave for the day."

"Thanks, KC, but if it's all the same to you, I'd like to stay."

"Why, April? I would think a young woman, like you, would want to head home or out to have some fun."

April Bennett, a woman in her mid-twenties smiled almost bashfully and shrugged her shoulders. "I was one of Judge Montgomery's legal secretaries right out of trade school when she was a founding member of her Alexander, Carter, Chandler, Charles, Lightfoot, and Towson, PA, law firm. I asked her to let me work for her here at the court and she agreed. She has been a wonderful role model for me and you're just like her. You're what I want to be.

"Judge Alexander-Montgomery said, if I want to go back to school to become a paralegal or if I want to go to law school, she'd help me. I enjoy working around all of you. You work so hard and so well together. I've learned a lot and I want to learn more. There aren't enough female judges, particularly young judges. People don't understand how hard it is to get to where you are and how hard it is to stay there. They also don't understand how important it is to have good judges in the court system. What you do affects millions of people who will never know what you do for them."

A soft, weary smile bowed Kristen's mouth. "Thanks, April, that's kind of you to say, but we're not role models, or, at least, I don't consider myself to be one. We're flesh and blood individuals just like anyone else, not idols. We have our strengths and our weaknesses, but, if you're interested in pursuing a legal career, Vivian Alexander-Montgomery isn't the only one you can depend on to help you. I'm pleased you agreed to stay on to help us while Vivian is away. It's good to know what you want and go after it."

"Thanks, KC. I'll order your food now," she said and left the office.

As soon as the door closed, Peter leaned back in his chair, briskly rubbed his face, and then pinned Kristen with an inquiring gaze. "Do you know what *you* want, KC?"

That question surprised her as much as it had alerted her to its double meaning. It seemed to have come from such a deep, tender part of Peter's soul and it was not to be taken lightly. She knew they had to talk about the feelings he expressed; feelings which seemed to be just below the surface of their relationship for several years. It surprised her that she never noticed those feelings before. Looking into Peter's eyes now, she knew they were always there. What she had thought was brotherly affection was entirely something more intimate. What was she thinking? she wondered. How could she have missed it? Peter was every woman's fantasy: young, intelligent, strong, handsome, virile, wealthy, and sensitive. He would make the right woman a wonderful husband and father to their children, but not her. She knew that with certainty.

There were few, if any, secrets between them, but even now she could not bring herself to tell him why they could never be more than best friends. All she could do was try to make him understand what they had between them was as much as she would ever be able to give him of herself. She didn't want to lose his friendship, because it meant everything to her, but she couldn't give him her love or the intimacy he deserved.

Rising from her deep leather chair, Kristen dug her hands into the pockets of her slacks and walked toward one of the windows in her office. She looked up into the sky and noted how the clouds seem to be gathering for a storm. They were nothing like the wispy breaths of clouds that passed over the enchanted Plaza de Masquerada Island. Fall was approaching and the trees were beginning to turn to wondrous colors; oranges, yellows, and reds. She barely noticed as she pondered Peter's question.

Did she really know what she wanted? When she was in Ashton's arms she was sure. Still, what did she know about him other than the mere thought of him took away her breath? When she was with him she felt as if she could do anything, be anything she wanted to be. No man ever made her feel so strong, so confident, so alive and simultaneously so full of lust and love. She thought she would never see him again and, although that thought constricted her heart, she was prepared to go on with her life knowing, at least, once in her life she had loved and felt unadulterated love in return. It was not long, less than three short weeks on a captivating island in the Polynesian Archipelagos. Still, unlike two ships that only pass in the night, their destinies had again brought them together.

Kristen longed to share that with someone. Under ordinary circumstances, that person would have been Peter, but now…

"Kristen," Peter said softly standing behind her. "Look, I know you didn't expect this from me, but I couldn't work with you day in and day out without finally telling you how I feel."

Kristen turned to look up into his handsome face. "Peter, I…"

Pete must have read something in her eyes. He held up one hand and shook his head. "I don't know what it is I'm feeling. I haven't labeled it. I don't want to put you on the spot or make you feel uncomfortable. I would resign if you wanted it that way. Tina or Cheryl could step in as your Chief of Staff and both could lead your legal staff. They are both that good."

"Was it something I said or something I did?" Kristen asked

Peter smiled at the thought. "No, you're not an overt seductress, if that's what you're asking. You haven't done or said anything to lead me on or make me think there could be anything more than friendship between us. Although that hasn't stopped me from wanting to explore the possibility of us moving our friendship to another level."

"Peter, you, Cheryl, and Tina are my best friends, my family…" she still couldn't find the right words to say to him.

Peter held up his hand to stop her again. "I know that, KC, and I feel the same way about the three of you." He shook his head with indecision. "Look, I just wanted to make my position clear, not to put more of a burden on you now. My thoughts may stem from all the work we did together to get you here. I admire you and, if there can be something more between us, I'm open to exploring it. However, it's also clear to me you've got something or maybe I should say *someone* else on your mind now and I don't think it's Briggs. Still, this is neither the time nor the place to have this conversation. Think it over, KC. Regardless of what you decide about our relationship, I'll still respect you and our friendship."

"Peter, I—."

"I'm going to take a walk and stretch my legs. I'll be back by the time the food arrives."

With that, Peter turned and walked out of the library door.

Too many things were hitting her all at one time. Kristen felt as if the walls were beginning to close in on her. Too many people making demands on her; her father, Strickland, Peter, and Ashton. Yet, what was up with her friend Cheryl? Kristin's usually agile mind stalled. She needed to get a grip on her emotions and on her life. She wouldn't be able to function if she didn't. Quickly, she found April and told her she was leaving for the day and to tell the others she would see them on Monday morning to finish reviewing the cases.

Kristin left her office carrying a copy of the _McElvoy v. Wayne_ case, her briefcase, coat and purse. She acknowledged people who she passed in the wide, busy hallway, even on a weekend, but kept her mind focused on the double doors at the end of the hall. When she reached the door, she took a deep, steadying breath, before she entered.

The receptionist's head came up when Kristen walked in.

"Good afternoon, Judge Bryant,"

"Good afternoon, Kitty. Is the Chief Judge available?"

"I'll check. Please have a seat."

Kristen had been waiting for about fifteen minutes when she heard the door to Judge Hathaway's office open and the sound of laughter coming from his law clerks as they filed out of the room. All casually dressed for a Saturday, they acknowledged her with friendly smiles and greetings as they filed by. Harold Hathaway followed them out, with his shirt sleeves rolled up to his elbows and wearing a pair of chinos and tennis shoes.

"Kristin," he said, smiling. "Sorry to keep you waiting. Please, come in."

Gathering her belongings, Kristin rose from her seat and preceded him into his office. He motioned her to a sofa and she took a seat at one end while he settled into a winged-back chair across from her. Gathering her thoughts, she began to outline her situation. Judge Hathaway carefully listened to her, occasionally nodding his understanding or raising questions when necessary. He even picked up his iPad and together they checked a few things on LexisNexis, a search engine used primarily by people involved in the law. Forty-five minutes later, they concluded their discussion.

Outside the courthouse, Kristen placed her briefcase in the waiting car and dismissed her driver. Then she began to walk. She was so deep in thought she did not notice she was being followed.

⁂

"Good evening, Judge Hathaway," Ashton said extending his hand to the judge.

"Good evening, Mr. Marshall. What is it that I can do for you?" he asked taking a seat in his den and motioning Ashton to have a seat. "When you called and asked to see me this evening, you said it was important."

"Yes, Your Honor, it is. I have a serious problem I must discuss with you off the record. You see—."

"Mr. Marshall," the judge interrupted. "If this is about any case that's pending before my court, I will not discuss it unless opposing counsel is present. However, if you want to relate a personal matter, say concerning a friend or colleague of your acquaintance or a hypothetical situation, I could then, ethically speaking, of course, treat this matter as wholly unrelated to any action pending or likely to be pending before my court. Do we have an understanding, Mr. Marshall?" the judge wisely asked.

Ashton understood completely as he began laying out a scenario in the third person. The judge listened while Ashton talked. Fifteen minutes later he was finishing up.

"Therefore, Judge, my friend had to act swiftly to avoid the hint of impropriety."

The judge thoughtfully nodded. "Your friend, Mr. Marshall, acted wisely. There may have been serious damage done to highly-respected careers."

"What would you advise my friend to do under the circumstances, Judge Hathaway?"

"I believe your friend is astute enough to make that determination on his or her own, Mr. Marshall. Don't you?"

Ashton nodded his agreement then rose from his seat extending his hand. "Thank you, Judge Hathaway, for allowing me to discuss my friend's dilemma with you and letting me intrude upon your Saturday evening."

The judge rose and shook Ashton's hand in return. As Ashton started toward the door, the judge stopped him.

"By the way, Mr. Marshall, one of the judges on the panel hearing your case, has asked to be withdrawn from the proceedings and I have granted that request. Since the case had not yet been heard, another judge will be empaneled when court resumes. Earlier today, I formally sent notice to Mr. Briggs and to you by messenger, so my telling you this is strictly within the bounds of proper court etiquette and will not compromise the pending litigation."

Ashton's face brightened considerably and the judge's wise and knowing smile bolstered his spirit. "Thank you, Judge Hathaway," Ashton said and proceeded to the front door just as a strikingly beautiful young woman entered followed by another woman of unbelievable beauty.

"Hello, Uncle Harold," said the first woman before planting a kiss on his cheek and then turning her gaze on Ash. "Hello, you're Thomas Marshall, aren't you?"

"I am, yes, but you have me at a disadvantage."

She chuckled. "I'm Emory Ardon. We've never met, but I've seen you before in Europe and Asia. You were with Slade Richardson," she said not mentioning that Slade had pulled her to safety when bullets flew in her direction. "This is my friend, Angelique Menendez-Gaza."

"Ah," said Ashton, "now I remember. You're both fashion models."

"At one time, yes, but we've both moved on."

"I need to keep up. It was nice to meet both of you," he said and shook their hands before he left. Once outside the judge's home, Ashton's excitement for a future with Kristen couldn't be contained. He yanked the air with his fist and said a very loud and boisterous, *"Yes!"* When he got into the limo he directed the driver to his next stop.

Kristen was sitting at her desk in the library of her home making notes about an upcoming case when she heard commotion, loud voices raised in anger outside her closed door. She recognized Shelton's voice raised in exasperation and the voice of another person she expected. Before she could rise from her seat, the library door burst open and Strickland Briggs stalked in raging at the top of his lungs.

"What the fuck do you think you're doing?"

Shelton stood by angrily clutching at Strickland's arm. "I'm sorry, Judge Bryant, but he bolted past me before I could stop him. I told him you were not accepting any visitors. I'll call the police—."

Kristen raised her hand. "Thank you, Shelton. I'll handle this. There's no need to call the police. Mr. Briggs will be leaving in a few moments."

"But, Judge Bryant—?"

"That will be all, Shelton," she calmly said.

"Very good, Miss," he stiffly nodded. "I'll be available should you need further assistance."

With that Shelton gave Strickland an angry appraisal and left the library.

Strickland stalked toward Kristen, but she held her ground. She had expected a visit from him.

"I asked you a question, damn it! What do you think you're doing by pulling this stunt?"

"I heard the question the first time. It isn't a stunt. I've withdrawn from the panel hearing the *Wayne* case."

Ashton had visited Vivian at her old home in Georgetown on the edge of Rock Creek Park many years ago. This visit to the large, four-story, corner brick house would be different. When the door opened, a tall, svelte, dignified-looking man stood starring down his nose at Ashton. He had seen pictures of Kristen's father and knew immediately the man standing before him could not be the venerable Judge Clarence Bryant.

"Yes, may I help you, Sir?" he asked with an air of superiority.

"Yes. I am Thomas Marshall. I'm here to see Kristen Mar...Judge Bryant."

"Is the Judge expecting you, Sir?"

"No, she isn't, but I'm sure she will see me."

"I'm sorry, Sir, but Judge Bryant cannot be disturbed. I suggest you make an appointment..." he began but was distracted by the ringing telephone.

When the man stepped away from the door leaving it open, Ashton took that opportunity to step inside. He heard Kristen's voice and the voice of someone else. When the butler knocked on what Ashton knew to be the library door to announce that her father was on the line, Ashton decided not to intrude. He placed a package on the hall table and quietly left closing the front door behind him.

Chapter 11

When the door to the suite opened, Judge Clarence Bryant could only mutely stand and stare. Never in his wildest imagination had he expected to see Sheila Duckworth standing before him looking not a day older than she did back in law school at Howard University. She was tall, svelte, and nicely rounded then as she was now. He suddenly vividly remembered kissing her subtle curves before burying himself between her creamy thighs. Their time together came back to him in a flash of lust and heartache.

"Clarence?" Sheila asked taken aback by her former classmate's and lover's sudden appearance at her son's hotel suite door. When the call came from the concierge announcing the arrival of Judge Bryant, Sheila assumed it was the younger female Judge K. Catherine Bryant. Although Ashton was not there, she permitted the judge to come to the suite. Jillian's somewhat frantic telephone call convinced Sheila something was seriously wrong with her son. She was determined to get to the bottom of Ashton's uncharacteristic behavior. So, she had her secretary call the airport to have one of their company jets readied for departure. Within two hours of Jillian's call, Sheila's plane lifted off from a private airstrip headed for Washington, DC. When she arrived, Ashton was not in his suite and he was not answering his cellphone.

Now with the arrival of her former lover, her concerns about her son went out of her mind completely.

"Sheila?" Clarence asked, surprised. "I thought…I was told this was Thomas Marshall's suite."

"It is," she said. "Why are you here, Clarence?"

"I wanted to have a word with him about my…" he trailed off. "Is he your husband?"

"My husband? For heaven's sake, Clarence. No, Thomas is not my husband; he's my son. What in the world gave you the idea he was my husband?"

"I haven't seen you since we graduated from law school. I heard you married a lawyer, Thomas Marshall, after you dumped me."

Sheila had the good grace to look chagrined. She stepped back and invited Clarence to enter the suite. After closing the door, Clarence followed her into the living space.

"Would you like something to drink?" She asked proceeding to the bar. Putting ice cubes in a short squat glass she poured two fingers of scotch. She needed a moment to regain her equilibrium. There were not many things in her life she regretted, but the way she treated Clarence Bryant was one of her most memorable disgraces.

"I'll have what you're having," Clarence said from behind her.

Sheila hadn't heard him come up behind her, but she didn't jolt. Rather she steeled herself, poured another drink, turned, and handed it to him looking him in the eyes.

"You look good, Clarence. I heard you married the prima ballerina, Lydia Martine, and then several years later, you tragically lost her. I'm sorry for your loss. Life has been good to you otherwise?"

"Yes, I have two sons, Clarence Jr. and George, both sports and entertainment lawyers in private practice and a daughter, Judge Kristen Catherine."

"Well, the hits just keep on coming," she derisively mumbled. "When the concierge called to announce Judge Bryant arrived, I thought it was your daughter here to see Thomas. I didn't know they knew each other."

"As far as I know they don't know each other. She has never mentioned him to me."

"Then I'm confused, Clarence. Why are you here?"

"Something is going on and I believe your son is the cause. His behavior in court last week and my daughter's recent behavior since she returned from vacation have—."

"Vacation?" Sheila asked, her attention and curiosity peaked. "When was this?"

"Approximately a month ago. Why?"

"Ashton hasn't been himself since he got back from *his* vacation."

"Where did he go?"

"I don't know. What about your daughter? Where was she?"

"I'm not sure, but I overheard part of a conversation Kristin had with Judge Vivian Alexander Montgomery. Something about an island resort in the Pacific and an airline she apparently owns. Kristen and Vivian were in undergrad together at Spelman College. They, along with Kristen's law clerks, Cheryl Lawrence and Constantina Justice, have been friends with the judge since their freshman year."

"I know Vivian Montgomery. She and Ashton are very good friends and argued several cases together at The Hague before she became a judge on the D.C. Circuit. She and my mother-in-law, Esmeralda Marshall, are also close friends and on several corporate boards together."

"Dr. Esmeralda Marshall?"

"Yes, she's my mother-in-law."

"I've followed her sterling career, but that's a topic for another time. What do you think is going on?"

"I haven't a clue, but I intend to find out."

"I have plans for my daughter. I don't want anything to interfere with her future. She's to be engaged to Strickland Briggs."

"I have plans for my son, too, Clarence. If things fall into place, my son will wed Jillian Harris."

"I've seen Ms. Harris and heard her speak at national political conventions. Her family is very prominent in the party."

"As is Strickland Briggs and his family. His father was in the Illinois state legislature and he and his wife are lobbyists. Nevertheless, I understand Senator Tollson is stepping down and Briggs wants to run for that slot. He has strong backing in the party, but I'm surprised his father doesn't run for that office. At least he has public service credentials and experience. I might be persuaded to contribute to his campaign if you can assure me your daughter plans to marry him."

"Kristen has always depended on my advice and guidance. I've given Strickland my blessing to marry my daughter. I fully expect they will marry within the year or before the next election."

"Good! That's good to hear, Clarence," Sheila said, pleased Kristen Bryant would not pose an obstacle to her plan to have Ashton marry Jillian and enter the political arena in Oregon.

"What about you, Sheila? How have you been?"

"I have no complaints. I, like you, lost my spouse many years ago. Thomas is my only child and I'm very proud of him."

"I'm sorry for your loss. I didn't know. I knew who your husband was, of course. He represented some big named clients, but I didn't know he died."

"We kept his death as low keyed as possible," she said, remembering her husband died between the thighs of some eighteen-year-old college student from a class where he had lectured often at the university. Even her son didn't know the true facts of Thomas Junior's death. Only Esmeralda, the student, whose tuition she had to agree to cover to keep her quiet, and a few others who worked for her knew and helped her cover it up. As far as anyone knew, her husband died in his sleep next to her at their home in his bed.

She believed, had she married Clarence Bryant, he never would have cheated on her. He was made of sterner stuff and was loyal to a fault. They were lovers through law school until their final year. They attended a National Attorneys Association convention just before graduation in Washington, DC, and she sat in on an international law speech given by the handsome and venerable Thomas Marshall, Jr., Esq. He had so inspired her she stayed after his presentation to talk with him. The next thing she knew, they were sharing coffee and croissants naked in his suite the next morning. Nine months later, Thomas Ashton Marshall, III, made his appearance much to the delight of his parents, Thomas and Sheila Duckworth Marshall. Sheila moved to Portland, Oregon, and began practicing law in her father-in-law's and husband's well-established law firm.

Though she regretted how she treated Clarence, she hadn't looked back once. Not even when evidence of her husband's philandering began to surface. He never lied to her and readily admitted that, although he loved her because she was the mother of his son and would never leave her for any other woman, he was not built to be faithful. However, he would be as discreet as possible and due to the vasectomy he had shortly after he got her pregnant, he would not father any children outside of their marriage.

He had kept his word. He had dinner at home with her, their son, and his parents nearly every night and continued to make love with her as if she was the only woman in his life. In public he was the quintessential husband, complementary, supportive, and attentive. She rarely knew when he was with another woman, but she knew he had, and he didn't deny the accusations.

Even though he cheated on her, she still loved him because of the family they created. Though she wanted more children, that was the one thing he denied her. After her husband's death, Sheila didn't have a desire to marry again. She occasionally might accept dates with interesting men, but never let those relations develop into anything of substance. Now looking at Clarence, she vividly remembered what a wonderful lover he had been.

"Uh, do you travel much?" Clarence asked. "I mean, have you been to Chicago?" he asked uncharacteristically off-centered.

Sheila softly smiled. "No, I don't travel much anymore. Once my son was born, I preferred to be at home each night and weekend with him. I've never been to Chicago. I'm the managing partner of my law firm, Marshall and Marshall, so I don't get out of the office very often. The firm is one of the largest in the US, so I'm kept fairly busy. My son is my partner in the firm and he's rarely in the office. He travels extensively."

"If you are ever in Chicago, I hope you will look me up, Sheila. I'd be happy to show the city to you."

He would, Clarence thought looking into the eyes of the first woman he ever truly loved. It took him years to get over Sheila Duckworth and even now she still had a vital part of his heart.

It took the special woman; the French Canadian prima ballerina Lydia Martine Booth, to mend his broken heart after Sheila dumped him. He met Lydia one snowy afternoon in a diner downstairs from the Chicago law firm where he worked. She was on tour with a stage production, but because of the adverse weather, that night's show was cancelled. She was sitting alone watching the snow fall in the nearly deserted diner across the street from her hotel where he often ate dinner before going back to work. When she was ready to leave, she discovered her wallet was missing. He had overheard her conversation with the waitress and offered to pay for her meal. That night was the beginning of their romance and eighteen months later, they married.

She was a beautiful young woman and with a sweet disposition he found delightful. She was only nineteen-years-old and when they married, he was eight years her senior, but her first lover as he discovered on their wedding night. Less than a year later, Clarence Junior was born and in quick succession the birth of George and then Kristen followed. He dearly loved Lydia and took care of her, but nothing between them burned quite as brightly as his love for Sheila Duckworth.

"I've thought of you often, Clarence. Wondered how you were. I even asked about you at law school reunions. However, you never attended."

"It took years for me to get past what you meant to me. I don't think I really ever did. So, when you signed up to attend class reunions, I decided not to torture myself and stayed away."

"I admit I'm ashamed of how I treated you. You didn't deserve that, and I've had my regrets about it."

"Why did you do it, Sheila? We made plans for a future together."

"Before you, I didn't have much experience with committed relationships. My parents weren't married and my maternal grandfather died when I was very young. Though my paternal family still lives in Mississippi, we never had a relationship. Though he's still very much alive, I've never so much as spoken with my father face-to-face.

"You opened up a new world for me. I believe I was truly in love with you, but I still wanted time to explore. I didn't want to settle down quite yet. Then I went to Thomas' lecture and I was mesmerized by his skill and ability. I thought I was a sophisticated woman who was about to become a lawyer, but I was no better than a silly, impressionable child. He talked me into his bed that same night and then I learned I was pregnant a few weeks later. My exploration time had run out. I knew the baby couldn't have been yours because we always used protection, but that night with Thomas we didn't use anything.

"I could say that was the reason I left you, because I was pregnant, but the truth was he just swept me off my feet as I learned he did with many women before and after our marriage."

"I'm sorry, Sheila. I can't image any man being unfaithful to you. I certainly never would have risked losing you."

"I know that, Clarence. You were always good to me. Your marriage was a good one?"

"Yes, very good. Lydia was very young when we met and married. She gave up her career to become my wife and the mother of our children."

"She was an incredible performer. I've seen some of her work on video and of course when any of her protégés are interviewed they talk about what an inspiration she is in their lives. I'm surprised none of your children followed in her footsteps."

"My daughter was training to go into…," he broke off. "I didn't… My wife died because she was teaching some children to dance. I didn't want anything to happen to Kristen the way it happened to Lydia. So, I discouraged dance as a career choice for my daughter. Of course, it was the right decision. She is one of the youngest attorneys to be robed in Illinois history and, because of Judge Alexander-Montgomery's sabbatical, Kristen was appointed by the President to the federal appellate circuit. She has a very bright future ahead of her."

"You mean the Supreme Court?"

"Yes, I do. She has the right credentials to be considered and with her fiancé as a US Senator, it's only a matter of time. That's why there cannot be a hint of scandal related to her."

Sheila nodded her understanding. Because she felt she owed him and knew him to be a principled man, she shared her plans for her son to become the next governor of Oregon, positioning him to one day at the end of his second successful term, run for the Presidency of the United States.

"Really? I'd say we're thinking along the same lines. When Strickland successfully assumes the position of the junior senator from Illinois and completes his first six-year term in office, his parents and I also plan for him to run for the presidency. Maybe we can work together to have your son and Strickland run on the same ticket."

"Perhaps. Otherwise they would be competing against each other," she said, the wheels beginning to turn.

However, when she smiled up at him, everything else went right out of his head. He saw recognition dawn in her eyes as they continued to search each other's face. When he caressed her chin, she went into his arms. Hastily, they went into the second bedroom in the suite, closed and locked the door.

Chapter 18

Strickland exited his bedroom and tied the belt more securely around his terrycloth robe. It was about time the agent showed up and gave his report, he silently groused. Reaching the door just as the second knock sounded, he let the agent in. He didn't shake hands or otherwise acknowledge the man. After all, he was just a servant, not someone to spend time and energy on overmuch. Though his price was steep, he had come highly recommended by a trusted frat brother.

"What did you find out?"

"The target has been circumspect in her dealings. Since you put me on this surveillance detail, she pretty much sticks to the same routine. Her driver picks her up at six-thirty and she's in her office by seven o'clock. If she's not hearing cases from the bench, then she works with her chief of staff and law clerks most of the day. Nothing unusual happens during lunch, unless she's got a spa appointment once a week. She leaves her office around six in the evening. She sometimes has outside meetings with her various organizations and speaking engagements."

"Visitors?"

"I've provided a list. The most notable was a small dinner party with women she was in undergrad at Spelman College with along with their spouses or plus ones."

"Yes, I see it here. Vivian Montgomery, Cheryl Lawrence, Constantina Justice, JaiHonnah Hawkins Baylor, Savannah Logan Flack and LaiLoni Hawkins Logan. I know who Judge Montgomery is and who Cheryl Lawrence and Tina Justice are, but who are the others?"

"JaiHonnah Hawkins Baylor and LaiLoni Skai Hawkins Logan are sisters. Their father is Ambassador Jake Hawkins, titular head of

BlackHawk Global. Their brothers are Jacob and Adam Hawkins, both in the hierarchy of the BlackHawk corporate structure. Though the one brother, Adam, also designs and races Formula One cars as a hobby."

"Ah," he breathed as recognition dawned. Big money, deep pockets, he thought. "This LaiLoni is the daughter who was kidnapped as an infant?"

"That's correct. She's now the wife of former Ambassador Jefferson Logan." What he didn't add and would never divulge was that his former handler, LaiLoni Skai was also once the covert operative Dakota Sinclair, aka code name: Wind Breeze. If this assignment threatened her in any way, he would immediately signal her and The Nursery of a potential hazard. Until he knew more about why this Briggs character was having Judge Bryant surveilled, he would keep his own counsel.

"What about the other one? Her sister, JaiHonnah?"

"She's an award-winning architect and civil engineer. She holds doctorates in both disciplines. Her husband, J. Roderick Baylor—."

"JRock, the basketball star?"

"Yes, they co-chair their own company, Baylor and Baylor Design and Developers and her father's vast holding in BlackHawk Global while he's in public service."

"Mmm, very deep pockets, indeed. Go on."

"Savannah Logan Flack is Ambassador Logan's younger sister; the wife of Ambassador Nathan Flack. Mr. Flack is an attorney, the US Ambassador to the United Nations, and a member of the Fitch-Townsend Pharmaceutical family. Dr. Logan-Flack is an obstetrician and gynecologist with a large practice in Georgetown."

"Big Pharma, this Nathan Flack."

"Yes, he is. His wife, Savannah, is associated, as a full partner, with Judge Alexander-Montgomery's former husband's, Dr. Derrick Jackson's, medical practice."

"*Wait! What?* Are you telling me that Judge Alexander-Montgomery is the former wife of basketball great, Derrick 'Dunk and Jam' Jackson?"

"Yes. They married just after she graduated from Georgetown Law and passed the bar. He died of a heart attack within the first year of their marriage. It happened on April 1st, April Fool's Day, the same day their only biological son, Derrick Junior, was born. In fact, he was reported to be holding their baby in his arms in the hospital nursery when he died. Chuck Montgomery discovered him, tried to resuscitate him, but it was too late. He was perhaps in his mid to late thirties. She was in her early twenties. They adopted abandoned, health-challenged children. After his death, she continued to adopt children with physical ailments. Then she married, Dr. Charles Montgomery. Together they've had several children and adopted more children. At last count they numbered twenty-four."

"A pity. A little young, but she would have been a perfect match for me. Vivian Alexander is one of the wealthiest women in the world. I didn't make the connection. The Montgomery surname instead of Jackson threw me off, but now I remember. She's a former Olympic Gold Medalist in basketball. Her current husband, Chuck Montgomery and Derrick Jackson were the Gale Sayers and Brian Piccolo of the basketball industry back in the day."

"Yes, all reports indicate Derrick Jackson and Charles Montgomery grew up together as best friends."

"Interesting that Montgomery would wed and bed his former best friend's wife."

The agent did not comment. He was beginning to like this client less and less. "Other than these women, Judge Bryant hasn't been particularly close to anyone else or on the social scene."

"Good, good! Keep up the surveillance on her and report any departure from the routine immediately."

"Yes, Sir. Anything else?"

"Yes, start a surveillance on a Thomas Ashton Marshall, III, Esq. He's a lawyer and partner in a Portland, Oregon, firm, Marshall and Marshall. I want a complete dossier."

Again, the agent didn't let on the firm's name meant anything to him, but it did. Slade Richardson, aka code name: Cobra Khan, was head of Marshall and Marshall's Investigations and Security Department and an outlier and sandbagger for The Nursery. This client was raising a lot of red flags that could not be ignored. He hadn't been active with The Nursery for several years, but he knew it was necessary to report this client.

"I want the intel on Marshall ASAP."

"I'll have another contract messengered to you for your signature before close of business."

When the agent left, Strickland returned to his bedroom where he had Shannon face down, spread eagle, and tied to the bedposts. "Now, where were we," he crooned as he took off his robe and picked up a riding crop running it through his long, spindly fingers. Her ass was still a rosy pink, he noticed. She moaned with pleasure, the ball gag still between her teeth as he rubbed his palm over her. He had to be careful where he spanked her or it might show during one of her photo shoots. She had the most beautiful skin. He liked the idea of having one of the top fashion models in the world at his beck and call. He wanted to get his hands on two other younger top models, Ardon and on Angelique, too, but Shannon would do for now. He fisted her long, beautiful, auburn-colored hair in his left hand, pulled hard to expose her long, graceful neck, and the dog collar and chains he clamped around her. She struggled to her knees, her shackles limited her movements just enough for him to mount her.

"*Yippeekayay!*" he shouted and proceeded to ride her hard.

Frustrated, Jillian paced her suite in the McCoy Regent. She knew Sheila Marshall had arrived, but the woman wasn't answering her cell phone. It had been hours. She generously tipped one of the hotel desk clerks to alert her when Ashton returned, but so far, he was still out and about. She wanted to meet with his mother to prepare a strategy to deal with his uncharacteristic behavior.

It didn't bother her overmuch that she would lead the legal team on behalf of her clients, her former boss. Although initially the company president was miffed that Ashton assigned the lead to her, once she said a few choice words to him in his bed, reminding him of the *special relationship* they shared over the past three years, she had him panting for her and as docile as a lamb. Little did the father know she also had his son often and continuously. She kept her bosses close and her lovers closer.

If she could get her hooks into Thomas Ashton Marshall, III, which was her intention, she would ease away from her current father-and-son lovers. The father was easy, but the son could be problematic. She believed, if the rumors about Thomas' prowess in bed were true, she would have to concentrate her focus on him. Still, she hadn't been successful in getting him into her bed, but, with Sheila in her corner, he couldn't evade her forever.

It was bothersome he seemed taken by Judge Bryant for some reason. She had Googled the woman and, although she found Judge Bryant's credentials laudable, she didn't seem to be Ashton's type. The woman was, at one time, a practicing civil litigator, a law school professor, and then a judge on the federal district judiciary in Illinois. She was a little over thirty. The daughter of an Illinois state jurist, Judge Clarence Bryant, Sr., and the sister of two sports and entertainment lawyers, Clarence, Junior and George Bryant. There was a sidebar about her mother, the famous French Canadian-born prima ballerina, Lydia Martine Booth, but beyond the impressive credentials, she seemed ordinary, non-descript. Her official photo did her no favors. Certainly not a woman to catch the eye of an urbane and worldly man, like Ashton.

Perhaps she could gather the information she needed out of Strickland Briggs. She had Googled him, too and found loads of information about him, his lobbyist parents, and Judge Bryant as well as the fashion model Shannon. It might be worth it to seduce the information she wanted out of Briggs…after she beat his pants off in court, pun intended. She laughed to herself. Men were so easy. Show them some tits and ass and they were putty in her hands. Everyone so far, except Thomas.

She wanted to dismiss Judge Catherine Bryant out of hand, yet something convinced her to continue to be vigilant where this woman was concerned. There had to be a connection somewhere between the

Judge and Ashton. His uncharacteristic behavior seemed to start when the judges were impaneled.

However, she was more concerned about this Casey woman Thomas was mooning over and desperately trying to find. She would have tried to seduce the information out of Slade Richardson, the Sendhil Ramamurthy clone. His svelte six-five, Arab or East Indian sex appeal was enormous, but his friendship with Thomas Marshall was iron-clad and impenetrable. She would have to find another route to that information as well.

Jillian called Sheila's cellphone again, but it went straight to voice mail. She didn't leave another message. She had already left several. Ashton was similarly unreachable. She was tired of pacing the suite and decided to go to one of the hotel bars to have a drink and then get some dinner. This waiting around was not how she envisioned her off-work hours. Rather, she thought she would have been spending time in Ashton's bed with room service.

She liked the McCoy Hotel chain. Their facilities were elegant and chic, but homey. The accommodations were top of the line and the food first class. She settled into the booth the maître d' suggested and ordered a drink from the highly-efficient server. As her eyes became accustomed to the dim lighting, she spied a very tall, handsome man come in with a very pregnant, but attractive woman who looked like a youthful Jada Pinkett-Smith, scanning the bar as if looking for someone. If the man were not so tall and handsome, a Johnny Depp look-alike, she probably wouldn't have paid much attention, but then people approached him, shaking his hand, and asking for an autograph.

Lacking anything better to attract her attention, Jillian continued to observe the couple until the maître d' directed them to a distant spot in the bar. When they reached the table, a man stood and embraced the pregnant woman and gave the tall man a brother's shoulder bump by way of warm greeting. She would recognize that fine physique anywhere. It was Ashton and he seemed extremely happy to see the interracial couple. They sat and began an animated conversation with smiles wreathing their faces and laughter. She called her server to her table.

"Who is the tall man who was just seated with the pregnant woman? He seemed to be signing autographs when he arrived."

"Oh, that's Chucky P. He used to play professional basketball in the NBA," the server informed all smiles.

Jillian didn't follow sports and was surprised Ashton would know an American basketball player. He spent years abroad practicing international law and was rarely stateside. Although he was taller than average, she knew he was an avid tennis player and he sometimes played with his mother in Pro-Am, mixed doubles tournaments in the Portland area, mostly for charity events. He was also a golfer with an enviable handicap. He liked to play the toughest courses all over the world. If he hadn't been an exceptional lawyer, he could have joined the professional golf tours. However, this social side of Ashton was new to her and unexpected. Other than Slade, she did not know Ashton to have close personal friendships.

"Would you care for another drink, Miss?" the server asked.

"I would, yes."

"I'll bring it right away," he pleasantly said and scurried away.

Jillian continued to watch Ashton and his companions from her relatively secluded vantage point. The threesome seemed to have a great deal to talk and laugh about. She wished she could move closer to hear their conversation or read lips, but were she to make any move, she would be spotted. So, she decided to bide her time and watch. If they appeared to be wrapping up their conversation, she would intervene to learn more about whom they were and what were they to Ashton. It was her intention to learn everything there was to know about Thomas Ashton Marshall, III. She had her sights set on the governor's mansion and later, in her opinion, she would make a terrific First Lady of the United States.

"So, you're really serious, Ash?" Chuck asked. "You're going to pull up stakes on the Left Coast and settle down in DC?"

"I am, yes. Other than the topic we cannot discuss, my mother is making moves that don't align with my plans. I was at one of her political soirees a month ago. People kept coming to me about my 'upcoming run for the governorship'. That seemed to be the buzz trending upward, but even if I were to stay in Portland, it wouldn't be because I wanted to run for public office. If anyone should be governor, it should be Mother."

"Well, if you're determined, here are the keys to my Watergate condo and the pass for the garage and the fitness center. The place is already furnished, but feel free to make any changes you want. When you called to accept my suggestion that you use the place, I had Housekeeping give it a thorough cleaning. Fresh linens are already there. I didn't order groceries, so you might want to do a little shopping on your own. Of course, the Watergate has food service and in-house chefs, and there are plenty of restaurants in the area within walking distance.

"Now, as to my law offices, you know and understand why I cannot advise you on that. I have to maintain a strict Chinese wall of separation between me and my former practice. However, since I am officially on sabbatical and not being paid by the federal courts, I can suggest you meet with the founding partners: Bill Chandler, Alan and Melissa Charles Lightfoot, and David and Gloria Towson Carter. If you're seriously interested in joining the law firm or simply being of counsel, they would, no doubt, be amenable.

"Otherwise, as I mentioned before, I still own the building and there is adequate office space there to house your own law practice. Your practice is mainly international contract and mediation law, so it should not conflict with anyone in my former firm. Everyone in the firm practices law on the domestic side. Bill practices sports and entertainment law on an international basis, but he's the only one. That's not an area you've been known to focus on. Alan is the Attorney General to the Native American Nation and rarely takes on other clients. His wife, Melissa Charles, is a corporate attorney mostly practicing contract law. David is the managing partner and the President of the National Attorneys Association. His wife, Gloria, has a family law practice. There are a multitude of senior partners who practice various other specialties, but no one in the international arena other than Bill Chandler."

"Thanks, Viv. I think this is a good move for me and I appreciate the fact you were willing to agree to this so quickly."

"You're welcome, Ash. Let me or Chuck know whether you need anything else."

"Well, there is one other thing."

"What is it?"

"Would you mention our conversation to our mutual friend whose name we cannot discuss?"

Vivian warmly smiled. "I'm sure I can work it into a conversation. However, your court case should be resolved…"

"Well, well, fancy meeting you here, Ashton," Jillian interrupted drink in hand. It took two drinks to bolster her Dutch courage to interrupt what appeared to be a cozy conversation. "I've been trying to reach you all day. Aren't you going to introduce me?"

Ashton and Chuck got to their feet. "Good afternoon, Jillian. I planned to contact you in an hour or so."

"Well, since you haven't introduced me, I'll have to do it myself. I'm Jillian Harris, Ashton's partner," she said extending her hand to Chuck, "and you're Chucky P, the basketball star."

"Former player, yes, and this is my wife, Vivian," Chuck indicated.

Jillian noted Ashton quickly pocketing keys and another device before she took a vacant chair and sat down as if invited to do so. "So how do you know Ash?"

"We're friends," said Chuck cryptically leaving her nowhere to go for follow-up questioning.

They sat through a weighty silence before Vivian rose from her seat. "We'll talk with you soon, Ash," she commented when he rose from his seat and embraced her.

"Come back out to the ranch when you have some free time," Chuck invited. "We're having some people over for a New England-style clambake. I'll text the date and time to you."

"Ms. Harris," Vivian said, by way of farewell and she and Chuck were gone.

"Not very talkative, were they?"

"We seemed to be doing just fine before you arrived," he said while looking through his call log and text messages hoping to find a message from KC. Instead, he found several messages from his mother. According to the last text message, she had arrived in DC and was waiting for him in his suite.

He shook his head at the revelation. He might as well get their conversation over with. It was not going to be an easy discussion. He also noted Slade had recently left a coded 911 text message for him. He was on his way to DC from Japan and would arrive the next day, Sunday.

Ashton's brows beetled with curiosity and concern. It was rare for Slade to leave a 911 message, but he would call him as soon as he could dislodge himself from Jillian's presence.

"Did you meet with Knight and Little?" asked Ashton.

"Yes, we're ready for court."

"Good, then I'll say goodnight and likely goodbye."

"You're not coming to court?"

"You're ready, am I correct?"

"We are, yes."

"Then you don't need me. I have other business to attend to."

"Don't you want to know why I've been trying to reach you?"

"Not if it doesn't have anything to do with the client and the court case."

"If it's about us, you and me?"

"Then I'm not interested." He shook his head and reached for a modicum of residual patience. "Look, Jillian, you've made it abundantly clear you're interested in a relationship with me outside of the office. I've repeatedly tried to let you know I'm not open or available."

"You've never explained why."

"I don't have to explain my decisions to you. However, let me be crystal clear. I don't sleep where I eat and I'm simply not into you."

"Are you involved with someone other than this Casey that I don't know about?"

"I won't debate my decision with you. Have a good day in court and safe trip back to Portland."

He rose from the table and walked away.

Jillian stared after him more determined than ever to get her way with him. She would find out more about this basketball player and his wife and who they were to Ashton. That was at best a place to start.

Chapter 19

When Ashton walked into his hotel suite, he was surprised to see the lights were out in the common area. He expected to find his mother pacing the floor impatiently waiting for his arrival. He flipped on the lights and went to his laptop on a desk. There he found a single heart and knew it had come from KC. She had received the encrypted, high security cellphone he had left at her home for her and had used it to communicate via text with him. That was enough for now to settle him down. The rest would come when they could openly announce their relationship. Until then, he would do nothing to jeopardize her standing in the judicial community or court.

A noise caused him to look up in time to see his mother ease out of the second bedroom on the other side of the suite. Her somewhat disheveled appearance momentarily took him aback, yet she seemed to be glowing somehow. Her appearance was a departure from the woman who would never let herself be seen without every hair in place.

"Are you well, Mother?" he asked, concerned.

"Yes, yes, of course," she testily said. "I just woke from a nap, that's all. Why are you here?"

His brows beetled. "Because this is my suite?" he asked confused. "Didn't you expect me to be here? I mean, you've been blowing up my voice and text messages for three days."

"Yes, of course, but as usual, you've ignored me," she stridently said.

He smirked at that. *She-who-must-be-obeyed* resented more being ignored. "Would you like to talk now or over dinner?"

"I'm starving, so we'll talk over dinner." Her critical eyes appraised him. "You are going to change your clothes, aren't you?"

This time he laughed. He was wearing clothes appropriate for eating in the best five-star restaurants, but for someone with Sheila's impeccable taste and style, *haute couture* was never quite good enough. "I'll shower and change just for you," he said and kissed her temple.

Sheila watched him go and then scurried back into the second bedroom. "He's taking a shower," she urgently said to Clarence. "You can leave now without him seeing you."

He held out his hand beckoning her to come back to bed. She moved toward him, took his hand, and sat on the edge of the bed facing him. He brought her knuckles to his lips eyeing her terrycloth clad body. "That means we have a few more precious moments to spend together, Sheila. It's been more than thirty years since I had the pleasure of loving you. Three hours isn't enough for me. Is it enough for you?"

"Oh, Clarence," she moaned, burying her face in his still firm chest. "A lifetime wouldn't be enough for me if I could have you, but you know we can't. There is still too much between us. My son's future in politics has to be my top priority now. I imagine you feel the same way about your daughter. That doesn't leave any room or time in our lives for us."

"We need more time, Sheila. I need more time with you. Please, let's plan to be together tonight. My daughter doesn't know I'm in town. I just flew in for the day and planned to return to Chicago tonight. I'll get a room in the hotel. Tell your son you're going back to Portland and then come to me."

"I don't know, Clarence."

"Think about it. I hadn't planned to stay in town overnight, but I'll go out and get a change of clothes, have some dinner, and meet you back here after you meet with your son. Or we can both just leave and go somewhere together. I haven't taken a vacation in years. I'd like to spend quality time alone somewhere with you."

"We can discuss it, Clarence, but I can't promise this rendezvous idea of yours will settle anything."

"It's a start, Sheila. That's all I'm asking for right now."

Thomas and his mother were finishing a delicious dinner at one of the finest restaurants, Angelique's Place, in the city. Reservations had to be made well in advance, but thanks to Vivian and Chuck, who knew the owner, one phone call was all it took to secure accommodations. He remembered meeting Angelique at Judge Hathaway's home with the Judge's niece, Ardon. At the time, he hadn't recognized that Angelique was the new restaurateur he read about. Fine dining was something he appreciated about Washington, DC, Ashton thought. He would be able to enjoy other attributes the city had to offer now that he was to become a resident, but his decisions going forward would be made jointly with Kristen. He wouldn't make any permanent decisions about where they would settle down until they could do so together. Still, he had to admit, he liked the expansive area where Chuck and Vivian lived outside of the city limits in the rural part of the county. When he mentioned it, Chuck suggested he look at a private, seventy-two-hole, golf community, Havenhurst Estates, that wasn't far from Chuck and Vivian's ranch. This was right up his alley since he was an avid golfer. Apparently, former basketball icon J. Roderick Baylor and his wife, architect and engineer, JaiHonnah Hawkins, owned the land, designed the golf course and built most of the homes in the gated community; each on a minimum of seven-acre parcels. That seemed adequate to him. Perfect for raising a family—

"Ashton?"

"Yes, Mother?"

"You seem somehow different, distracted, I'd say. You've been sitting here with a smile on your face. What's that about?"

"Happiness, Mother. I'm very happy."

Sheila wasn't expecting that response from her son. Maybe Jillian had finally gotten through Ashton's resistance and he would be amenable to more of her plan for his future. Yet she had some thinking to do about her own needs. She checked her watch. If she was going to spend more time with Clarence, she needed to move her conversation with her son along.

"I'm happy for you, Son. Jillian will be a staunchly supportive wife for you. Just the kind of woman you need in the political…why are you laughing?"

"Give it up, Mother. I'm not interested in Jillian."

"You just said that you're happy," she protested.

"I am, however, my happiness has nothing to do with your protégée. Rather, I'm making moves to open a practice here in Washington. I have a place to live temporarily until I can firm up a more permanent arrangement. Before the end of the week, I'll close out my affairs in Portland, shut down my house there, and ship my car and some other things here.

"I actually have you to thank for helping me make this move. If you hadn't brought Jillian into the firm without my knowledge or consent and insisted I come to assist her with this case, I probably would still be in Portland existing on little or no real affection that women I've known intimately have to offer. So, thank you, Mother, for helping me reach this level of euphoria," Ashton said and smiled at his mother whose stunned, but animated expression resembled a guppy.

Sheila couldn't quite get her thoughts together. Her eyes bucked and her mouth kept opening and closing, but no sound came out. Her son, her only offspring couldn't be planning to leave his home, their law firm, and all the networking they had done to build a campaign treasure trove in Oregon to throw it all away and move to Washington, DC. This is not what she had been grooming him for all of his life and planning for his future. He needed to have his permanent residence in Oregon in order to become governor of the state and then run for the presidency in eight years. Her son was extremely intelligent, but perhaps he didn't understand what she had sacrificed for his future; what she would still have to sacrifice with Clarence; and what a monumental accomplishment it would be for them to have a legacy of a governorship and a presidency to add to the Marshall brand in the state, in this country, in the world.

The resulting benefits to their law firm would be unlimited. They could recruit from the best law schools in the country and attract the largest clients from around the world. Somehow, she had failed to clearly explain…*what the hell?*

Finally finding her voice and her outrage, she vehemently exploded, *"Nonsense!* You're talking absolute nonsense, Thomas! You have a duty to your namesakes to take your career to the highest levels and provide a sterling legacy for my grandchildren! I have tirelessly worked to insure you are positioned to become more than your father and grandfather or their ancestors ever could have aspired to become!"

"And, you, Mother? Is that it? Do you want to show off a son who came through you from the most financially challenged parts of Mississippi? A woman raised by her grandmother on the money she made cleaning houses? Honest money, made from giving an honest day's work? Is it my paternal father's and grandfather's legacy you want to elevate or is it Sheila Amelia Duckworth's genealogy you want to holdup for public jubilation?

"You're the illegitimate daughter of a man from a prominent Mississippi family who continuously had sex with his housekeeper's under-aged daughter and then refused to claim you as his child. The daughter of a fifteen-year-old who ran away and left you one night when you were still a babe in arms without saying goodbye. A woman you have not seen or heard from since.

"Mother, you've got to buy a clue. I love you and I don't want to hurt you, but I will not be sacrificed to atone for your ill treatment. I did not live through what you have, so I can only empathize with what you've suffered. I can't go back and make your biological parents responsible or take away the disrespect my father brought to your marriage. I will live with the woman of my own choosing, have a family with her, and be faithful to our bonds of matrimony. As for my career, I've never been interested in going into politics. I enjoy what I do, but I don't have to be a lawyer to be happy. I can live without it. Fortunately, if I didn't want to work another day for the rest of my life, I could do so very comfortably.

"So, there is nothing you can threaten me with to coerce me into your plan for my life."

"Perhaps we could compromise," Sheila said. "Take this one step at a time. If you agree not to leave the firm and remain in Portland, I'll not insist you marry Jillian. We'll find someone else suitable with the right pedigree, background, and breeding to be a Marshall."

Ashton shook his head at her attempt to negotiate when she had no hand to play in the deal. "No, Mother. I gave you an opportunity to get Jillian out of the firm. So far, you have chosen not to do that. Now I've made my decision."

"I'll just speak to your grandmother about this!" she fumed quickly rising from the table and strutting away.

He had never seen his mother upset and anxious, but if there was one thing he knew about Sheila Duckworth Marshall, it was she wasn't finished with him yet. He drew an uneasy breath and ordered a nightcap. He'd give her time to cool off, pack his things, and head to the condo shortly leaving the hotel suite for her use.

⁂

It was still the middle of the night when Slade let himself into the hotel suite Ash used at the McCoy Regent. Since one bedroom door, in the two-bedroom suite, was closed, he took the other. When he got a call from a former member of The Nursery, he called in other investigators from his company and was fortunate to catch a military transport arranged by one of his Nursery handlers, code name: Explorer One, out of Japan headed directly for Andrews Air Force Base located a few miles outside the Washington, DC, city limits. He wished he could have taken the female pilot up on her offer to spend the night, but a woman with her attributes would unerringly lead to encompass all four days of her layover in the city. Regrettably, duty called and he heeded the message. His friend, Ashton, was under surveillance arranged by Strickland Briggs as was Judge Kristin Catherine Bryant. He couldn't trust conventional communications systems had not been compromised between him and his boyhood friend. For this reason, despite Sheila's directive, Slade dropped his remaining tasks on others on his staff and made it back to talk face-to-face with Ashton.

First, he needed a shower and some sleep. He could still smell Judith's unique scent on his clothes and skin from their impromptu coupling at sixty-thousand feet in the cramped cargo bay while her subordinate pilots manned the controls of the giant Boeing C-17 Globemaster III military transport. He stripped and headed for the shower to wash her out of his system. He really needed to consider settling down the way Ashton was planning to do, but so far only one woman, Code Name: Satin Doll, spiked his interest and she was still in The Nursery with zero interest in doing anything else for the rest of her life. He didn't know why he was still thinking about her except she was like no other woman he had ever known.

Feeling refreshed after his shower, Slade left the bedroom to get a cold bottle of water from the fridge in the kitchenette. He felt the dehydration from the long hours of flying and sex, and knew he needed to hydrate. The door to the other bedroom opened and a man, whose voice Slade didn't recognize, started into the common area before being beckoned back into the bedroom by a female voice he did recognize. He stood absolutely still until the man returned to the bedroom and closed the door. "Well, hell," groaned Slade.

Chapter 20

"What do you mean he's checked out!" demanded Jillian of the hotel desk clerk.

"I'm not sure what else I can say, Ms. Harris. According to our records, Mr. Marshall checked out of the McCoy Regent last night."

"Where did he go?"

"I do not have that information, ma'am."

This was getting her nowhere, Jillian fumed. She had to be in court this morning and as she checked her watch, she realized she was running out of time. Attorneys Ben Knight and Von Little were already inside the town car waiting for her. Without further comment, she turned from the hotel clerk and stalked to the car, cursing every step of the way. Both attorneys ignored her arrival when the chauffer closed the car door behind her. One was texting while the other talked on the phone. She wondered whether either one of them knew where Ashton was and what he planned. After all, they did work for him. Still, she would not ask because she felt doing so would make her seem needy for Ashton's support.

As usual, the courthouse steps were mobbed with reporters yelling questions at her. She and the other attorneys moved as swiftly as possible snaking their way into the stately building. Once inside the courtroom, they were met with another crowd. At least this one included Sheila Marshall standing next to the defendant's table and their client inside a gated area speaking into a cell phone. She looked for Ashton, but he was nowhere in sight. They still had fifteen minutes before the session would begin, so she sent another text message to him.

After laying out her documents on the table in the order of her presentation, she looked up to see whether Sheila finished her phone call, but discovered opposing counsel, Strickland Briggs, intently watching her. When she stared back at him, he didn't look away. He wasn't a bad-looking man; a little too much on the pretty-boy side for her taste, but not unmanly so. She had seen him at political conventions but didn't bother to make his acquaintance. However, his parents she did make time to meet. They were influential in the party hierarchy. She made it her business to know all the right people. She never knew when certain connections would prove beneficial. She used that ploy to ingratiate herself with Sheila Marshall. Power recognized power and it landed her right where she wanted to be…one step closer to becoming the First Lady of Oregon and eventually the wife of the President of the United States.

Jillian's attention was diverted when Sheila ended her call and looked around as if searching for someone.

"Where is Ashton?" asked Sheila of Jillian and the other attorneys.

Jillian's brows beetled. "He withdrew from the proceedings. Didn't you know?"

"Withdrew?" asked Sheila, annoyed. "Then who's handling the case?"

"I am, with the agreement of the client, of course. Ashton cleared it and arranged for Knight and Little to sit second chair."

The clerk called the room to order ending all discussion. When the three-judge panel was seated, Sheila noticed Judge Bryant was not among them. Not only had her son withdrawn from the case, but also Clarence's daughter as well. Ashton never did anything like this before, and Sheila sensed it had something to do with Judge Catherine Bryant. She would get to the bottom of this.

Ashton waited until the room had settled down and been called to order before slipping into the court and taking a seat in the back which was held in reserve for him. Since Briggs was the petitioner, he was allowed to go first. Then he listened to Jillian's surgical annihilation of Briggs and his blustering, blundering, blowhard attempts to defend his indefensible arguments. Two hours after it started, court ended with Jillian Harris the clear victor of the day.

He slipped out just before court recessed and took a rear exit away from the media. He was to meet with Slade at the condo as soon as court was over. Catching a cab a block over, he headed to a large department store where he boarded an elevator up and got off when no one else got off at that floor. Then he took a service elevator back down to the loading dock. Heeding Slade's warning, he used other methods to avoid being followed before heading for the Watergate Complex. When he entered the condo, Slade was already there working and talking on his cell phone.

"How was your flight?" asked Ashton of his friend.

"Eventful," said Slade, a grin bowing his mouth.

"Anyone I know?"

"I hope not. Judith Merritt, Air Force pilot, stationed in Japan. She's under General Benjamin Alexander's command." He didn't bring it up, but she was also a friend of a missing pilot from the Plaza de Masquerade.

"No, the name doesn't ring any bells for me."

"Good. However, I doubt I'll see her again. I won't need to return to Japan anytime soon. I was able to identify the Japanese hacker and shut him and his operation down. I destroyed his databases and confiscated his equipment. Pieces of it will end up as paper weights or door stops. His bank accounts under every one of his pseudonyms have been divested of all funds and donated to Save the Children campaigns worldwide. He no longer has a pot to piss in or a window to throw it out of. I relieved him of his pocket identity, credit cards, and cash and trashed every alias he used. We had a come-to-Buddha meeting before I left. I put a few more of my investigators on tracking his movements for the next few months. Sheila's clients won't have a hacker problem from him again. I've met Sheila's dictates and the client is pleased."

"No doubt. *She-who-must-be-obeyed* is in town, by the way."

"Uh, yes, I know. I went to the hotel and learned quite accidentally and uncomfortably that she was in the midst of a romantic interlude."

"Mother?" Ashton asked and grinned at Slade's nod. "Well, go Mom!"

"Not so fast, brother. I looped a photo of her man from the hotel surveillance system and sent it through facial recognition. The man in question is none other than—wait for it—Judge Clarence Edward Bryant, Sr."

The grin melted from Ashton's face. "You've got to be shitting me."

"No joke. I had a background check and complete dossier run on him. He and your mother were an item during law school when they were both students at Howard University. Suddenly, after being lovers for several years, she up and dumped him. Nine months later you were born. I checked with my uncle in Portland. He and my aunt were working for the Marshall family back then. He confirmed Sheila was pregnant when she married Thomas Junior. Because I know how important this would be to you, I had DNA comparisons run on the sheets in Sheila's room after she left for court this morning before housekeeping arrived. I used the residue on the sheets and compared it to yours. Sheila is without question your mother, however, Clarence Bryant is not your biological father and Kristen Bryant is not your sister."

Ashton released a breath and noticeably relaxed. "You've been busy."

"I have, yes. Thanks to a heads up I received from an old acquaintance, I was able to find out that Strickland Briggs has Judge KC Bryant under surveillance and now believes you're also under surveillance. I convinced my contact, the investigator, your activities should never include contact with Kristen Bryant. Otherwise he's free to surveil you."

"Thanks, Slade. I withdrew from the case and Kristen was replaced in court today. Briggs apparently gave her a perfect out. He and his parents showed up at Kristin's home for dinner. Then Briggs showed up again angry because she's been excused from deliberations on this case. Kristin used that and Briggs' claim he wanted to renew their former relationship and engagement as her rationale for withdrawing from hearing the case. Kristin never mentioned me to Briggs, but obviously he's suspicious of whether she and I know each other. Otherwise, he would have no reason to have me followed. I just came from court. KC wasn't on the bench and

Jillian Harris annihilated Briggs in court. This case should be over as soon as the Appellate Court renders an opinion. Then Kristen and I will not have to avoid seeing each other."

"Briggs could appeal the decision to the US Supreme Court," Slade suggested.

"True, but I doubt the high court would even grant certiorari and agree to hear the case. In any event, I'm moving forward with opening an office here. Vivian has ideal space in one of her buildings in the city where her former law firm is located. I'm also going to look at properties where Kristin and I will have some privacy and security once the case is over. I'm scheduled to sit down with Vivian's founding law firm partners next week. I'll either accept a partnership with her former law firm or open Marshall International and Associates, PA.

"On that note, I want you to consider moving your operation to Washington. I'm not suggesting you leave Sheila completely; just telecommute from here."

Slade laughed. "You think my very protective uncle and aunt, Harold and Millicent Turner, would let me move this far away from them? To ground zero at that?" he smirked. "They don't like it when I travel for business. They are terrified I'll be the victim of a terrorist attack just like my parents were or be mistaken for a terrorist because of my skin color."

"You're right and I understand, but still consider it."

He shrugged, but his uncle and aunt, who had no children of their own, raised him as if he was their biological child after his parents were killed when he was a toddler. He never considered moving away from them for any long period of time. However, for his friend, he would consider it. After all, it was Ashton who, along with others, set him up in business. He owed Ash and Vivian's brother, Kenneth Alexander, a huge debt of gratitude.

In their wild youth, he used to hang out with Vivian's other brother, Air Force fighter jet pilot and astronaut, Benjamin Alexander and their cousin Donald Dixon, aka code name: Delta Dawn. It was Delta who recruited him from his naval military career as a Navy SEAL into The

Nursery and handed him over to Explorer One for Mossad training. Were it not for them, he might have left The Nursery completely.

Although from time to time, he was called to handle missions for The Nursery, he liked running his own operation. He trained new recruits for The Nursery on Plaza de Masquerada and other deserted Polynesian islands in the Archipelagos for his operation. He considered moving his training facility site permanently to a deserted island. The disappearance of women he was recruiting had him concerned. Moreover, it might not be a bad idea to expand his investigation and personal security business with an East Coast office. He had enough staff and new recruits to fully populate a second location. He admitted to himself the idea was gaining momentum. Bottom line, it would put him in closer proximity to Satin. She was reason enough to make the move.

"I need you to put a team together to run a background check and surveil Briggs."

"Fair exchange ain't no robbery. What's good for the goose is good for the gander."

"If you're spouting clichés, you must still be jet-lagged. Get some rest."

Slade shook his head. "Later. Now I have work to do." He looked around the condo. "This is a great place and location. Central to everything. Do you think Vivian would be interested in selling it?"

"I doubt it. I offered to buy it from her, but she said it holds too many good memories for her. Her first husband, Derrick Jackson, owned it when they married. This was their first home together."

"Derrick was a great basketball talent. It's good he and Chuck are both now in the Basketball Legends Hall of Fame."

"Derrick and Chuck were best friends; as close as family. You rarely saw one without the other."

"Sort of like us," said Slade.

"Very much so. We were raised together from toddlers. Now I'm at a point in my life where I want children of my own with Kristen."

"Uncle Slade," he said testing the sound of that. "Yes, that just might work," he said laughing.

Chapter 21

"Holy shit!" fumed Jillian in a terse whisper as she read the information she found on line about Ashton's friend, Charles "Chucky P" Montgomery, basketball legend; now a medical doctor who owned Physician's Hospital in the rural area in Maryland outside of Washington, DC. Then she found information about his wife, Vivian Alexander Jackson Montgomery, sister of Kenneth Alexander, former two-term governor of California, and head of the giant multibillion dollar research and technology firm CompuCorrect Global based in Santa Barbara and San Francisco, California. His wife, JeNelle Towson Alexander, the junior US Senator from California.

To add insult to injury, Vivian is not only an Appellate Court Judge, but also the sister of astronaut, Air Force jet fighter pilot, and five-star General Benjamin Alexander, who is married to Admiral Stacy Greene Alexander. They are siblings of basketball player of the year, Gregory Alexander, known in the sports world as "Alexander the Great." Even she had heard of him. There was a fifth child, Aretha Grace Alexander, a scholar at Harvard and at Eton University in England. The five Alexander offspring were the children of Dr. Bernard and Sylvia Benson Alexander. The father, a PhD in education and business management and State Senator in South Carolina, and the mother, current president of the South Carolina Nurses Association and Dean of Summer County Nursing School.

All of their stellar accomplishments were available on the internet and Vivian and Ashton shared cases in international courts before Vivian became a judge at the Federal Appellate Court level. That was the position she was taking a sabbatical from, and her college chum Catherine Bryant was assuming in Vivian's absence. *Could it be as simple as that?* Jillian wondered. *Could Ashton know Judge Bryant through his pals Dr. Charles P. and Vivian Alexander Montgomery?*

She continued to follow the links finding out Judge Montgomery was an Olympic gold medalist in basketball. Her family was fascinating and she and her first and second husbands adopted health-challenged children. One of their daughters, Linda, is a prima ballerina which reminded her that Catherine Bryant's mother was also a world-class dancer which seemed like another anomaly. According to all accounts, Chuck and Vivian had twenty-four children and didn't appear to be slowing down. They were über wealthy and were very private people except with close personal friends…like Ashton. No wonder they clammed up when she approached the table. She had made a huge tactical mistake approaching them that way.

A plan began to hatch to find a way to get into the Alexander-Montgomery's good graces. She couldn't afford to alienate people of their stature, particularly because they were obviously friends of Ashton's. She needed them as allies to win Ashton over. The way to do that was to take another approach through Judge Bryant.

"Hello, Ali, this is Jillian Harris."

"How are you, Jillian? I haven't spoken with you since the last sorority convention over a year ago. What's up?"

"You're still the head of the National Women's Alliance, right?"

"I am, yes. Executive Director. Why?"

"Have you heard of Judges Vivian Alexander Montgomery and Catherine Bryant?"

Ali laughed. "You're kidding, right?"

"No, I'm serious. Do you know them?"

"I wish. The Alliance has been trying to book them for one of our conferences for some time. They're both hot commodities."

"Have you tried to get them recently?"

"We pretty much gave up hope. They are entirely too popular right now and are booked months in advance. They are said to be collaborating on a new book about women in the legal profession starting with Charlotte E. Ray, the first woman of colour to be admitted to the DC bar in 1872. Of course, you would already know all that."

Actually, she didn't, but she wasn't a historian, so who cared about the details. "I'll make a sizable donation to the Alliance if you'll keep trying to book them."

"How sizable?"

Jillian mentioned an amount that had Ali whistling. "For that type of money, we'll try to reach out to them again."

"Good. I'll, of course, do what I can to help through my connections. Let me know when you're successful."

"Will do," she said and disconnected.

Now, with the Alliance as an intro, I'll go see this Judge and pitch the idea, she thought as she left the hotel suite.

"Yes, may I help you?" asked a woman in Judge Bryant's chamber.

For a moment, Jillian had to admire the interior décor of the outer office. After taking it in, she leveled her eyes on the young, stylish woman. "I wondered whether Judge Bryant has a moment to speak with me? My name is Jillian Harris. I'm a member of the National Women's Alliance."

"Is Judge Bryant expecting you?"

"No, I was just in the building and thought I'd stop by."

"I see. Have a seat. I'll contact her Chief of Staff."

Jillian did as asked while the young woman made the call. Shortly, a tall, handsome man came out into the reception area and directly to her.

"Good morning, Ms. Harris. I'm Peter Brock, Judge Bryant's Chief of Staff. Please step into my office," he said extending his hand. "I understand you're here to see Judge Bryant without an appointment. May I ask what this is about?" he closed his office door, showed her to a seat, and then sat down behind his very orderly desk.

"Yes, thank you for seeing me. I represent the National Women's Alliance. We have been trying to arrange for Judge Bryant and Judge Montgomery to be guest speakers at an upcoming conference, but we haven't been successful in getting through to either one of them. Our Executive Director and I are making a personal appeal in the hope we can change their minds."

"I see."

"Is it possible to speak with Judge Bryant for a few moments?"

"No, it isn't. Especially since you represent Wayne Agra Industry; a case currently pending before this Appellate Court."

"This has nothing to do with the court case, I assure you, Mr. Brock. Besides the oral arguments concluded on Monday."

"Regardless, you must realize this contact is wholly inappropriate and ill-timed."

"You're recording this conversation, aren't you?"

"I am, yes, every word. Moments before you arrived, I received a call from Ali Joyce about this issue. She said nothing of enlisting your assistance with this effort. So, what is your reason for coming here today?"

"I assure you, Mr. Brock, my reasons are as I stated."

The telephone rang, cutting into their conversation.

"Pardon me," he said to Jillian and then picked up the phone. "Yes?" Peter answered; then checked his watch.

Handsome and intuitive, too, thought Jillian observing him more closely. He was a feast for the eyes. She spied pictures on the wall of groups of people laughing. She stood and casually wandered the room while he continued his telephone conversation. She recognized the judge and Peter Brock, but not the others. She pretended to check her phone but took pictures of the groups instead. His wall of credentials was so impressive she took as many pictures as she could while he continued to speak quietly.

"Yes, that will be fine. I'll see you there," he said ending his call.

Jillian turned and extended her hand. "Thank you, Mr. Brock. I've taken up enough of your time."

"Let me have your cell phone, Ms. Harris."

Busted, she handed it over. He set about deleting each of the pictures she had taken. When finished, he handed it back to her and without further commentary showed her out of the office.

Shortly thereafter, Tina and Cheryl entered Peter's office.

"Did it work?" asked Cheryl.

"It did, yes. As soon as she thought I was distracted, she took pictures of my wall."

"What do you think this is about, Peter?" asked Cheryl.

"It may be about her client, Wayne Agra Industries, trying to discover why the Chief Judge withdrew Kristen's name from the panel of judges…"

"Or about Thomas Marshall," surmised Tina. "There is definitely something going on with KC and she's not sharing that information with us."

"She has been somewhat secretive since she returned from vacation," commented Cheryl. She turned to Peter. "Has she said anything to you, Peter? About where she went on her secret vacation or who she may have gone with?"

He had his suspicions, but no conclusive evidence. For the time being, he would keep his own counsel. "No, she hasn't. When she's ready, she'll tell us what's going on. For now, I'm running behind for a lunch meeting."

"Are you still seeing Denise Lombard?" asked Tina.

Peter's brows beetled. "Why?"

"There was something in the society pages about the two of you."

He shrugged. "Some."

"She's a little older than you, isn't she? Not quite cougar country," teased Tina.

Peter grinned at her. "What is it I heard about you and…"

"Never mind," Tina quipped cutting off Peter."

"I'm outta here," said Cheryl. "I have a lunch appointment to get my hair cut. I may be a little late getting back.

She was gone so quickly Tina and Peter just stared.

"Talk about someone who's a little off these past months," commented Tina, then she turned back to Peter. "Where is KC anyway?"

"She and Savannah Logan Brock have a lunch meeting."

"It must be a brunch. It's barely past breakfast."

Peter had no comment.

Chapter 22

"Are you sure, Savannah?" asked Kristen of her friend and OB/GYN specialist.

"The tests don't lie," said Dr. Savannah Logan Flack. "I'm positive."

"Oh, hell," Kristen moaned.

"You thought it was something else?"

"I've been somewhat lethargic lately. Because I've been out of the country recently, I thought I was coming down with something."

"Well, for the next seven to eight months, you will be. According to your lab results, you're healthy, KC, and in great physical shape. I see no reason you will not deliver a healthy baby. Do you have reason for concern there is something troubling in your partner's medical history?"

She shook her head. "No, nothing like that. It's just that this is the worst possible time for this to happen."

"Hey, it was fun at the beginning, right?" Savannah teased.

Kristen rubbed her abdomen where she had just learned a fetus was growing. She was going to be a mother. Yet her happiness was tempered by how devastating a blow this would be to her father. He was her only parent since her mother's untimely death. He had such high hopes for her and her future. She stood the chance of alienating him to the point he would not be able to forgive her. They didn't see eye-to-eye about many things, but to embarrass her father would break her heart. Her brothers would take it in stride and would probably be happy about becoming uncles.

Then what of Ashton? she wondered. They barely had time to really get to know each other. How would he feel about this ill-timed turn of events? She believed him to be a good man. Heaven knew he was a passionate one, but what if he didn't want children? Or maybe this would be too soon for him. She really wanted time with him unencumbered by the weight of her public office and the stresses her life had become. She wanted what they had at Plaza de Masquerade Island; a perpetual honeymoon.

"You're overthinking this, KC," Savannah chided. "Talk with your partner. Let him share the good news with you. You are happy about this, right?"

"I am, yes, but I'm a little blown away by the news. It is totally unexpected." She thought a moment; almost wistfully. "Do you remember, when we were back in college? We used to talk about marriage and family as something off in the distant future after we accomplished everything we felt we were meant to do as career women."

"How well I remember those sessions with Vivian, JaiHonnah, Cheryl, Tina, you, and me. We were so serious and centered. Still, we've done what we started out to do. Now here we are ten years later in our thirties and raising families."

"Not quite all of us. Cheryl and Tina are still single, remember."

"They're both seriously dating, aren't they?"

"Cheryl perhaps, but she's being very secretive about this man she's seeing. However, as usual, a man would have to drag Tina kicking and screaming into a committed relationship. Oh, hell! I'm going to have to tell them and Peter about this!"

"You'll handle it, KC. You always do. Come on, let's go to an early lunch. You don't have to be in court today, do you?"

"No, I don't. Now that I know I'm eating for two, I'm famished."

After lunch with her friend, Kristen headed back to her office. Just as she entered, Peter was leaving for lunch. "Got a minute?" she asked him.

He checked his watch. "Sure," he said, though he was running very late and followed her to her office.

Once inside, she closed the door and paced with her hands in her suit trouser pockets.

Peter waited patiently for a while, checked the time again, and then asked, "What is it, KC? What's wrong?"

She finally stopped pacing and leaned her butt against her desk, arms akimbo, legs crossed at the ankles. "I, um, have a favor to ask."

"Sure, okay shoot."

"You have feelings for me and I wouldn't ask if it weren't important."

His brows beetled in question. "Uh, yeah, I have feelings for you. We're friends and have always been, but you know that. Short of asking me to do something illegal or immoral, there is nothing I wouldn't do for you, Tina or Cheryl. So, spit it out, KC. What do you need me to do for you?"

"Would you marry me?"

Peter stared intently at her without shifting his gaze as he pulled his cellphone from his pocket. He pressed one button and his assistant answered on the second ring. "Janet, this is Peter. Call my one o'clock and postpone lunch, again, please. Tell her I apologize and I'll call to reschedule. Thanks," he said and disconnected never taking his eyes from KCs. "As marriage proposals go, that one lacked a bit of passion, KC. Now, tell me what's going on."

"Would you believe Strickland is putting pressure on me? When he and his parents came to my home with the insane demand we renew our relationship and marry him, he issued ultimatums. Threats really against me and my father to ruin our reputations in the state. You were there so you know how he led everyone to believe we are still a couple. Then when Judge Hathaway withdrew me from the panel, Strickland was livid and stormed in issuing more threats."

"Would I believe it, yes, I would. That's just the kind of person he is. Do I believe you would allow anyone to intimidate you into doing something you did not want to do? No, I would not."

"Then, I take it you won't marry me?"

"Yes, I will marry you, but there are conditions, KC."

She slumped at that proviso. Of course, there would be conditions with Peter. He was not a man to go blindly into any situation.

"First, I want you to be completely honest with me. You had a visit from Jillian Harris today while you were out of the office."

Confusion covered Kristen's face. "Why did she come to see me?'

"I suspect to size up the competition." He explained he had caught her snooping. "After she left, I checked with a few contacts I have who know her. She makes no secret of the fact she's interested in a non-platonic relationship with Thomas Marshall. Her name has been linked with the head of Wayne Agra Industries *and* his son. She is purported to be a very able and competent trial litigator, but she's been known to sleep her way through her professional career with her clients. Granted, this is all rumor, conjecture, and innuendo, but it comes from more than one impeccable and unimpeachable source."

"Is there any truth to the rumor she and Thomas Marshall are an item?"

"None, so far, but they have been working together on this case for some time. His rep is that he does have an active social life, but not with women in his employ."

"I see."

"Do you really, KC?"

She looked up at him. "What do you mean, Peter?"

"I've never been anything but up front with you. As one of the conditions of your request, I want the same open and honest response from you."

She turned and walked away. "Ask your question, Peter."

"Is there a relationship going on between you and Thomas Marshall?"

She exhaled and shook her head. He had asked for honesty and she felt she owed him that, but it was not just her secret to keep. Furthermore, in light of this news about a possible liaison between Ashton and Jillian, she couldn't take Peter into her confidence until she had time to talk with Ashton. "I will answer you, Peter. Not today, but soon."

"All right. I'll accept that for now, but if I'm to have your back and protect you from people, like Jillian Harris, you've got to level with me."

She nodded her understanding, then Peter left her office. Taking the secure phone from her pocket, she asked, "Did you hear all of that?"

"I did, yes, but I'm not involved with Jillian Harris. However, first and foremost, I'm in love with you and you're in love with me. I've never been in love with any woman before you. Just ask my grandmother, Esmerelda Marshall."

She lightly laughed. "I'm an admirer of your grandmother's collected works. I even have some autographed copies of her books. She's a phenomenal woman."

"She is. I'm glad you believe in her works. I'll arrange for you to meet her. She wants to meet you and she'll assure you that you need not involve Peter Brock in this relationship between us. Please be patient, Kristen. The time will come when these days will be only a footnote in our history."

"I don't know, Ashton. I have to do something to get Strickland off of me and my father. If my father and your mother link up, on an intimate basis, as you say they have, we could be in for a long battle on more fronts. This is tough enough as it is for me."

"For the time being, your father and my mother are on The Vineyard staying somewhere they wouldn't be easily recognized. As I mentioned last night, my mother was in a fit of anger I have not witnessed in her behavior before. The report has it he was waiting for her when she returned from dinner with me. They discreetly left right away."

"How do you know this?"

"Trust me, KC, I know they are together."

"I do trust you, Ashton, but this is so out of character for my father. What are the chances, after all this time, your mother and my father accidentally came together?"

"Don't conjure up any conspiracy theories. I'm just glad they did. We can deal with the fallout later. For now, they aren't concerned about us or our lives. We only have Strickland and Jillian to contend with for the time being."

They continued to talk while others plotted around them.

Chapter 23

Strickland, the day after the court appearance, was still in a fit of temper over his poor showing. His parents were disappointed in him and were out trying to mend fences with the conservative party hierarchy. That spitfire, Jillian Harris, had disgraced him before the press and news media. He was making the nighttime television talk show hosts very popular at his expense. He needed relief and he didn't have Shannon around to slake his needs. She was away at a photo shoot in Mexico for two weeks.

He wished he could get his hands on the supermodels Angelique or Ardon. They were both a step up from Shannon; the kind of women who deserved to be seen with him. He looked at himself in the full-length mirror, removing his robe for a full-frontal view. Nearing forty, he believed his body was still nice and tight. Not an extra ounce of fat or flab anywhere. Posing for a side view while stroking himself into a full erection, he liked what he saw. His ass was still high and firm. He would keep it that way with his daily workout routines.

Shannon's body was well sculptured, but the truth be told, Kristen's daily dance routines were pure poetry in motion. Her ankles and calves were perfection. She could crack walnuts with the strength in her thighs alone. She had a grace that was not matched by any of the models he desired, but she was not a biddable woman. If she would become a submissive to his dominance, perhaps he could tolerate her for a while as his wife. His parents were expecting him to close the deal and marry her. She was the most high-profile, eligible woman in the State of Illinois with a spotless reputation. Prime to become a Supreme Court Justice and First Lady of the United States with her laudable credentials. Kristin and her brothers had instant name recognition. Both of her brothers were standout athletes inducted into the Illinois State Hall of Fame. They had an impressive client list of young, highly-touted professional athletes in their joint stable. Judge Clarence Bryant was a well-respected jurist hailed by the local and state law enforcement community as the leader of the conservative elements and a strict constructionist when it came to handing down sentences. There was not a whisper of scandal associated with the Bryant name and brand in the State of Illinois. Their name and support were worth at least ten to fifteen percentage election points. He had to keep them in his hip pocket. However, this damn case could lose him every benefit he had gained if he didn't win.

He didn't have Kristen firmly in his grasp either. If she were still one of the empaneled judges on his case, then he would have been sure of one secure vote for his client's cause of action. However, she found a way to be withdrawn from the panel. He wanted to know how she did it and, more importantly, whether there was something going on between her and Thomas Marshall.

He had a direct link to Marshall via that spitfire Jillian Harris. Now, there was a tasty morsel if ever he saw one. She was not particularly or classically beautiful, like Kristen or her two best friends, Tina and Cheryl, but she would do.

When there was a knock at the door, he put on his robe and stopped his self-gratification. When he opened his door, in strolled the object of his thoughts. None other than Jillian Harris.

Jillian's eyes dropped to the tent in the front of Strickland's robe and grinned. "Busy?"

"I have time. How can I help you, Ms. Harris?"

She had definite ideas on how he could be of service to her, but for the moment, she strolled around the hotel suite noting the doors to the two bedrooms were open indicating he was alone in the suite. Yeah, she could figure out what he was doing alone. Men, she thought, have sex on their brains fifty times a day. This man would be easy to control. She had taken the precaution of paying a housekeeper to let her know when the model Shannon departed. She hadn't expected to find Strickland Briggs barefoot and wearing a short terrycloth robe in the middle of the day. As she continued to stroll, she spotted a riding crop, picked it up, and grinned up at him. She clamped her eyes on his and approached while slowly running the crop through her fingers. When close enough, she lightly ran the wand down his torso separating the folds of his robe wide enough for his member to jut out hard and ready. Arms folded across his chest, he made no move to stop her exploration. She ran the crop up between his thighs. One little sharp slap and his eyes began to glaze with pleasure.

Oh, yeah! It was time to play.

Two and a half hours later, like combatants in a high school wrestling match, they had taken each other in every conceivable way known to mankind. He was face down, spread eagle on the rumpled sheets exhausted, his back and buttocks still showing signs of red whelps. Yet, he was still wearing some of the toys he introduced into the session.

Jillian properly assessed, from the way he scrutinized her in court, he was a playa. No way was she ever wrong about men and their peccadillos. She could teach Christian Grey from the E. L. James novels something about female dominatrix. She'd cherish the day she could get a strong man, like Thomas Marshall, to bend to her will. So far, she hadn't even succeeded in getting him between her sheets. She would remedy that if she could figure out whether there was a relationship between Ashton and Judge Bryant. Since Strickland knew the judge intimately, he was a good place to start. They were taking a break while waiting for room service meals to arrive, so she continued the seemingly innocuous interrogation she began during their mutually satisfying session.

"So, you were saying you've known Judge Bryant for about five years?"

"Give or take. I met her when she was a tenured professor at the Chicago School of Law. She was a panelist at a conference I attended and Law Review president. Youngest woman to ever hold that post," he mumbled, his face buried in a pillow. "She was appointed to the Illinois Federal District Court, but she still continued to periodically lecture.

"In all of that time, she never mentioned knowing Thomas Marshall?"

"She's not the type of woman who finds celebrity interesting. She may have cited his cases for class assignments, but other than that, she wouldn't know him from a can of paint. Yet, her reaction to him in court was out of character for her. I wondered about that at the time, but so far, I have no evidence she knows him."

"It is curious, but he represents clients worldwide and is usually out of the country. He fluently speaks an incredible number of languages and is an international law expert, but he doesn't have many domestic law clients. None in Illinois that I've found. Ashton usually assigns those cases to his staff of attorneys. He doesn't do college or university lecture tours or write extensively about his cases. However, I recently discovered that he is close to Dr. Charles Montgomery and his wife, Vivian Alexander."

"Yes, I know. Judge Montgomery and Kristen were in undergrad together."

"Could that be the connection? Could Judge Bryant know Ashton through Vivian Montgomery?"

"Anything is possible," he said gingerly rolling over and slowly getting to his feet to answer the knock at the suite door. "With KC Bryant, she's the soul of discretion. She would not let any judicial indiscretion tarnish her sterling reputation. If she had a personal relationship with a defendant or petitioner, she'd put it on the record."

Jillian was intently watching Strickland's taunt muscles ease slowly into his robe and almost missed the name he called Judge Bryant. KC for Kristen Catherine. She remembered the night after Sheila's party when she went to Ashton's home. She thought she was succeeding with seducing him when he moaned the name Casey. At the time, she thought that was what he was saying, but maybe the woman he was dreaming about and desperately trying to locate was KC for Kristen Catherine. That would, at least, account for their reaction toward each other in court; particularly if they hadn't expected to see each other. It was after that encounter both Ashton and Judge Bryant withdrew from the case.

All of this excessive interest in one woman seemed to start after Ashton returned from his vacation… She wondered whether Judge

Bryant had taken any recent trips? When she walked bare bodied into the common area of the suite, Strickland had removed his robe and was waiting for her.

She positioned him in a chair so they would have access to the food, sheathed him in a condom, and impaled herself on his impressive hard on, breasts to chest.

"So, has Judge Bryant been away recently?"

Strickland found the question odd, but dug eight inches deep and being simultaneously fed, he really didn't care why she asked. "In fact, yes, she was away for a time before she came to DC. I tried to find out where she was, but her friends either didn't know or were just unwilling to tell me."

Bingo! thought Jillian. That had to be it. Ashton and Kristen Catherine must have had a romantic rendezvous somewhere. She could feel she was on to something besides Strickland's impressive cock.

Knowing Ashton, it would have to be somewhere private and exclusive. She knew just the person to ask about such places. Her former boss' son, Wallace Wayne, frequently traveled to all the hottest and most exclusive spots around the world. In fact, he was due back from a long voyage on one of his yachts any day now. He owned several private islands and traveled via his several yachts or airplanes island hopping. He was into extremes in everything he did, mountain climbing, sky diving, etc., but he tested out of both high school and college studies beyond genius level. Added to the fact he was a multi-billionaire, handsome, and virile, he was hard to ignore. However, he always seemed to be competing with his father on every level. That's why it was so easy to seduce him. He wanted everything his father had and more. A more brilliant, complicated man she never met. He was remotely following the trial proceeding and wanted to see her. She agreed, but for the moment, Strickland Briggs had her undivided attention.

"Tell me more about Judge Bryant."

"Why are you fixated on her?"

"Unlike you, I believe she and Ashton know each other intimately."

He laughed. "Kristen and I have been lovers for the past two years. She's loyal and committed; not the type of woman to sleep around. If she did, which I'm sure she didn't, it would likely be with her Chief of Staff. They are as close as siblings, but for him, I believe it goes deeper."

"Peter Brock?" she smirked. "I can see why. He's a nice piece of flesh."

Strickland smacked her on her naked, still tender buttocks. She tensed and grinned at him. He did it again and then lifted her, carrying her back to bed without breaking their intimate union.

∞∞ ∞∞

Jillian still didn't know where Ashton went after he checked out of the McCoy Regent, but he had not yet returned to Portland. Of that she was sure. Even Sheila seemed to be uncharacteristically off the grid. For the moment, she was at a loss for what to do with all the intelligence she had acquired. Little bits and pieces were helping her connect the dots. All toward locking down a marriage to Thomas Ashton Marshall, III, becoming First Lady of the State of Oregon, and then the country, because, if there was one thing she knew without question about Thomas Marshall, it was that he had the drive and ambition to be anything he wanted to be. The problem was she didn't know what it was he wanted or what it would take to maneuver him into her and Sheila's plan. She hadn't succeeded in pinning him down long enough to figure him out. He was a man, so she expected him to respond to her on a sexual level. She had been miffed and then intrigued that he didn't. So, she tried to redouble her efforts, but, so far, he wasn't taking her up on her offers.

Perhaps Judge Bryant was his Achilles Heel. However, she couldn't make a run at KC Bryant. The woman was too well insulated by her friends and position. Blackmailing her, if caught, could lead to disbarment or worse, a prison sentence. Still, getting Ashton to the altar might be enhanced if he felt protective of his precious "KC". That was a better way to go about accomplishing her goal and didn't hold the risks threatening a sitting US appellate court judge would rain down on her. As threat assessments went, she had few options. However, she first had to find Ashton to start laying the groundwork for her plan.

She also wanted to spend time with Wallace Wayne, firming up the places where Ashton and Kristen may have had a rendezvous a few months ago. She had a taste for Wallace Wayne and his extreme kind of off-the-chain erotica. The more information and evidence she had to trap Ashton, the better and Wallace was the key.

Strickland Briggs turned out to be a surprisingly tasty afternoon delight. They made plans to see each other again later. Technically, what they were doing together wasn't prohibited. The *Wayne v. McElvoy* case was under consideration. They only had to wait now for the court to hand down an opinion. Their opposing clients may have been bothered by their connection, but what they didn't know wasn't quite considered sleeping with the enemy. Particularly since they rarely slept.

As she went about her shopping errands, she didn't notice she was being followed.

Chapter 24

Ashton and Slade were working on the weight machines, both sweaty with exertion and unknowingly giving the women in the Watergate Fitness Center a little beefcake thrill. When Slade's cellphone chirped, he eased it out of his pocket and read the text message.

"Something important?" asked Ashton when he noticed a strange expression cross Slade's face.

"Could be. There may be a lead on the missing women from Plaza de Masquerada."

"Are you following up for a Richardson client?"

Slade shrugged, "Something like that," he absently said. He and Ashton were like brothers, but there were still things Slade couldn't share with someone he trusted as much as he did Ashton; particularly when it involved missions for The Nursery.

Ashton understood. Slade Richardson was the head of Marshall and Marshall's Security and Investigations Division, but he also headed his own Richardson Associates; a high tech private security firm. There were certain things Slade was honor bound not to reveal about his clients and what he did for them. Still, Slade's operation seamlessly fit into the Marshall and Marshall law firm. Every case required the law firm to have a clear picture of the issues and the players involved. They didn't take on cases for everyone who walked through their doors. It was why they had a high win record and a spotless reputation.

"I'll see you back upstairs," said Slade as he headed for the locker room.

Watching him go were a number of women and even some envious men, Ashton noticed. Slade was probably aware of it, too. Slade's keen sense of his surroundings at all times had saved them both from being attacked in some out-of-the-way locations, like Dubai, the back-alley ways of Calcutta, and a particularly sticky situation in the West End of Paris, France. They were both skilled in hand-to-hand combat, the martial arts, and the use of a wide range of weaponry, but didn't relish a fight. Slade's uncle, Walter Turner, was their Mr. Miyagi. He was a former Special Forces warrior and had trained the two boys how to protect themselves since they were toddlers.

Ashton continued his workout while simultaneously working out plans to close down his Oregon operation. He was meeting with Roderick and JaiHonnah Hawkins Baylor later that day at their offices to view the topography maps of their Havenhurst Estates development. Once he identified a few sites which met his needs, they would then go out to the site before joining Chuck and Vivian at their home for an old-fashioned, New England clam bake. He wanted to lock down an option on several parcels of land on which he and Kristen could begin to build a home and future.

He admitted to himself his concern that KC would move independently of him because of the amount of pressure Strickland Briggs was bringing to her doorstep. Next, her father was a force to be reckoned with, and, finally, Peter Brock, one of her best friends, who KC admitted she respected, trusted, and loved like a brother. He didn't know how much more pressure she could take before she felt trapped. He wanted to lift the burden from her shoulders and his need to be with her was also growing. He hadn't been able to touch her in some time. He had to be patient, though, and await the court's decision before he could put any permanent plans into action.

He smiled at the phone he slipped from his pocket. "Good morning," he said while wiping the perspiration from his face with a towel around his neck. "I'm in the gym getting some exercise. What about you?" He laughed at her ribald comment and settled in to enjoy a few moments that would set up his day.

191

"This is a good spot," said Ashton as he and Roderick and JaiHonnah Hawkins Baylor walked a seven-acre parcel of land that had a spectacular view of one of the contiguous lakes at Havenhurst Estates. The seventy-two-hole golf club community had great amenities, including a state-of-the-art security system supplied by Kenneth Alexander's CompuCorrect Company and monitored by Slade's Richardson's Technology and Security Company. The land was flat and sparsely forested with old-growth trees that would enhance the landscape once their home was properly set on the pristine acreage. He could see it in his mind's eye. He only had to know what type of home KC would want to begin planning.

"I think it's ideal because you'll have a southern exposure for your solar panels. Everyone is off the grid here," said JaiHonnah proudly. "We use geothermal, solar, and wind to power the homes and businesses. A rain barrel system supplies the potable water supply, well and septic system and propane for those who prefer to cook with gas. We're completely green."

He smiled at the beautiful woman who he remembered was the first runner up in a Miss America Pageant years earlier when she was still in school at Spelman College. She hadn't lost any of her splendor; rather she looked even lovelier and contented with Roderick holding her hand. He wanted that for himself and Kristen; for her to be happy with him and guilt free.

JaiHonnah was also a classmate of Vivian and Kristen's at Spelman. Roderick and JaiHonnah were quite the team with their Baylor and Baylor Design and Development Company. JaiHonnah, a PhD architect and civil and structural engineer, designed unique, custom homes and businesses and Roderick's construction company built them. Again, Ashton had Vivian and Chuck to thank for putting him in touch with the much in-demand Baylor team.

"When are you thinking of breaking ground?" asked Roderick, accepting Ashton's check for the parcel of land.

"Probably early spring. I like the homes here and I'd like to get on your schedule, JaiHonnah, for the design phase of the construction."

"I think that's doable. Do you have something in mind?"

"Not yet. I wanted to walk the property first." What he didn't say was now that he had bought the land, he would bring Kristen to see it as soon as possible.

"That's good thinking," said JaiHonnah. "You should come several more times at different times of the day. The country club and restaurant, The Foxes Lair, are a big hit here as is the championship golf course. Membership to all comes with your land ownership. You can lease a condo here or a townhouse for the short term if it's more convenient for you."

"That's good to know. I'll take advantage of the amenities and especially the golf course and club house."

"You're also not far from Vivian and Chuck's ranch. They're going to provide riding stables and horses for Havenhurst Estates. If you're into polo, a field will be going in during the spring over on the northern area of the Estates. The residents voted for a quarter mile exercise track and bridle paths through the forested areas that surround the Estates. The land here backs up to a permanent green space we contracted with the county to use for grazing and riding."

"I'm impressed with what you're doing with the land."

"Thank you, Ashton. We're pleased to welcome you to Maryland."

Roderick checked his watch. "If you've seen enough for now, Ashton, Chuck and Vivian are waiting for us to join them for that sea-food lunch."

He took another long look around the property he just bought; nodded, pleased with his selection, and joined Roderick and JaiHonnah on the walk back to their car.

⚬⚬⚬

Kristen and Peter shared a significant look before he cleared his throat. "I have an announcement," he said while cracking the shell of a large lobster.

"Not today, brotherman," said Tina as she dipped a thick chunk of crab meat into a bowl of hot sauce. "We're off the clock and these hot crabs are hittin' and holdin'. Is there any more cocktail sauce?"

"Here you go," said Cheryl shoving the half empty jar in her direction. "The next round should be ready by now." She rose from the back patio table and disappeared into the kitchen of Kristen's home.

When she returned carrying a large, hot pot of freshly steamed shrimp, crabs, mussels, clams, and lobsters, Peter stood to clear a space on the long newspaper-covered, trestle table.

Tina picked up a pair of tongs and lifted the lid to get a grip on a steamy hot lobster. She dug deeper for an ear of corn and some clams, oysters, and crabs.

When Peter sat again, he wiped his hands and took a long drink of his beer, eyeing Kristen. He cleared his throat again, turned down the music using a remote-control device, and, at Kristen's nod of encouragement, spoke up. "This is important," he said significantly to Tina and Cheryl.

"Okay, if you must, son," said Cheryl while adding hot sauce to her steamed clam.

"On Friday, in two weeks, Kristen and I are getting married."

Silence reigned. Cheryl and Tina both stopped eating and stared.

"To each other?" asked Cheryl.

At their joint nod, Tina deadpanned, "What the hell? Why?"

"We want to be together," said Peter simply.

"You're serious?" asked Cheryl.

Kristen nodded when Cheryl and Tina both turned to look at her; both women were frowning.

"Since when have you two been an item?" asked Tina.

"Does that really matter?" asked Peter.

"It does if you expect us to believe you suddenly got a wild hair and went down on bended knee, brotherman. Last week you were out and about with Denise what's-her-face, the cougar-in-training chick. Now you're going to marry KC in two weeks on Friday?" She shook her head. "I'll admit you've got jokes, son. Now I'm waiting for the punchline."

Again, silence reigned until Cheryl stood and hugged Kristen and then Peter. "Well, congrats," she said smiling weakly with little to no enthusiasm. "I guess this is the perfect time to announce that I'm engaged to be married too."

Everyone turned to regard Cheryl with a Prozac stare.

"Oh, for pity's sake! Has the whole Chicago Crew gone crazy?" exclaimed Tina morosely tossing her hand towel on the pile of crustacean carcasses on the table before her.

"Are you going to stand up with me?" Cheryl asked Tina.

"Of course, but pick a lane, would you? Who the hell are you going to marry?"

"Oh, I forgot. I'm marrying Wilbur Hardy."

"You have *got* to be kidding me, Cheryl," Tina exclaimed. "Isn't he your old college ethics professor who you discovered had no ethics and was servicing the sexual needs of women in the Washington, Virginia, and Maryland standard metropolitan area? The one you left Maryland University to get away from and then joined me and KC at Spelman? *That Wilbur Hardy?* You're planning to marry him? On purpose?"

"He's changed, Tina. We ran into each other a few months ago at a cocktail party. We've been seeing each other exclusively since then."

"Leopards don't change their spots, Cheryl," commented Tina drolly and just shook her head.

Cheryl turned to look at Kristen taking her hand and then Peter's. "Will you stand up with me, too, KC? You and Peter?"

Kristen squeezed Cheryl's hand, nodded, and extended her other hand to Tina.

After a disquieting moment, Tina on a huff of breath linked hands with Kristen and then with Peter around the table signifying the four life-long friends were still each other's support system.

They tucked back into their meal, but the atmosphere was quieter and much less animated.

Chapter 25

The wedding of Cheryl Lawrence and Wilbur Hardy on the following Saturday afternoon was a subdued, quiet affair. The bride wore a Vera Wang original, but didn't sparkle when wedding pictures were taken. Her father, Cuban-born print and television journalist, columnist, and renowned investigative reporter, Farrow Lawrence, seemed as perplexed by his daughter's hasty nuptials as did her mother; an equally renowned, Southside Chicago-born columnist and reporter, Helen Kendall Lawrence. Other guests included the usual suspects from a lifetime of close friendships, Tina's parents, Redmond and Marguerite Alanza Dela Vega Justice, her six older brothers, and both sets of grandparents, Rev. Ellis and Anna Lettie Outlaw Justice, and Raphael Alanza and Alicia Diaz Vasquez Dela Vega. Peter's parents, Peter and Cassia Brock, Sr., and Clarence Bryant and his sons, Clarence Junior and George were there. Chuck and Vivian, Roderick and JaiHonnah, and Nathan and Savannah attended rounding out the family and close friends for the event.

No guests attended from the groom's family.

The wedding was held at the Maryland House; a colonial built in the early 1800s on the University campus. Wilbur Hardy, a tenured professor, was able to bump a student-sponsored poetry reading scheduled for the facility and snag it for three hours for his and Cheryl's wedding. The guests dined on an awesome array of foods catered by world renowned super model and Le Cordon Bleu-trained Chef Angelique in person, but despite the sumptuous food, great environment, and enticing music, nothing seemed up beat or happy about the event. Tina and Kristen stood as Cheryl's maids-of-honor, while Peter stood as Wilbur's best man. They performed their duties as was expected of the close friends, but none seemed to enjoy their roles. No one, not Tina, Cheryl, Kristen or Peter, mentioned the impending nuptials scheduled to take place in Judge Hathaway's chambers the following Friday.

After the wedding and reception, the newlyweds left for the rest of the weekend to spend time at a beach cottage Cheryl recently purchased on the Maryland Eastern shore. Not to anyone's surprise, she expected to be at work on Monday morning as usual.

Attending to details for Cheryl's wedding was difficult for Kristen, she admitted to herself. She still believed there was more to her friend's rationale for the impromptu wedding. The fact Cheryl kept her renewed relationship with Wilbur Hardy a secret was the first inkling she had that her friend's behavior was out of character. They were friends far too long for Kristen to believe Cheryl was in love with Wilbur Hardy, a man twelve-years Cheryl's senior. Nevertheless, she wished the couple the very best and hoped her upcoming marriage to Peter Brock would prove that two, long-term, purely platonic friends could build a loving relationship.

⁂

Ashton had just settled into the Watergate condo after getting off of a long flight back to DC from Portland. He was surprised to receive a visit he hadn't expected but was none-the-less pleased at the outcome. He immediately swung into action. Now he had completed the details of shutting down his home base, he was free to move full steam ahead with his relocation plans.

That same afternoon, he again met with Vivian's former founding law firm partners and decided to utilize their well-established operation and to open a contiguous firm, Marshall International and Associates, as a sole proprietorship. He would be "of counsel" to Alexander, Carter, Chandler, Charles, Lightfoot, and Townson, PA, on matters involving international affairs.

When news of his decision to leave the Marshall and Marshall law firm was announced, everyone in his division, except Jillian Harris, asked to relocate with him to Washington. Taking the entire International

Division might have devastated Marshall and Marshall, so he planned to remain of counsel to Marshall and Marshall, too, for a year until he could help his mother rebuild that department. In the meantime, Baylor and Baylor subcontracted work on his new office space to JaiHonnah's uncle and cousin, Alroy Lowry, Sr., and his daughter, architect and interior designer Lizelle Fiona Lowry. One design meeting is all it took, and work began. He was pleased with Lowry Builders efficiency and creativity. Apparently, Lowry Builders was a family firm populated by Alroy Lowry, his six sons and one daughter. Each of the sons had a builder's specialty and their individual businesses but came together to coordinate projects with their father and sister. Ashton, after only one meeting with them, felt confident the Lowry Builders would meet and exceed his requirements. He knew Roderick and JaiHonnah would not have recommended them if they were not top-of-the-line builders.

Now everything was falling into place, he dispatched the rest of his plans with finesse and efficiency. He was ready to get on with the rest of his life. One last detail had to be addressed, but to do so, he needed to speak with Jillian Harris. However, after months of having to avoid her, she was strangely not around. Calls to her cellphone went straight to voice mail. He checked with both Ben Knight and Von Little, who were still in the area taking advantage of vacation time and the early fall weather in the Shenandoah Mountains watching the leaves turn with a couple of women they recently met. They suggested he join them with a lady *du jour* at a quaint bed and breakfast, an invitation which he declined. However, neither Knight nor Little had communicated with Jillian Harris since court adjourned several weeks earlier. He had enough on his plate as it was. He didn't have the time or inclination to try to track Jillian down. However, if she didn't return his call by the following week, he would put Slade on her trail.

For the time being, he set up temporary operations in the Watergate's instant-office facility and began taking meetings with both old and new clients. It kept him busy from early morning to late at night.

⁕⁕⁕

Jillian rolled off of Strickland's moist body and lay beside him. He slowly turned in her direction feeling limp and exhausted. For the better part of a few weeks, they were on Martha's Vineyard sequestered at a private residence owned by a friend of his. The ocean rolled up on shore just outside their bedroom window in West Chop on the Tisbury Peninsula. There were beautiful yachts skimming across the water in plain view. When Strickland's phone chirped, he ignored it and commenced to pleasuring Jillian as she had pleasured him to the point he was beyond relaxed. The minx knew what she was doing in bed. He had never been with a woman who matched his needs so precisely. She was even more sexually adventurous than he; a fact he found intriguing. There was nothing she wouldn't consider. She proved it when he arranged a *ménage a trois* one night in an Oak Bluff bar with an heiress of a prominent Boston family. They spent three days and nights together and made plans to meet again during the holidays at a villa the heiress owned in Cancun. He was looking forward to the new adventure before he took up the roll of devoted husband to Kristen, though he fully intended to continue his liaison with Jillian even after he married Kristen and Jillian married Thomas Marshall.

In short order, Strickland had Jillian in a mindless euphoria again while the waves pounded the shore.

"I'm starving," said Sheila as she dried her hair in the bathroom of the little cottage.

Clarence stepped out of the shower stall and dried his face with a fluffy white towel.

Sheila eyed his nude body in the mirror and smiled. He was still built well and firm in all of the right places. He ran for exercise every day. They ran together enjoying being away on a New England Island having an adventure. She realized she needed this respite from the years when she did not take so much as a weekend off to rest, relax, and decompress.

Each and every day was devoted to making Marshall and Marshall an enviable brand in Oregon and the USA. She still had ambition, but without her son's enthusiastic participation, what was the future to be for her? She worked around the clock to serve Marshall and Marshall clients, but was that to be all there was for the rest of her life? The days and nights she spent with Clarence were evidence there could be more for her and her life.

What of Clarence? He admitted he never stopped loving her. He loved his wife and the family they shared, but he never got over what he felt for her. No man, not even her husband, cherished her the way Clarence Bryant did.

She turned from watching him dry his body in the mirror and smiled at him.

"What?" he asked, when he saw her watching him closely. Walking toward her, he tossed the towel aside and palmed her face for a warm, slow kiss. "If you keep looking at me like that, Sheila, I'm going to have to take you back to bed and dinner will have to wait a while."

She grinned at him. "Does the restaurant deliver?" she asked winking at him.

He laughed at her antics. "No, my love, but we can eat really fast," he teased.

She demurely sighed and hugged him close. "Then let's hurry. Dinner isn't the only thing I have a taste for tonight."

Hours later, as Clarence and Sheila were leaving Lola's five-star restaurant in Oak Bluffs, they were chatting as they made their way to their rental car.

"I didn't know this is one of former President Clinton's favorite restaurants," commented Sheila.

"It must be with all of the pictures of him on the restaurant wall. The food was beyond my expectation. I enjoyed the Louisiana-style atmosphere here, too. It is unexpected to find this type of dining on a New England island."

"Did you know the movies, *Inkwell* and *Jaws*, were filmed here?"

"I didn't, no. I haven't made time to see movies. I've had my hands full raising three …" he stopped talking when he heard moaning and grunting as they proceeded through the restaurant parking lot.

Sheila apparently heard it, too, and turned toward the sounds. She initially thought the woman against the hood of the car with the man at her back with his trousers down around his ankles may have been assaulting her, so she stepped up boldly and grabbed the man to pull him off the woman.

Clarence was two steps behind her when she grabbed the man.

"What the hell?" exclaimed the man, incensed that someone was interfering with his near cataclysmic eruption. *"Mind your own damn business, lady!"*

"Strickland?" asked Clarence unbelieving what he was seeing.

When the woman against the car looked up over her shoulder annoyed at the intrusion, she too froze.

"Jillian?" said Sheila, equally as stunned as Clarence.

"Well, hell, this is awkward," proclaimed Strickland.

"Awkward!" thundered Clarence. "Put that thing away," he said turning his head while gesturing to Strickland's phallus swinging limply in the cool evening air.

"It's not what you think, Sheila," Jillian averred without much conviction. She hastily pulled down her skirt over her bare bottom. Strickland handed her thong to her. She snatched it out of his hand and stuffed it in her pocket.

"I know what it is, Ms. Harris, and you're fired. To think I wanted *you* to be Ashton's wife!" She turned on her heels and strode away.

Clarence malevolently regarded the couple and then strode away following Sheila.

No one noticed the camera with night-vision technology trained on the two couples as they parted company.

Chapter 26

"Frankly, KC, I don't understand any of this," said Tina as she paced Judge Hathaway's private office, her hands planted on her impressive hips and a frown marring her gamine face. "We've been friends with Peter since we were all in diapers, but not once in all of that time have you two had that type of chemistry between you."

"I noticed it a time or two," said Cheryl as she sat with her feet up in another chair, arms crossed.

"You never said anything," scowled Tina. "I'm supposed to know when two of my best friends start bumping uglies."

"We haven't," said Kristen as she nervously paced the well-appointed Chief Judge's chambers waiting for Peter to arrive.

"Wait! What?" exclaimed Tina. "You mean you're marrying a man you haven't taken out for a test drive? Even *I* thought of tapping that a time or two!"

Kristen frowned at her friend. "Did you?"

Tina shook her head, "Never touched him," she pledged holding up three fingers, "Scouts honor."

"She's not the only one," admitted Cheryl, her tone dry as dust. "You have to agree Peter is a walking wet dream."

"I never looked at him that way. We were like sister and brother."

"Yet, you're going to marry him? A man you don't have amorous feeling for? Oh, come *on*, KC! Why are you and Peter really doing this?"

Kristen looked from one best friend to the other, then heavily sighed. "I'm pregnant," she said on an exhausted breath. She sat on a sofa next to Cheryl while her friends gathered on each side of her.

"It's Peter's baby?" Cheryl asked, stunned.

"No, no," denied Kristen. "I wasn't lying. Peter and I haven't slept together."

"Strickland?" questioned Tina, horrified.

"No, I haven't been with him in more than six months."

"Then who?" asked Tina, perplexed. "You're a saint, kid, but I'll bet this was not the Immaculate Conception."

Kristin pursed her lips smirking at her friend. "I can't tell you that right now."

"It happened on your vacation, didn't it? Were you attacked, KC? Is that it? Did someone hurt you?" demanded Tina becoming enraged.

"No, Tina, no. I wasn't sexually assaulted."

"Does Peter know?" asked Cheryl.

Kristen shook her head.

"Yet, he's going to marry you?"

"He's a good friend, Cheryl."

"I'll say. He's been dating that clinical psychologist, Denise Lombard, since we came to town," Tina offered.

"I think that's more her doing than his. He said he's not serious about her or we wouldn't be doing this," said KC.

Just then the door opened and in walked Judge Hathaway and Peter.

"Sorry to keep you waiting so long, my dear. I had a bit of business to dispense with," the Judge said taking Kristen's hands, drawing her to her feet. "Now, I think we're ready to proceed."

"Thank you, Harold, for doing this," said Kristen.

"Happy to do so. Now if you two would sign the witness statement," the Judge said indicating papers on his desk.

Cheryl selected a pen and quickly signed the document, but Tina took time to read it. Her eyes brightened and then connected with Peter's. She grinned at him and added her signature to the sheet.

"All right," said the Judge, collecting the sheets of paper, before donning his judicial robe. "You're here, Peter" said the Judge positioning him and Kristen on Peter's left with Tina and Cheryl flanking them at their backs.

Just as he was about to proceed, the chamber door opened.

"A little redundant, wouldn't you say, KC?" Ashton asked as he strolled in.

Kristen's shoulders slumped at hearing Ashton's voice behind her. "You shouldn't be here," she pleadingly said, not turning to look at him.

Cheryl and Tina parted so that Ashton could arrange himself at Kristen's back. Without physically touching her, he said. "Remember the love song they sang to us on the white sandy beach? We wore traditional Pāreu; native wedding attire. The priest was a stout man with an ingratiating smile and big laugh. Remember, KC? He thought you were beautiful, and I agreed. When he tied us together with seaweed and then signed the wedding certificate on tapa. It was a pledge we made together. I have that certificate with me today. I brought it here from Portland. I had it encased in glass so that it would never be damaged. I also have the crowns, leis, and Pāreu we wore on that magical afternoon."

"It wasn't legally binding, Ashton," she sighed shaking her head in denial.

"Oh, but that's where you're wrong, my beautiful, KC. I'm an expert on international law. Weddings on the Polynesian Islands are now legally binding for American and Canadian nationals. There are one-hundred-and-eighteen islands in the archipelagos and we're husband and wife on each and every one of them, including the Plaza de Masquerada, Mrs. Marshall. It was thirty minutes that transformed my life. I still smell the coconut leaves and hibiscus flowers we wore. The priest declared me your tańe, husband, and you my vahinè, wife. We exchanged leis and crowns symbolizing harmony for the rest of our lives together. We drank the sacred coconut milk to toast our wedding in the islands and sealed our union. We were wrapped in a tifaifai, paddled aboard an outrigger to an overwater bungalow where we spent our first night as a married couple. After loving you, when I woke up the next morning, you were gone."

"I had to go, Ashton. My obligations …"

"*Our* obligations, KC. You're not alone in this marriage."

The chamber door opened again, and Slade ushered Sheila and Clarence into the room. Esmerelda Marshall followed with Clarence Junior and George Bryant on her heels.

"What's the meaning of this?" thundered Clarence, Senior. "What's going on here, Kristin?"

"Ashton?" asked Sheila, perplexed.

"Hello, Mother," he said kissing his mother's temple. "Judge Bryant," he said extending his hand. "What's going on here, Judge Bryant, is the second and last wedding I and your daughter will ever have to participate in."

"Second wedding?" asked Sheila. "What do you mean, Ashton?"

"This lovely lady and I were married on the Plaza de Masquerada by a Polynesian Priest while we were on vacation. Today, in an abundance of caution and before our family and friends, Judge Hathaway is going to perform the second ceremony, isn't he, KC?"

Though her eyes dripped with tears, she turned to face Ashton. "Yes," she whispered and then went into his arms. "I'm sorry, Dad, but I'm in love with him…and, I'm, uh, pregnant with his child."

Pandemonium erupted when Ashton swooped her up in his arms to kiss her like there was no tomorrow.

Epilogue

"How did this happen," asked Kristen snug in her husband's arms in bed at the Watergate.

"Peter, actually," Ashton said, rubbing his hand along her bare bottom.

"Peter?"

"Yes, he tracked me down through Vivian. He came here to the condo and asked me what I felt for you. I told him the truth…that I'm in love for the first time in my life. He told me he was going to talk with the other judges' law clerks and try to expedite the _Wayne_ case. Since you weren't hearing that case, his actions couldn't be construed as an indiscretion. Still, we didn't want a hint of impropriety to affect you. The other clerks prioritized the _Wayne_ case to the top of the pile and sealed the opinion. Judge Hathaway signed the order denying the Petition for Stay and had it messengered to Briggs and Jillian just before he entered his chambers to conduct the ceremony. That was the business he and Peter were taking care of while you were waiting."

"You were so sure I would agree to marry you that you had the witness statement include your name instead of Peter's?"

"Peter handled that as well. I arranged to get your father, your brothers, my mother, and grandmother there in time to witness the marriage. We couldn't get Tina's, Peter's and Cheryl's families there without tipping our hand. Peter told me they are all very important to you. We'll have to arrange some type of reception, so they can look me over and pass judgment on my suitability to marry into your extended family."

"They are family, Ashton. Our parents and grandparents have been friends for many years. They all started out in the old Southside neighborhood and remained friends through college, marriage, and raising their next generation together. My mother was the newest addition."

"Peter told me what a tragedy it was when she died. You and your brothers were still very young."

"You and Peter must have had quite a conversation."

"We did, yes. He cares very deeply for you, but he sacrificed his feelings because he wants you to be happy. He believed you wanted to be with me instead of with him."

"Yes, he is right about my wanting to be with you. He is also right about my brothers and me. We were young when our mother died. Now I believe I know why my father never remarried. He was still in love with your mother."

"So, he said when he took me aside to have 'the chat' with me," he said, smiling.

"I hope it wasn't too bad."

"He tried for stern, but he was too giddy about becoming a grandfather."

"So was your mother, grandmother, and my brothers about our pregnancy. Ours will be the first born for the next generation of Brocks, Justices, Lawrences, and Bryants."

"For my family, too. Sheila will be in a deadly tug of war to get her hands on our child."

"Children. I expect you to do your duty and keep me barefoot and pregnant for several more years."

"You're serious about wanting to go live on Plaza de Masquerada?"

"I am, yes, but not until after our baby is born. I'm planning to remain on the bench for a year, at least. I want to be with you, do ordinary things with you. Go to the movies, have family and friends over for fun; take you to Chicago and show you the city I grew up in. I want you to take me to Portland and walk me through each step and stage of your life. You've travelled the globe, so I want to travel with you when we can before we have to put our children in school. I don't want my career to take over my life, Ashton. Being a judge is my day job. Something I do between nine and five, but for the rest of that time, I want to enjoy being the wife of Thomas Ashton Marshall, III, and the mother of our child."

"You said children as in more than one. That fits with my plan to be the husband of Kristin Catherine Bryant Marshall and the father of our children."

"What about your law practice?"

"I've already set up shop here in DC. However, I'll manage the Marshall and Marshall practice from here. I don't have to take cases out of the country. That's what I have a staff of attorneys for. I want to spend time doing extraordinary things with you. I want to sleep beside you every night, rub your back while we watch your belly rise with our children, and sit across a table and share our day and adventures with each other."

"This happened so fast, Ashton. Six months ago, I didn't even know you existed. Now I can't imagine my life without you in it and we're expecting a child."

"Don't fret, KC. This marriage was the right fit for both of us. All I want is your love and your happiness."

⊱⋆⊰

"Don't fret, dallin' Jillian," crooned one of the voices she could not see for the blindfold over her eyes. She was tied to something and spread eagle on a bed. There was the feel of a boat or ship of some kind cutting through the water and the smell of salt sea air, but she had no sense of where she was other than that. Voices were bidding on her she knew. She could hear the voices; some spoke in languages she had never heard before and thus could not understand. However, the ones who spoke in English were clearly understood. She was being auctioned off to the highest bidder! No one intervened to stop this craziness. She didn't know how she got here. All she remembered was being found in the parking lot with Strickland by Sheila and another man. When she walked away she smelled something in the air and everything went black. She didn't know how long it took her to come around, but when she did, she was disoriented, naked, blindfolded, and tied down. She didn't like what was going on as terror began to fill her head and heart before she noticed that same smell and everything faded to black again.

About the Author

Ann Jeffries, the critically acclaimed author of the Family Reunion—Wisdom of the Ancestors Series, is a native of Washington, DC. As an only child, she enjoyed the benefits of a private school education at Allen in Asheville, North Carolina, and a public education at the University of Maryland. Ann began writing fiction for her own amusement.

Ms. Jeffries is the recipient of many awards for leadership and public service. A keynote speaker at colleges, universities, conferences, and conventions, she has extensively traveled the North American continent, Asia, and Europe. Among other endeavors, she is an entrepreneur, an avid supporter of public television, a genealogist, and a voracious reader.

Her pride and joy are her family, particularly her Fabulous Four grands. She lives in Maryland and South Carolina.

Follow Ann on her website: www.annjeffries.net, Facebook @ Ann Jeffries, on Twitter @Ann Jeffries and her publishing house site: www.newviewliterature.com. Her novels are available in both e-book and paperback. Her autographed copies can be found through annjeffries.net and also un-autographed on Amazon.com and barnesandnoble.com.